Capitol Hill L

OCT 23

D0762045

NO LONGER PROPERTY OF
SEATTLE PUBLIC LIBRARY

Capitol Hill Library

AUG 26 2016

THE WRONG SIDE
OF MAGIC

Capitol Hill Library

AUG 26 2016

THE WRONG SIDE OF MAGIC

JANETTE RALLISON

Feiwel and Friends
New York

A Feiwel and Friends Book

An Imprint of Macmillan

The Wrong Side of Magic. Copyright © 2016 by Janette Rallison. All rights reserved.
Map illustration by Peter Donnelly. Printed in the United States of America
by R. R. Donnelley & Sons Company, Harrisonburg, Virginia. For information, address
Feiwel and Friends, 175 Fifth Avenue, New York, N.Y. 10010.

Our books may be purchased in bulk for promotional, educational, or business use. Please
contact your local bookseller or the Macmillan Corporate and Premium Sales Department at
(800) 221-7945 ext. 5442 or by e-mail at MacmillanSpecialMarkets@macmillan.com.

Library of Congress Cataloging-in-Publication Data
Names: Rallison, Janette, 1966– author.
Title: The wrong side of magic / Janette Rallison.
Description: First edition. | New York : Feiwel & Friends, 2016. |
Summary: "Eighth-grader Hudson stopped believing in magic long ago. Until
the day he is whisked away to the magical land of Logos—a land ruled by words,
thoughts, and memories. Upon arrival, Hudson is quickly saddled with a troll curse,
and only his friend Charlotte can help rid him of the curse. But she has an agenda
of her own—find and rescue the missing Princess of Logos"—Provided by publisher.
Identifiers: LCCN 2015036148 |
ISBN 9781250074287 (hardback) | ISBN 9781250086815 (e-book)
Subjects: | CYAC: Fantasy. | Magic—Fiction. |
BISAC: JUVENILE FICTION / Fantasy & Magic. | JUVENILE FICTION /
Humorous Stories. | JUVENILE FICTION / Social Issues / Friendship.
Classification: LCC PZ7.R13455 Wr 2016 | DDC [Fic]—dc23
LC record available at https://lccn.loc.gov/2015036148

Book design by Eileen Savage

Feiwel and Friends logo designed by Filomena Tuosto

First Edition—2016

1   3   5   7   9   10   8   6   4   2

mackids.com

To Norton Juster, who wrote my favorite childhood book, *The Phantom Tollbooth*. Also to Michael Kuykendall, my fifth-grade teacher, who read the book to our class. You opened up a world of magic to so many people!

1

SOMETIMES MAGIC SNEAKS up on a person like a sudden rainstorm, or bad news, or a mugger wearing really quiet shoes. That's what happened to Hudson Brown. He was an average eighth grader, with average brown hair that usually needed to be cut and average brown eyes that didn't always pay attention to his teachers. He lived in an average bedroom that needed to be cleaned and had average friends—many of whom also needed to be cleaned.

In short, Hudson was the type who hadn't believed in magic for years. Truth be told, magic hadn't believed in Hudson for even longer, but boys are often getting tangled in trouble, and Hudson was no exception. Except his trouble involved trolls, wizards, and several other things that wanted to kill him.

It started with a cat. Many problems do, which is why dogs, mice, and grumpy old men don't like them.

Hudson's little sister, Bonnie, however, adored them. Cats,

that is, not grumpy old men. When she found a stray kitten cowering in the bushes near their house, it was love at first drag-a-furry-black-creature-out-of-the-junipers-so-she-could-tell-what-it-was sight. Bonnie brought the kitten inside, fed her tuna casserole, and named her Sunshine.

She begged their mother to let Sunshine be their official pet. (Bonnie occasionally captured bugs and made them unofficial pets.)

Perhaps their mother didn't turn the cat away because she was tired of Bonnie bringing crickets and spiders inside, some of which later escaped into unknown parts of the house. Or perhaps their mother relented because Sunshine actually liked her tuna casserole, whereas Bonnie and Hudson only poked at it whenever it was put on their plates.

The important thing was, Sunshine stayed.

The cat spent the next week pouncing, purring, and attempting to change everyone's hearts into soft, kitten-shaped objects. Then just as abruptly, Sunshine got sick and hardly ate for two days. She lay among the unmade covers of Bonnie's bed in a limp, pathetic heap.

On the third morning, Hudson woke to the sound of Bonnie in the kitchen pleading with their mother. "Can we take her to the vet? I'll pay for it. I've got eighteen dollars."

Dishes clanked about in the sink noisily. Mrs. Brown made a daily heroic attempt to keep the kitchen clean. "A vet wouldn't pet your cat for eighteen dollars. Maybe we should bring her to a shelter and let them take care of her."

"But I love Sunshine. I'll earn more money and pay you back."

Mrs. Brown let out a grunt. "Honey, vet bills can be thousands of dollars. Besides, I hardly have the time to take *you* to the doctor when you're sick. I can just imagine what my manager would say if I asked for time off for a stray cat."

"Pleeeeease?" Bonnie insisted. No one could drag out a word like Bonnie could.

The dishwasher snapped shut. "I've got to get ready for work. Wake up Hudson and tell him to get a move on, or you'll both be late for school."

Hudson pulled himself out of bed and staggered into the shower. By the time he walked into the kitchen, his mother was picking up her jacket and purse, about to go out the door.

Mrs. Brown was tall, with curly brown hair that she pinned up when she went to work. She was pretty in a motherly way, no-nonsense in every other way. She never wore the sorts of clothes you saw on department-store mannequins. No frills or bling. And her philosophy on shoes was: If a woman couldn't comfortably run after a bus in them, there was no point in buying them.

Bonnie stood by the table, the kitten in her arms and a worried frown on her face.

Mrs. Brown walked over to Hudson and gave him a kiss on the cheek. "You have a good day at school." Next, she went to Bonnie, kissed her on the head, and smoothed down Bonnie's hair. "The cat will probably get better on her own."

Bonnie didn't answer, just petted Sunshine's ears.

Their mother sighed and gave Bonnie an extra kiss. "You have a good day at school, too."

As their mother slipped on her jacket, she asked her usual morning question. "And why do you need a good education?"

Bonnie gave the standard answer. "So we can have jobs where we don't have to listen to people complain all day."

"That's right, baby." Mrs. Brown gave them one last wave before she headed out the door. Ever since Mr. Brown's Marine unit had deployed overseas, she'd worked in customer service at a department store.

Bonnie opened a can of wet cat food and sat down at the table with Sunshine cradled in her arms. Using one of her doll spoons, she tried to slip food into the kitten's mouth. Mostly she just managed to get fish-smelling mush all over Sunshine's fur.

Hudson walked to the cupboard and took out a cereal bowl. "Bonnie, what are you doing that for?"

"She's got to eat something or she'll die."

And if Bonnie didn't eat breakfast, she'd be hungry later. He didn't tell her this. She didn't listen to him when he said anything that sounded vaguely parental. Which made Hudson's job twice as hard. His mom had put him in charge of making sure Bonnie got to school on time, walking her home afterward, and helping her with her homework.

He sat down, placed a bowl in front of Bonnie, and poured her a bowl of generic Cheerios. Their mom never bought the real kind. She bought the cheap brand in the big bags that were shoved on the bottom shelf of the cereal aisle. Generic might not be so bad if she bought the generic Froot Loops, but she said those had too much sugar. She only bought cheap and healthy stuff, which was never going to be a good combination.

Hudson poured the milk on his and Bonnie's cereal, then dumped spoonfuls of sugar on the floating circles. They bobbed around his bowl, and he pretended they were fleeing from his spoon with their little mouths opened in O's of horrified surprise. "No one escapes the spoon of death," he told Bonnie, and shoveled a dripping pile from his bowl.

Bonnie ignored him and kept trying to feed Sunshine. By the time they had to leave for school, she'd managed to get cat food on the table, the floor, and all over the kitten's black fur. "Well," he said, "at least if she licks herself off, she'll get some nutrients."

"We have to get money for a vet." Bonnie's eyes were big and full of eight-year-old innocence. She had the sort of adorable little-girl face you saw on the cover of parenting magazines. "We could rob a bank," she said hopefully.

"No, no, we couldn't." Hudson took the breakfast dishes to the sink. He had fifty-five dollars stashed in his sock drawer. Money he'd earned last summer mowing lawns. He was saving up for a gaming system. "I can give you ten dollars."

Bonnie blinked at him sadly. She knew it wasn't enough.

"Okay," he said, "twenty."

"Won't Sunshine need some medicine?"

"I'll ask around and see if anyone needs yard work done. . . ."

"I could mow lawns, too," she said, just as enthusiastic about this possibility as about robbing banks.

"You're too young. Lawn mowers eat eight-year-olds."

Bonnie laid a dish towel in their mother's biggest mixing bowl and set the kitten inside to rest. Hudson didn't point out that this new sleeping arrangement wouldn't make their mother happy.

He picked up his backpack. "If your cat dies in that bowl, I'm never eating out of it again."

Bonnie set the bowl near the front door and cooed at the kitten. "We'll take you to the vet after school, Sunshine. 'Cause I'm robbing a bank on the way home."

Hudson let out a sigh. The money in his sock drawer was in serious danger. Sometimes it was easier to give in to Bonnie than to argue with her or keep her out of trouble.

Then again, maybe he could put some of her cuteness to good use. It was, after all, her best asset. Hudson turned the idea around in his mind. "I know how we can make some money," he said. "After school, we can go to a busy intersection somewhere, wash people's car windows, and then ask for a donation for your sick kitten."

Cute kid plus sick kitten: irresistible. And much better than taking up a life of crime.

Bonnie brightened at the idea. "Mom will be so surprised."

Yeah. And mortified, too. Their mother expected many things from her children. Panhandling wasn't on that list.

Bonnie ran to the laundry room and came back with a squee-gee and an empty bucket. "We can do it right after school. There are lots of cars around then."

While Bonnie swung the bucket back and forth, Hudson tucked the squeegee into her backpack. "Mom probably shouldn't know about this."

They headed down the sidewalk toward the school. The

early-November morning was whispering of winter in a way that made you keep your hands in your pockets and wish for afternoon sun. Hudson didn't mind. Winter could go ahead and shout, for all he cared. Cold meant Thanksgiving was almost here, and his dad had said he would be home for it.

Before long, Hudson and Bonnie came to Charlotte Fantasmo's yard. Her real last name was Smith, but everyone at school called her Fantasmo because her dad was Mr. Fantasmo, Magician Extraordinaire. *Extraordinaire* in this case meaning weird.

He wore brightly colored corduroy pants and loud Hawaiian shirts, and every once in a while he fixed people with a stare so complete it felt like a bushy-eyebrowed X-ray. He claimed to be an actual wizard, banished from the magical land of Logos.

It was one thing to say that sort of thing when you were onstage, busy turning balloons into handkerchiefs, but he also talked that way when he came to pick up Charlotte from school.

And this from a man who wasn't even a big-name magician. Mostly he performed at kids' birthday parties. At the back-to-school night, he put on a show right in the parking lot—producing oranges and radishes and then a dazed-looking sparrow from his hat. When the crowd got big enough, he took a few bows and handed out flyers advertising his rates.

Mrs. Brown said the whole I'm-a-wizard-from-Logos thing was part of his act—his persona—but that didn't explain why half the time Charlotte also talked like she'd just taken a taxi from Crazyville.

In the four months since Charlotte had moved to town, she

hadn't made any friends. You could say something perfectly normal like, "Hey, what's up?"

She'd spout off, "The ceiling. The price of gasoline. Two-thirds of the letters in the word *UPS*." And she wasn't joking.

This morning Charlotte lay on her stomach on the lawn, fingering through the grass. Her long red hair was pulled into a ponytail at the top of her head, and she wore a pair of faded jeans and a man's plaid flannel shirt.

She might have been pretty if she tried. Well, pretty in an elfish sort of way. That's the impression you got from her upturned eyes, pixie nose, and pointed chin. She looked like she'd just wandered out of Santa's workshop and would momentarily be returning to make toy sleighs for good little girls and boys.

She saw Hudson and Bonnie and then waved at them.

Bonnie waved back enthusiastically. She just liked the fact that an eighth grader knew who she was. Hudson took hold of Bonnie's jacket sleeve and pulled her forward. "We don't have time to stop and talk."

It was too late. Charlotte got up and came toward them, bouncing with excitement. She held up a clover. "Look, it's the second four-leaf one I've found since I moved to Houston. I can't believe nobody else picked it first."

Bonnie leaned closer for a better look. "What are you going to do with it?"

"Dip it in silver," Charlotte said, as though the answer should be obvious. "So it can protect against wizard spells."

"Oh," Bonnie said. "I found one once, and my mom put it in between the pages of a book to dry."

Charlotte tilted her head until her ponytail rested against her shoulder. "What good does that do?"

"Well," Hudson said, smiling, "wizards haven't ever attacked our bookcase, so it must be doing its job." He nudged Bonnie in the direction of the school. "We've got to go, or we'll be late for school."

Charlotte's eyes widened. "Oh, right. I forgot—school." She turned and ran back to her house. "Thanks for reminding me!" She dashed inside, leaving the screen door swinging wildly.

What sort of person forgot they had school in the morning? *Hello*, had she not done this every morning for, like, nine years? Hudson walked on, shaking his head.

A few minutes later, Charlotte caught up to them, breathless because she'd been running. She slipped her arms into a bright blue sweater that was too big. No one said anything for a moment. Hudson was thinking of their after-school plans, his mind busy sifting through ideas to bring in more of those elusive dollar signs.

"So," Charlotte said, "do you really care about the weather?"

"What?" Hudson asked.

"The weather. You know, clouds, wind, that sort of thing."

"Why would I care about that?"

Charlotte let out a humph of triumph. "I knew it. I knew people didn't really care about the weather. Well, you know, not unless there's a drought or something."

Hudson stared at her, wondering if it was worth it to ask the next question. "Charlotte, what are you talking about?"

"That's what I'm trying to figure out," she said. Then nothing else.

He knew he shouldn't have asked.

Bonnie gazed up at the sky. Her bucket banged against her legs as she walked. "Is there something wrong with the weather?"

"Pollution. Acid rain. The occasional hurricane." Charlotte fiddled with her sweater, turning the cuffs inward instead of outward.

Bonnie cocked her head and didn't let the subject drop. "So why did you ask about the weather?"

"My dad said that when people here don't know what to talk about, they talk about the weather. But I don't think I should, because no one actually cares about the weather. Why not talk about something people care about?"

Bonnie nodded in agreement. "I never talk about the weather."

"Let's talk about soda pop," Charlotte said. "I saw three soda pop commercials last night, so it must be a hot topic."

Hudson looked at her to see if she was serious. He didn't know why he bothered. It's not like you could tell anything from her expression. She always looked either intrigued or distracted.

"That doesn't make them hot topics," he said. "That makes them advertisements."

"Right," Charlotte agreed. "The soda companies want to get their message out. It sort of makes me feel sad—all those commercials. So many people urgently want to educate us about laundry detergent, cell phone coverage, car insurance—I can barely keep it all in my mind."

"You're not supposed to . . ." he started, and then figured she was being sarcastic about it anyway.

"Soda pop," Charlotte went on. "How exactly is it connected to happiness? I mean, do they pour a little bit of happiness into each can, or does that only come in the liter sizes?"

"Probably just the liter sizes," he said.

Her eyebrows scrunched together. "I must not be buying the right brand, then."

"Okay . . ." Hudson said, and then didn't know what else to say. This was most likely why people talked about the weather. It was hard to mess up a conversation about the temperature.

Bonnie walked closer to Charlotte. "Aren't you happy?"

The words hung in the air. The question was too personal. Anyone else would have brushed off the subject with a laugh. Charlotte looked at the lawn they were passing and sighed. "Sometimes." She didn't sound very convincing.

"You probably need a kitten," Bonnie said.

"We could give her ours," Hudson said.

Bonnie scowled and swung the bucket at him, trying to hit his leg. "No, we couldn't."

Instead of commenting on kittens, Charlotte paused in front of a patch of clover as though she wanted to search through it, then she resumed walking beside Hudson. "Would you willingly face danger to save someone important, even if you didn't know them?"

He shrugged. "How much danger?"

"Wizards. Dragons. Soldiers. Possibly giants—"

"Nope."

Charlotte frowned. "What if the person you need to save was *really* important?"

"Still, nope."

Charlotte's frown stayed firmly fixed on her lips and was joined by a dip in her eyebrows. "Do you think I could find someone that brave?"

Hudson let out a snort. "You don't need someone who's brave. You need someone who's stupid. And most people aren't that stupid." He didn't bother asking for details about who Charlotte thought needed to be saved from dragons, wizards, and possibly giants. None of those things existed, so it didn't matter.

The group was close enough to school now that other people converged on the sidewalk, heading their way. Hudson spotted his best friend, Trevor, walking toward the parking lot. He was thin with dark hair and an unmistakable slouch that proclaimed, *I'm only here because I have to be.*

"Trevor!" Hudson called. To Bonnie and Charlotte he said, "I'll see you all later."

"Probably," Charlotte said. "Although you never can tell when sudden blindness will strike."

Really, she was too weird.

Before Hudson had gone more than a couple of steps away, he heard footsteps on the sidewalk behind him.

"Hey, Charlotte," a guy said, "can your dad really do magic?"

Hudson glanced over his shoulder and saw Andy and Caidan, two of the popular guys in the eighth grade. Both were grinning at Charlotte in a way that was supposed to look nice but somehow didn't.

"Of course he can do magic," Charlotte said. "That's what wizards do."

Andy looked Charlotte up and down, taking in her oversize sweater. "Well, then, maybe the next time he's doing tricks, he can make you disappear for good."

Andy and Caidan both laughed, then pushed past Charlotte and went down the sidewalk toward the school. For a moment, Hudson wanted to yell at them and tell them they didn't need to be jerks. He didn't, though. It wouldn't do any good and would just make Andy and Caidan mad at him. Hudson kept walking without saying anything.

And then regretted it for the rest of the day.

2

SCHOOL WENT NORMALLY enough. No wizards, dragons, or giants put Hudson's bravery or stupidity to the test. If there was magic lurking around, Hudson didn't notice it. The biggest news of the day was that some guys from room 10 challenged a few guys from room 12 to a basketball game in the park an hour after school ended. Everybody was going to watch it, even the girls.

Of course, only the popular guys were playing. Guys like Andy and Caidan, who lived the deluxe version of life while everyone else struggled along with the regular edition. They were tall, athletic, and good-looking enough that it didn't matter what sort of jerk-wad things they did; the girls still liked them.

By the time school ended, Hudson had forgotten about his window-washing plans. When he got to the spot where he usually met Bonnie, she wasn't there. Instead, one of her friends handed him a note from her.

It read, *Hudson, I decided to start working right away. I got soap and water from the school bathroom, and I'm at the parent pickup line washing windows.*

What? Hudson's stomach lurched. It was one thing to ask strangers for money in an intersection where no one recognized them. It was completely different to ask for money at school, where the entire eighth grade would openly mock him for it.

He hurried over to the parent pickup line to explain this subtle difference to his sister. There she was at the back of the row of cars, bouncing around cleaning windows with a sign taped to her jacket that read SICK KITTEN FUND-RAISER.

Bonnie saw him, smiled, and waved at him.

He slunk over, self-conscious with every step. "What are you doing? We can't do this at school."

Bonnie dunked her squeegee into the bucket, then slapped the sponge side onto the nearest car window. A stream of water dripped down the glass. "Here is better because Mom doesn't like me to go near busy intersections."

"No, actually, here isn't better." He looked over his shoulder to check for disapproving teachers. He didn't see any—not yet.

"I've already made ten dollars," she told him happily.

"I don't want you to get into trouble," Hudson said.

"Aren't you going to help?" she asked.

That's when he saw a group of popular kids coming his way. Andy and Caidan were walking with Isabella Stanton, the undisputed prettiest girl in the eighth grade. She had starlet blonde hair and a way of blinking her blue eyes that sort of hypnotized you into staring at her. Someday, maybe when Hudson was older, or cooler, or stuck in an elevator with her, he would talk to her.

As though Isabella felt his stare, she turned and glanced in Hudson's direction.

He turned away quickly. Bonnie was holding the squeegee out. "You wanna do a few cars? I can give you my sign."

He couldn't. Not when Andy, Caidan, and Isabella were watching him. He might as well make a sign that read FREAK and attach it to his forehead until high school graduation.

Hudson stepped away from his sister. "No, I have stuff to do. Go home as soon as you're done."

He felt bad about leaving her, but he didn't stay around to hear more protests. He turned and hurried back across the parking lot.

When Hudson reached home, Sunshine still lay limply in the bowl. Just to prove he wasn't a horrible brother, he took her to the sink and tried to get her to drink some water.

His mother would yell at him if she knew he had left Bonnie at the school to walk home by herself. Then again, she'd yell even more if she knew Bonnie was panhandling at school. If one of their mom's friends got her windshield cleaned . . . or if the teachers doing traffic duty caught on . . .

Stupid cat.

Sunshine didn't drink any water, just let out a few pitiful meows. The minutes plodded by, and Bonnie still didn't come home. A hard ball of worry formed in Hudson's stomach. The line of cars picking kids up at school had to be gone by now.

What was Bonnie doing? Probably something that would get both of them in trouble. He should have just given her all his money.

Finally, Hudson's worry propelled him toward the door. He would go find his sister—had to. Just as he grabbed his jacket, Bonnie burst in the door. She was breathlessly excited, her eyes shining.

He was so relieved, he nearly hugged her. Instead, he tossed his jacket on the couch. "What took you so long?"

"I got caught." Still smiling, she dropped her backpack and bucket on the floor. "My teacher came by, but she has a cat of her own, so she was real nice and gave me twenty dollars. Then she told me to go on home."

Twenty dollars? Third-grade teachers were a soft bunch. Hudson chuckled and followed his sister into the kitchen. "So how much did you make?"

"Thirty-three dollars." Bonnie leaned over the bowl and gave Sunshine a kiss on the top of the head. Sunshine opened her eyes but didn't move. Didn't even meow.

Hudson added the sum out loud. "Thirty-three plus the twenty I'm giving you and the eighteen you already have . . . that's seventy-one dollars. I bet it's enough to see a vet."

Bonnie stopped petting Sunshine and straightened up. "I don't have the money anymore. I gave it to Charlotte for this." She reached into her pocket and pulled out a dented and scratched compass. "It's magic."

He blinked at her. "You did what?"

"It's a magic compass. Charlotte promised."

Hudson put his hands on his hips. "Wait—you gave your money to Charlotte?"

A flash of hurt passed over Bonnie's expression. "She's just keeping my money until Sunshine is better and I return the compass." Bonnie held out the compass for him to see. "Charlotte had to make me trade something for it. Magic is expensive."

It could have been worse, Hudson realized. Bonnie could have lost more than her money. Someone could have grabbed her and kidnapped her, because apparently she didn't have a lick of common sense.

Hudson put his hands out, palms lifted in exasperation. "Why were you even talking to Charlotte?"

The smile dropped from Bonnie's face. She clutched the compass defensively, as though Hudson would grab it. "Charlotte stayed after school to finish an assignment, so we were both walking home at the same time. I told her about Sunshine, and she said I could use the magic compass as long as I promised to return it when I'm done."

Yeah, and Charlotte probably had a great deal on magic beans, too.

"In Logos," Bonnie went on, "there's a plant called catflower that makes sick cats better. The compass will take me there."

"Let me see it."

Bonnie reluctantly handed him the compass. It was a worn gold color, completely scuffed, with a few dents and deep scratches. A knob stuck out of one side, making it look like it had started its life as a pocket watch. Instead of letters indicating north, south, east, and west, there were four lines. One of the lines read THE LAND OF BANISHMENT. The needle pointed firmly there. Hudson turned the compass to his left and then to his right, but the needle didn't budge.

He flipped the compass over. "This is a piece of junk. It doesn't even show directions, and the needle is stuck."

Bonnie grabbed the compass back and examined it more closely. "Maybe it doesn't work for you because it's magic."

She turned the compass with the same results.

"If that compass was really magic," he pointed out, "why didn't Mr. Fantasmo get a bunch of catflower and become a vet instead of a magician? Vets make way more money."

Bonnie tilted her chin down, a miniature teacher. "'Cause he got kicked out of Logos when he refused to work for the new tyrant king. He tells that story every time he does his tricks."

Hudson tried again to show her the logic. "Then why doesn't Fantasmo hire someone else to get catflower for him?"

Bonnie bent over the kitten, petting its fur reassuringly. "Charlotte said only people with pure hearts can travel safely in the kingdom of Logos. Unicorns pick them up and take them wherever they want to go. Everybody else has to look out for the trolls and stuff. I'll be all right, though, because I have a pure heart."

And, unfortunately, she also had a gullible mind. Only Hudson didn't come out and say that. He just sighed. "Charlotte lied to you. Magic doesn't really exist. It's all tricks and pretend."

Bonnie gripped the compass and set her jaw.

"You don't believe me?" Hudson picked up the phone from the countertop and held it out. "Call and ask somebody: Mom,

Grandpa, your teacher. I'm sorry, but Charlotte took advantage of you."

Bonnie stared at the phone for a moment, then looked down at the compass. Her eyes puffed up with tears. "Charlotte promised. She said when I pull the knob up, I'll go to Logos. I only came home to drop off my backpack and to tell you so you wouldn't worry. . . ."

Hudson gently took the compass from her hand. Maybe he hadn't done the right thing by letting her walk home by herself, but he would fix his mistake. "Yeah, well, I'm going to talk to Charlotte. Don't worry, I'll get your money back."

Hudson put on his jacket. The last image he saw as he went out the door was Bonnie, her shoulders slumped as she cradled the mixing bowl.

Hudson walked quickly, his feet making an angry rhythm down the sidewalk. Charlotte had gone too far this time. It was one thing to come up with stories about magic; it was another to use them to take money from little kids. He turned the compass over in his hand, squeezing it.

Charlotte's house came into view. He could see her lying on her stomach in the grass, sorting through the clover again. Pull up the knob and he'd be in a magical kingdom, huh? What kind of compass had a knob on it, anyway?

Hudson jerked up the knob with his thumbnail. A few angry words had been heading toward his lips. These stopped, faltered, and completely toppled off his tongue.

He no longer stood on his street. He was on a meandering dirt path in the middle of a thick forest. Huge trees towered over him, their leafy canopies nearly crowding out the sky. He had seen autumn trees with their yellow, orange, and red leaves. This forest not only had those sorts of trees, but it also had purple, light blue, and dark blue ones. The place looked like a rainbow had fallen to earth and toppled color everywhere.

Hudson let out a startled scream. He blinked and then blinked harder in case the last time hadn't worked. He checked behind him. The trees there looked as though they'd sprouted out of a box of Crayolas. He had landed in freaking Candy Land.

This couldn't be real. It was an illusion of some sort, a trick. A really good trick, since Hudson could even *smell* the forest. He was surrounded by the scent of trees, bushes, and soil. Every once in a while, he caught a whiff of something flowery. "Hello?" he called.

He heard nothing except birds chirping to one another. Even that sounded strange. The chirps had a trilling noise to them like someone playing a piano.

"Charlotte?"

No answer.

Hudson turned in a circle, searching for anything familiar. "Hey, Charlotte, where are you? How did you do this?"

The wind blew through the trees. It made the forest seem like a parade, with thousands of leaves fluttering like colorful confetti. *Don't panic*, he told himself. *This isn't real.*

Hudson stepped over to a blue bush, whose featherlike leaves swayed in the wind, and he ran a finger along a leaf. It felt as soft as velvet. He drew his hand away quickly. A magic trick couldn't have turned his neighborhood into a forest. He shouldn't be able to see, smell, or feel this place if it didn't exist. His heart beat faster, half with excitement and half with fear. The compass had really done something, had taken him somewhere new. Charlotte hadn't lied about the compass's magic. Cool. Beyond cool. Magic was real. Logos actually existed.

Why hadn't Charlotte shown people this before? She should have taken a few people here so everyone would know she and her father weren't crazy. As soon as Hudson got home, he was going to talk to her about it. And apologize.

He looked down at the compass still gripped in his hand. The phrase LAND OF BANISHMENT had disappeared from the face. The settings now read FOREST OF POSSIBILITIES, SEA OF LIFE, GRAMMARIA, and GIGANTICA. The needle pointed to FOREST OF POSSIBILITIES. Apparently, the compass pointed to where you were instead of telling you directions.

He glanced around at all the bushes and trees. How would he find catflower in this place, and more important, how would he get back home once he had? Charlotte had probably told Bonnie these details, but Hudson didn't know them.

He'd pulled the knob up to get here, so pushing the knob down might take him back. He wouldn't try it yet. First he would find catflower. Since he didn't know what it looked like, maybe he should just pick every type of flower he saw. It would take a while, but hopefully he'd end up finding the right plant.

A thudding noise from somewhere in the forest interrupted his thoughts. It sounded like several footsteps. Not human footsteps—larger, heavier, probably scarier. Behind the curtain of trees, something was moving around. He couldn't tell exactly where. The sound seemed to echo around him.

"Hello?" Hudson called.

No one called back.

Come to think of it, magic and being in the land of Logos probably had its drawbacks. He suddenly remembered all the fairy tales he'd read—stories about dragons, witches, and giants.

Hudson heard a grunt of some sort, low and grumbly, like something was hungry. The noise brought him to the immediate and urgent conclusion that he couldn't stay here, not even to find catflower. He pushed the compass knob back down.

Nothing happened. He still stood on the dirt path in the forest.

Hudson lifted up the compass knob and pushed it back down a second time. Still nothing.

The noise came again. More footsteps were rustling through the forest. He considered running off the path and hiding, but he still wasn't sure where the noise had come from, and besides, who knew what strange creatures lived in this place? Maybe multicolored lions and bears were skulking around behind the trees, waiting to pounce. Maybe they already had him in their sights.

Hudson's gaze darted around the trees, searching one side and then the other. What was he facing? He tried to remember everything Mr. Fantasmo had said about Logos. There was that bit about King Vaygran, the tyrant, taking over. Charlotte had mentioned giants, although if one of those was lumbering around, Hudson probably would have noticed it by now.

What else? Oh yeah, trolls. Monstrous trolls lived in Logos. You always had to be on your guard against them. What sounds did trolls make?

Hudson had no way to defend himself. He didn't see even a stick or rock lying on the ground that he could pick up and use to ward off an attack.

He turned the compass over in his hand, fumbling as he looked for instructions, anything that would help him. The only words on the compass were the settings on its face: FOREST OF POSSIBILITIES, SEA OF LIFE, GRAMMARIA, and GIGANTICA.

Another grunt echoed through the forest. Probably trolls. Time to panic. He pushed the knob up so hard it popped off and fell to the ground.

He stared at the place the knob had been. Shouldn't magic compasses be built better than that? If he had any chance of making this thing work, he needed all the pieces. He dropped to his knees and searched the ground, looking for a glint of gold. He ran his hands frantically over dirt and bits of dried leaves, all the while cursing magic compasses.

Hudson heard another low, rumbling noise, this time directly over his shoulder. He wouldn't become troll dinner without a fight. He spun around, swinging his arm as he did. His fist didn't connect with anything. The noise hadn't been a troll. Two unicorns stood on the path behind him, their heads lifted too high to be hit by the arc of his swing.

Hudson let out another startled scream. He was getting quite good at those. He put his hand to his chest and sat back down on the ground, too relieved and surprised to speak.

One unicorn was a gray color—not the gray of rocks or dirty sidewalks. It was the soft gray of morning mist. The other unicorn was the tawny brown of glistening honey.

The gray unicorn took a step back and turned to the unicorn beside him. "Did you see that, Nigel? That human tried to strike me."

"Most uncivil," the tawny unicorn agreed. Both spoke with a sort of British-sounding accent.

Hudson got to his feet, gaping at them. "You can talk?"

The gray unicorn tossed his mane, warily keeping an eye on Hudson. He still spoke only to the other unicorn. "What sort of incantation do you suppose the boy was performing on the road a moment ago?"

The tawny unicorn leaned his head toward his companion. "I don't think that was an incantation. It sounded distinctly like cursing to me."

"He was cursing the road?" the gray unicorn asked. "How barbaric."

"You don't understand," Hudson said, still so surprised that it was hard to think straight. He held up the compass for them to see. "I accidentally flipped the knob off the compass because, well, I heard you grunting and I thought you were going to eat me or something—"

The unicorns let out a simultaneous "Hmmph!" and turned back toward each other. In a lowered voice, the tawny unicorn said, "All those who vote that the human boy is impure in heart, raise their horn."

The gray unicorn immediately raised his head so his horn

stood straight up. The tawny unicorn lifted his head, as well. "Impure it is, then."

They trotted around Hudson, noses twitching.

It was only when the unicorns declared Hudson to be impure that he remembered Bonnie's insistence that unicorns helped travelers who were pure in heart.

"Wait!" Hudson turned and walked after them. "I've got a pure heart. Really, I do!" He hurried to catch up. He had to convince them that he was good. Otherwise, he had no idea how to get home.

The unicorns didn't stop. As they continued down the path, the gray one glanced over his shoulder. "It's following us now."

"Don't make eye contact with it, Cecil. That just encourages them."

At that, the unicorns went from trot to canter. Hudson ran, plodding uselessly after them. "Come back!" he called. "I'm pure!"

They swished their tails to shoo him off and galloped away, disappearing as they went around a twist in the path.

There was no use in trying to catch up with them. Hudson stopped running and looked down the path, panting. What did a person do when he was stuck in a magic forest with trolls, giants, and no idea of how to get home? Somehow, none of his schoolteachers had ever covered this topic. Ditto for the stories he'd read.

He would have to retrace his steps, find the missing knob to the compass, and hope he could figure out a way to make it take him home.

He walked back along the path, past pink bushes, tufts of purple grass, and green ferns that seemed out of place for looking so ordinary. Several types of flowers grew along the way: orange ones that shot up like miniature flames on stems, white ones that resembled upside-down jellyfish, and pink striped ones whose petals twirled in the wind like pinwheels. Were any of them catflowers? Then again, catflower might be like cauliflower—something that didn't look like a flower at all.

Hudson stared at the plants, hoping they might produce name tags. Finally, he reached out and touched a white one. The petals immediately drew inward, disappearing into the stem like a sea anemone.

Hudson drew his hand away almost as quickly. Maybe he shouldn't pick random flowers. What if some were poisonous, or venomous, or something equally troubling? It would be safer to go back home, ask Charlotte what catflower looked like, and then come back for some.

He traced the unicorns' footsteps along the path to the place where they'd gone from a trot to a canter. Then he found the spot where he'd knelt on the dirt. At least he thought it was the right place. He slipped the compass into his jacket pocket and crawled around on his hands and knees searching for the knob. His hands kept getting dirtier. Minutes passed by. He would have given up if he could think of anything else to do. What if he couldn't find the knob? What if he found it and the compass still couldn't take him back home? He could be stuck here indefinitely.

He heard a voice coming from down the path. "What curse do you suppose has got hold of that boy? Look, he thinks he's some sort of beast."

3

HUDSON GLANCED UP and was relieved to see a girl and boy coming around a bend in the path. The two looked to be about Hudson's age. Both had pale green eyes, sleek brown hair, and high cheekbones. Strings of light blue flowers were woven into the girl's long hair, and her dress's scalloped edges mimicked leaves. The guy's hair was tied behind his head in a short ponytail, and he wore a long green shirt, tight yellow pants, and bright blue boots. The sort of clothing forest elves might wear.

As the two made their way down the path, they watched Hudson with a mixture of disdain and humor. "My guess is," the guy said, "he thinks he's a dirt-sifting badger."

The girl tilted her head, studying Hudson. "My guess is, he thinks he's a dog, and he sadly never learned how to dig holes properly."

"We'll ask him," the guy said, "and see who wins this round."

Hudson sat up and wiped his hands on his jeans, his cheeks

flushing in embarrassment. "I don't think I'm anything. I'm just trying to find something I lost."

"You don't think you're anything?" the guy repeated. He was almost to Hudson now. "What would that make you, then—talking air?"

"Well," the girl said, "we both lost that round, but you lost worse than I did. A dirt-sifting badger wasn't even close."

Hudson didn't know whether the two were making fun of him or just joking around with him. Judging from the guy's smirk, Hudson suspected it was the first.

The girl scanned the path near Hudson. "What did you lose?"

Before Hudson could answer, the guy said, "His wits."

The girl shot her companion an exasperated look.

"What?" he asked. "I thought we were still playing the guessing game."

Hudson ignored the guy and spoke to the girl. "I lost the knob to my compass. It's gold and"—he held his thumb and forefinger close together—"about this big. Do you see it anywhere? I really need to find it." The girl took a few steps around Hudson, checking among the pebbles that lined the road. The guy didn't move.

"Is it real gold?" he asked, sounding doubtful.

"I don't know," Hudson said. "It goes to this." He pulled the compass from his pocket. As he held it up, he noticed that smaller print had appeared in between the lines for FOREST OF POSSIBILITIES, SEA OF LIFE, GRAMMARIA, and GIGANTICA. The lines read BEWARE OF TROLLS, BEWARE OF WAVES, BEWARE OF KING VAY-GRAN, and BEWARE OF GIANTS. The needle pointed at BEWARE OF TROLLS.

Hudson scanned the surrounding forest. He didn't see anything suspicious among the trees. "Huh," he said, and squinted, looking harder.

"Is something wrong with your compass?" the guy asked.

"It says 'Beware of Trolls.' "

"Oh, I found it." The girl plucked the compass's knob from the side of the path, where it must have rolled and been hidden in a scattering of yellow leaves. She walked over to Hudson and handed him the knob.

"Thanks!" Hudson got to his feet with relief. He pushed the knob back onto the compass, then moved it to see which direction the trolls were. Regardless of where he pointed it, the warning remained the same.

For a compass, it didn't do a very good job of showing you where things were.

"Maybe it really is broken," he said. Before the other two could ask why he kept turning in circles, he added, "No matter where I stand, the compass says 'Beware of Trolls.' " He peered into the forest, trying to see beyond the shifting shadows the trees cast. "Did you see any signs of trolls along the road?"

The guy and girl exchanged a look that indicated they didn't think him to be terribly bright. "What sort of signs do you think trolls leave?" the boy asked.

Hudson shrugged. "Footprints . . . fleeing animals . . . troll calls . . ." He had no idea what trolls sounded like, or even if they made noise, and hoped he hadn't made himself appear stupider.

"I wouldn't trouble yourself about trolls." The girl took a closer look at the compass. "They're not as bad as everyone thinks."

"Really?" Hudson couldn't tell if she was serious. "Aren't they dangerous?"

"Everything can be dangerous," the guy said. "Especially people—but you probably don't worry about running into them."

Hudson supposed this was a valid point, since he had been relieved when he saw the two of them coming down the path.

The girl brushed some remaining flecks of dirt from her fingers. "That reminds me, we never introduced ourselves. I'm Glamora. This is my twin brother, Proval."

"She always tells people we're twins," Proval added, "because she doesn't want anyone to think I'm older."

"He's not," Glamora said.

"I am, too," Proval said. "By three brays of a donkey."

Glamora turned away from her brother, ending that discussion. "What's your name?"

"I'm Hudson. Hudson Brown."

Proval cocked his head. "HudsonHudsonBrown. A rather long name. Is that standard in your family, or did your mum not care for you much?"

"It's just one Hudson, and you don't have to say the Brown part. That's my last name."

Glamora's eyebrows drew together. "If it's your most recent name, shouldn't it be the one you use?"

Suddenly a lot of things about Charlotte became clearer. People in Logos seemed to take what you said literally. "You can call me whatever you want," Hudson said.

"Yes," Proval said with a flicker of mockery. "I bet people do."

Glamora nudged her brother to be quiet. "We're on our way to our village. Do you have a place to stay for the night?"

"I can't stay that long," Hudson said. "I'd like to find some catflower, and then I have to figure out a way to go back home." He needed help, and perhaps these two could offer some, so he added, "I'm from a different world. Do either of you know how to travel by compass?"

A smug smile broke across Proval's face. "I knew you were from the Land of Banishment." He said the sentence as though Hudson had been hiding it. "I recognized your sacred symbols."

"What sacred symbols?" Hudson asked.

Proval pointed to Hudson's tennis shoes. "The sign of the Nike and"—Proval nodded at Hudson's jeans—"the sign of the Levis."

"Oh, um . . ." Obviously, brand names were like trolls, a subject of misinformation between the two worlds. "Those aren't really sacred." Instead of explaining, he asked, "Do a lot of people travel between our worlds?"

"Not many," Proval said. "Most people in your world don't have the magic to get here." He looked over Hudson a bit more closely. "You're pretty young for a wizard."

Hudson meant to explain that he wasn't, that he'd gotten the compass from a girl at school, but he didn't know how much he should say about Charlotte. She and her father had left Logos to get away from King Vaygran. She probably didn't want Hudson telling people where they'd gone.

"If you need catflower," Glamora said, "you can get some at our village. It's only a half hour walk from here." She sent him a knowing smile. "You can buy about anything you want there."

Glamora and Proval started down the path, clearly expecting Hudson to follow. He stayed where he was, clutching the compass in his hand. "But how am I going to get back home?"

"Oh, getting back home is easy." Glamora turned to wait for him. "You just have to find a magical exit. There's one in our village."

A magical exit? Awesome. Hudson joined them, relief making his footsteps light. "Really? It's easy?"

"Well, it's up the thorn tree," Proval clarified. "You'll have to climb the tree."

"Are there thorns on it?"

"Yeah," Proval said. "If it had apples on it, we'd call it an apple tree."

Suddenly, getting to a magical exit sounded less like something that was easy and more like something that was painful.

Glamora let out an airy laugh. "A wizard like yourself shouldn't be afraid. You can change yourself into an owl and fly up."

Or he could climb up and get scratched. It looked like Hudson would be stuck with option B.

The three of them kept heading down the path, with Glamora walking next to him and Proval on her other side. They told him about a bonfire their village was having that night, and then they each made guesses about what would be served, who would be there, and who would end up accidentally singeing their hat.

Finally, Glamora looked over at him, including him in the conversation. "You should stay for the party. Everyone loves to meet a new wizard."

Hudson shook his head. "I need to leave as soon as possible."

His mother would worry about him if she came home and he wasn't there.

Glamora shrugged, and she and Proval went back to guessing things about the bonfire.

Hudson was still holding the compass, and he checked it again. The entire time the three of them had been walking, the compass's needle had determinedly pointed at BEWARE OF TROLLS.

He glanced around the forest but saw no signs of anything lurking in the trees, no shadows darting between trunks that would indicate that they were being followed. The birds chirped out their pianolike songs as calmly as ever. But still. How could he not be nervous?

During a break in Glamora and Proval's conversation, Hudson said, "I've never seen a troll before. What are they like?"

Proval rolled his eyes. "Are you still worrying about that?"

Glamora waved her hand at her brother to silence him. "Guess what they're like."

Hudson thought about the trolls in the stories he'd read. "Big, ugly, bad-tempered, slow-moving, stupid—"

"They're actually very clever," Glamora cut in. "That's what makes them dangerous. Well, that and they can tell—just by looking at you—the things about yourself that you want to hide."

What an odd ability. What good did it do trolls to know what you were hiding unless you were hiding from them? That, Hudson decided, was probably what Glamora meant. Trolls could find you when you hid from them.

Proval patted Hudson on the shoulder. "You, my friend, lose the guessing game."

Glamora pushed a strand of hair behind her ear. "The important thing to know about trolls is that if you meet some, you should give them whatever they want."

Hudson considered this advice. "So you're saying I couldn't outrun one?"

Glamora shrugged. "I don't know. I've never seen you run."

"It doesn't matter," Proval put in. "We're almost home."

They'd gone over a bend in the road, and a village came into sight. It was smaller than Hudson had expected. Three or four dozen cottages lined circular streets that ringed an open market area. The wooden homes had green, yellow, and pink vines growing up their walls, twisting and stretching over doors and around windows so they looked as if they had been painted with leaves.

"The plants are so colorful here," Hudson said, picking up his pace. Glamora and Proval were walking faster now that they were almost home. "Plants are mostly green where I'm from."

"Why?" Proval asked.

"It has to do with chlorophyll." Hudson had learned about photosynthesis in science class, and he tried to remember the information. "You know, because plants convert light into . . . themselves." He wasn't explaining it right, but Proval and Glamora didn't seem confused.

"Yes," Glamora said. "And thousands of colors make up the light spectrum, which is why plants are so many different colors."

"I don't think that's how it works," Hudson said. He didn't say more. Proval and Glamora were exchanging looks again— the sort that indicated they thought he was an idiot.

Really, Hudson was going to be much more patient with Charlotte when he got back home. Compared with these two, she was really nice.

Several people milled around the village streets, all wearing clothes that looked like they came from some brightly colored and completely tasteless period in the Middle Ages. Half the people wore strange, elaborate hats. One had horns like a bull; another had feathered wings that flapped up and down. A woman strolled by sporting a pink turban with a pig snout in the front and a curly tail in the back. She looked like she was wearing a legless pig on her head.

Apparently, Hudson had come to town on Creepy Hat Day.

He didn't comment on the fashion. He just walked beside Glamora and Proval as they made their way down the street. Several trees grew among the houses and shops, but none had the thorns to indicate it was a thorn tree. "Where is the magical exit?" he asked.

"I'm taking you to our father's store first," Glamora said. "That way you can buy catflower before you go."

Hudson felt his pockets even though he knew he hadn't brought his wallet. He was hoping to find some forgotten bills. His pockets were empty. "I don't have any money with me."

Glamora shrugged. "You can always trade something."

Hudson only had his clothes and shoes. He hoped catflower wasn't expensive.

The group passed a man unloading a wagon full of barrels and a woman scolding her children for getting their clothes dirty. None of the villagers paid much attention to Hudson beyond giving him brief, inquisitive looks.

They came to a shop with round, carved shutters that twirled in on themselves like snail shells. "This is our father's shop," Glamora said, and she and Proval strode up to its curved door. They didn't go in.

Glamora planted her hands on her hips in frustration. "Where did the doorknob wander off to?"

Hudson thought she was joking until he saw that the door had no knob. It also didn't have a hole where one had been. It was just a flat, wooden door.

"It can't have gone far," Proval said, searching the edges of the door trim.

Glamora checked the ground. "Here it is." She bent over and picked up a fist-size snail.

It waved its jellylike antennae at her, protesting its change in location. Glamora let out a small, indignant humph. "Quit lying about and see to your job." She placed it firmly on the door.

The snail immediately inched—in what was probably the equivalent of a snail sprint—toward the bottom of the door.

"Slacker," Proval said, and gave the snail a twist like it was a knob. Not only did the snail stop moving, but the door swung open. Proval and Glamora stepped inside without another glance at the animal.

Hudson followed them, giving the doorknob on the inside— also snail-shaped—a long stare. It didn't move. That either meant it was a job-conscious snail or an inanimate object. The fact that Hudson didn't know which made him want to get home all the more quickly.

A counter stood at one end of the shop, and shelves lined every available space on the wall. They were covered with bottles, boxes, tongs, knives, and jars full of things that sparkled and glowed. The whole room smelled like it had rained inside and things had never really dried out.

Over in one corner, a stout man with arms as thick as tree trunks was stacking copper plates on a shelf. He wore black boots, red pants, and a long medieval shirt as the other men in the village wore. But instead of a regular belt, a snake was wrapped around his middle. It turned its head toward Hudson and licked the air with a forked tongue.

"Father," Glamora said, traipsing over to him, "we've brought someone to trade with you."

The man's gaze slid over Hudson, sizing him up. "Have you?" He had the same glossy brown hair and green eyes as his children, but the resemblance stopped there. No one would think he was a forest elf. He looked more like a lion tamer with a snake-belt sidekick.

"This is Hudson," Glamora said. "He's a wizard from the other realm."

Hudson felt oddly like he should bow after such an introduction. He nodded awkwardly instead.

"You can call me Rex." The man reached out and shook Hudson's hand, a motion that brought the snake closer to Hudson than he liked. "My children's friends are always welcome here."

Glamora sashayed over to the counter and leaned against it. "Hudson came to our village to buy catflower. Then he's going to climb the thorn tree to return back to his world."

"Ahh," Rex said, and a smile split his face apart. "I never tire of watching wizards from your world. Such an entertaining bunch, the lot of you are."

How many people from Hudson's world had come here? And why hadn't any of them told anyone that this place existed? Then again, maybe some people had, and everyone thought they were crazy. After all, what would the guys at Hudson's school think if he told them talking unicorns had snubbed him?

Rex wiped his hands against the sides of his pants, his eagerness evident. "What did you bring to trade?"

Hudson looked down at his clothes as though hoping to find something of value. Would his jacket be worth anything? What did catflower cost?

Before he could ask, Glamora said, "He has a magic compass."

Well, yeah, but it was Charlotte's, and besides, Hudson didn't know whether it did any magic beyond bringing people here. As far as its compass capabilities, it didn't seem to point the way anywhere except where you already were. Plus, it obviously had a strong phobia of trolls. He glanced down at it and noticed an exclamation mark had joined the BEWARE OF TROLLS warning.

Rex took a step closer to examine the compass in Hudson's hand. "A fine piece of work, and it has a troll warning, too. That's handy for common folk. It's worth much more than a bunch of catflower."

"I can't sell the compass," Hudson said, fingering it. "I'm just borrowing it from a friend."

Rex frowned. "Then what did you bring to trade?"

Hudson shifted his weight uncomfortably. "I could give you my shoes, my shirt, or my jacket." He wasn't taking off his pants and climbing a tree in his underwear, though, not even for Bonnie's kitten.

Rex shook his head, still frowning. "We don't wear clothes

from the Land of Banishment." He peered at the compass again. "You can always tell your friend you lost the compass. It won't even be a lie. You'll lose it and gain something from my shop." He stepped behind the counter and gestured to the cupboards behind him. "I keep the truly fine merchandise back here. Things worthy of a magic compass."

Rex opened a cupboard and pulled out a leather belt, complete with scabbard and sword. With fluid grace, he unsheathed the sword and pointed it in Hudson's direction. Hudson took an unsteady step backward. For one gasping moment, he thought Rex was about to strike him.

"If you want power," Rex said, "you need this magic sword. As long as you hold it, your enemies will run."

And if Hudson ever brought it to school, they'd run right to the principal's office and have him expelled. "I came to get catflower for my sister. If you tell me where it grows, maybe I can find some."

"Your sister is a cat?" Rex frowned. "How unfortunate."

"No, my sister has a sick cat."

Rex sheathed the sword and put it back into the cupboard. "Well, you can easily buy her a new cat, once"—he pulled a velvet bag from underneath the counter—"you own this magic purse." Rex took a silver coin from his pocket, placed it into the bag, and pulled the drawstring tight. He shook the purse dramatically, then opened it and turned it upside down. Two silver coins fell out. "Instant and continuous wealth." Rex held the purse out to Hudson, offering it to him.

Hudson wasn't sure the purse was even a good trick, let alone magic. A silver coin could have already been inside the purse to begin with.

He didn't reach for the purse. "I could get something from my home to trade and bring it back here." The problem with this suggestion was that Hudson had no idea what sort of things the people here wanted. "I could give you some food," he said. "Or maybe a doorknob that won't wander off. . . ."

Rex flicked his hand, waving away Hudson's words. As far as salesman went, he was determined. "Wealth and swords don't interest you. I should have known as much. Fine wizards have enough of those. But I bet I can guess what you do want. Admiration." He pulled a round mirror, no bigger than Hudson's palm, from a drawer. He put it on the counter, rubbing away some dust that coated the tiny golden leaves twining around the mirror's rim. "Perhaps there is a fair lady, someone whose attention you want to catch. Once you own this magic mirror, you'll always be the most handsome person around."

From behind Hudson, Proval whispered, "Take my advice and choose that one. You need it." Then he snickered at his own joke.

Hudson opened his mouth to refuse the offer, then paused. The mirror's magic seemed to rise from it the same way scents rose from fresh-baked cookies—warm and delicious. He leaned over the counter to get a better look. From the mirror, his eyes gazed back at him hopefully. What would it be like to be the best-looking guy at school—to be tall, muscular, and always have girls hanging around? To have Isabella hanging around?

Before Hudson could change his mind, he put the compass in his pocket. "I'm just here for catflower."

Glamora gave him a forced smile. "What a good brother you are."

Rex nodded, undeterred. "True enough, and good brothers should be rewarded." He picked up the mirror from the counter. "I'm so sure you'll appreciate the fine nature of my wares, I'll give you this one for free. That way, when you come back again, you'll want to do business with me." He held out the mirror to Hudson. It gleamed, shining with promises.

"Won't people notice if I suddenly look different?"

"That's the beauty of this magic," Rex said. "They won't think your appearance has changed." He leaned closer to Hudson. "So, do you accept my gift?"

Hudson nearly didn't. He wasn't going to come back here, so it didn't seem right. Besides, something was vaguely unsettling about Rex's smile. It was the smile of a person who was keeping secrets.

But a magic mirror—when would Hudson ever get that sort of gift again? He reached out and took it. "Sure, thanks." After all, if Rex wanted to give the mirror away, why shouldn't Hudson be the most handsome guy in his school? He slipped the mirror into his pocket.

Rex smiled again and motioned to his children. "Why don't you find some catflower for our guest and show him the way home."

Glamora and Proval turned and walked from the room without comment. Hudson followed after them, remembering to throw in a "Thanks again for the mirror" as he left.

Once outside, Glamora walked over to a clump of orange

flowers growing next to the dirt road—the ones that looked like flames on a stem. She picked a flower and handed it to Hudson. "This should be enough for one cat."

The orange flower? The one he'd seen dotting the path all the way here? "Why didn't you tell me before that this was cat-flower?" he asked.

Glamora shrugged. "I never thought about it."

Right. He knew she was lying but didn't argue with her. It was best just to go back home as quickly as he could. "Thanks." He added the flower to the other things in his pockets. "Which way to the thorn tree?"

"This way." Glamora turned, and she and Proval led him through the streets of vine-bound cottages.

The thorn tree stood towering over the buildings in the middle of the town square—or, in this case, the town circle. The tree hadn't been misnamed. Every few inches along the branches, clawlike thorns protruded between the tree's bright red leaves.

Glamora pointed at a large wooden box up in some high branches. "That's the exit. As you go through the door, say the location you want, and you'll end up there as long as it's in your home city."

Hudson touched one of the thorns on a low branch. Needle-sharp, it pricked his finger. He didn't like the idea of navigating up a tree full of these things. "Are there any other doorways back to my world?"

"Yes," Proval said, "but you'd have to wander all over the countryside to find one. This one is right here."

He had a point. Hudson gingerly reached toward a branch,

spreading his fingers apart so he wasn't impaled in the process. "Have either of you ever gone through the door?"

"Of course not," Proval said with a scoff. "It's an *exit*. To get to your world, we'd need a magical *entrance*, and those are nearly impossible to find."

"Oh," Hudson said, not quite sure how that made sense.

Glamora must have seen his confusion. "An exit always takes a person to his homeland. Our home is here."

"Oh," Hudson said again. Magical doorways must not follow regular laws of physics. He reached for a second branch, testing it to make sure it would hold his weight.

Proval put his hands in his pockets and leaned back on the heels of his boots. "If you don't want to risk the thorns, you can always fly up. Even mediocre wizards should be able to conjure that sort of spell."

And that was one more disadvantage of not being even a mediocre wizard. Hudson started up the tree, carefully placing each hand and foot. He wondered if Proval had ever seen anyone from his world fly up this tree, or whether he was just goading Hudson because he knew people from his world didn't have any magical abilities.

Hudson avoided the thorns for the first few branches. The farther he went up the tree, the harder it became. He kept brushing his knees and elbows into branches, and every time he did, thorns caught on his clothes, holding him tight. He had to yank himself free, and more than once he ripped the sleeves of his jacket. Better his jacket than his skin, he told himself.

As he climbed, the wind blew some of the smaller branches toward him, piercing the skin on his wrists and hands. Each time it happened, Hudson let out a yelp. Which—although he couldn't be sure—seemed to make Proval laugh. Once or twice Proval called out, "Careful not to fall!"

Hudson hoped this wasn't some horrible practical joke. If the box didn't lead anywhere and he had to climb back down this tree, he would not be happy.

Finally, after pricking and pulling himself over a dozen more branches, Hudson reached a platform and the dresser-size box that sat there. It was made of twisted tree branches, and leaves and thorns still covered many of them. The door was smooth— modern-looking, as though it belonged to Hudson's world instead of this one. Well, with one notable difference. A bird's nest protruded where the doorknob should have been. Its owner, a red-and-white-striped bird, squawked angrily at Hudson and flew away.

Three candy-cane-striped eggs sat in the nest. Hudson took them out so they wouldn't break, then twisted the bird's nest to open the door. He kept the door open with his foot, replaced the eggs, and waved good-bye to Glamora and Proval.

They waved back.

Hudson crouched his way inside the box, and as he said his address, the door closed shut behind him.

It was completely dark. He wondered again if this box would really take him home, or whether Proval and Glamora were playing a prank. Only one way to find out. Slowly, he got on his hands and knees and eased his way farther into the box. He still couldn't see anything. The floor under his hands felt smooth and cool. He took a few more crawling steps forward.

Hudson had never thought about the different kinds of

darkness before, but he knew them: The annoying black that happened when somebody accidentally turned off the light on you. The peaceful obscurity that came from shutting your eyes to go to sleep. And there was the pressing dimness—fear curling its edges—that happened when you had to walk somewhere alone in the night.

Hudson had never felt magical darkness before. It was a spinning sort of blackness that made him feel as if he were falling down and rushing upward, and he had no idea where he would land.

4

AFTER A FEW moments, the magical darkness faded into a general freaked-out blackness, which would have been worse except Hudson saw a crack of light ahead of him—the outline of a small door. He crawled forward, and his hand clanged into something. He scooted to the right and bumped into more things, all of them scattering and clanking in a scolding chorus. He had no idea what any of them were, and he lunged forward out of the door.

He found himself sprawled on his kitchen floor surrounded by pots and pans he'd knocked out of the cupboard.

He lay there, startled, and took deep breaths.

Bonnie sat at the table, holding the mixing bowl in her lap. She cocked her head with confusion when she saw him. "Hudson, what were you doing in the cupboard?"

How could he even begin to answer that question? He sat up and brushed himself off. A few little red leaves from the thorn tree fluttered to the floor. "So it turns out I was wrong about that compass," he said. "It was magic after all."

Bonnie's mouth dropped open. "Did it magic you into the cupboard?"

"It magicked me into Charlotte's world. I just came home through the cupboard." He pulled the now crumpled stem of catflower from his pocket and held it out. "I got your catflower."

Her eyes widened, and she grabbed the flower from his hand. "This is it?"

Hudson nodded. "I don't know how we're supposed to feed it to Sunshine. Maybe if we tear it up into pieces and . . ."

He didn't finish, because Bonnie had put the flower near the kitten's face. Sunshine opened her eyes, licked the flower several times, then chewed on the end. After a few moments of this, she purred and chomped down the whole flower. Then, as if she'd only just noticed how bedraggled she was, she set about giving herself a thorough lick-down.

"Look at that," Hudson said. "She's getting better already."

Bonnie petted Sunshine's head happily. "I knew Charlotte was telling the truth." Bonnie paused, apparently remembering the other things Charlotte had told her about Logos. "Were there unicorns?"

"Yep. I met two."

Bonnie's lips scrunched together, and she let out a huff of irritation. "I wanted to go and ride them, but you wouldn't let me. You said it was pretend."

Hudson did feel bad about it, when she put it that way. "The unicorns weren't as nice as you'd think. Actually, they were sort of snooty."

Bonnie's lips remained unhappily scrunched together.

"And I had to climb a thorny tree to get back here." He held up his hands so she could see the scratches the thorns had left across his palms. That's when he noticed the kitchen clock. He'd been gone for over an hour. "I'd better give Charlotte her compass back."

Before Bonnie could go on and on about how he'd made her miss riding a unicorn, Hudson slipped out the door and headed down the sidewalk to Charlotte's house. He hadn't gone far when Isabella and her friend Macy turned onto the sidewalk a little ways ahead of him. It was only then that he remembered about the basketball game. All the oddities of the past couple of hours had chased mundane things like basketball from his mind.

Normally, Hudson wouldn't have said anything to a group of girls on the sidewalk—especially if Isabella was one of those girls. But he felt the weight of the magic mirror in his pocket. It was a cool, gleaming disk full of confidence.

He wanted to take the mirror out of his pocket and check his appearance. Was he taller now? Stronger? His nose probably wasn't so wide, and his teeth were probably straight, too, which meant he wouldn't have to wear braces. His mom could stop saving money for them. Win-win, all the way.

He left the mirror in his pocket. He didn't want Isabella and Macy to glance over their shoulders and catch him staring at his reflection for no apparent reason.

Instead, he caught up with the girls. "Hey," he said, smiling. "Are you all going to the basketball game?"

Isabella gazed at him casually. She didn't seem to notice his new handsomeness. "Yeah. We promised Andy and Caidan we'd cheer for them."

Macy was holding her phone and texting someone. "I hope it doesn't last long. I don't know why boys get such a kick out of running around bouncing a ball."

"It's fun," Hudson said. He was a decent basketball player. Maybe now that he was taller, the other guys would ask him to play.

The group reached Charlotte's house. Hudson didn't stop. He could return the compass to her after the game. It would be safe in his pocket for an hour or so.

Isabella looked Hudson over questioningly, and he wondered if she'd finally noticed his recent switch to hotness. "What happened to your jacket?" she asked.

Hudson glanced down at his jacket. It was not only ripped in places, but it was also peppered with flecks of bark. He brushed those away. "I climbed a thorn tree. It messed up my clothes."

Isabella scrunched her nose. "Thorn tree? What's that?"

"And why would you climb one?" Macy added.

Hudson considered telling them the truth about Logos and quickly dismissed that idea. Good looks could only earn you forgiveness for so much craziness. Case in point: Charlotte. She was pretty enough, but the popular girls avoided her. And Andy and Caidan had made fun of her to her face today.

Besides, if Hudson told Isabella and Macy about Logos, they'd want to see the compass—maybe even use it—and it belonged to Charlotte.

"Uh, I was goofing around. You know, climbing stuff." Hudson wiped his jacket some more. His mom wouldn't be happy he'd ruined it. She'd just bought it for him.

"Is that how you scratched your hands?" Isabella asked.

The skin around his scratches was tinted an angry red, and the scratches stung a little, too. "Yeah," he said.

Macy shook her head. "I will never understand boys."

Isabella kept peering at his hands. "Those scratches look infected. Maybe you should put something on them."

"I will," Hudson said. "Later." He didn't want to go home now, not when he was having his first real conversation with Isabella. She had to have noticed by now the handsomeness oozing off him. Any moment now, she'd start flirting.

Macy stared at his hands, too. "Was there any poison ivy around? I walked through poison ivy once, and my legs got red like that."

"No." Hudson put his hands in his jacket pockets, so the girls would stop gaping at them. "Just thorns."

"If you say so." Macy clearly didn't believe him.

After that, Macy talked to Isabella about the social studies Civil War assignment. Macy thought it would be fun to dress up like a Southern belle for her report, and she wanted Isabella to go dress shopping with her.

Really, Macy thought boys didn't make sense? At least they didn't go on and on about hoop skirts.

When the group got to the park, the game had already started. People lined both sides of the court, sitting in the grass there. Some of them shouted out instructions to the players.

"Steal the ball! C'mon!"

"Make the shot!"

Out on the court, Andy dodged around another player and went for a layup. The ball swooshed effortlessly into the basket, and a cheer went up from the crowd on the far side.

Without saying good-bye to Hudson, Macy and Isabella walked off, heading toward a group of girls sitting in a cluster behind one of the baskets.

So much for the power of his new good looks. Hudson spotted Trevor and went to sit with him. Did the mirror even work? He slipped it out of his pocket, shifting it one way and then the other to look at his face. From what he could tell, he looked exactly the same. Wide nose and crooked teeth. Maybe the magic took a while to kick in. He put the mirror back in his pocket, watched the game, and forgot about it.

A half an hour later, Macy and Isabella made their way over to Hudson. He was so engrossed in the game he didn't see them until Isabella snapped out, "Hudson!"

He looked at her and gasped. Small red boils dotted both girls' faces and arms. "What happened to you?" he asked.

"That's what we want to know," Isabella said stiffly. "What plants did you tromp around in? Because whatever it was, we've got an allergic reaction to it."

Hudson checked his own arms. No spots. No boils, just the scratches on his hands. "It couldn't be from me," he said, and then stopped. He noticed faint pink spots blooming on Trevor's cheeks—the beginnings of boils.

Macy saw them, as well. "It *is* you! Trevor is getting them, too!"

Trevor put his hands to his face, worried. "What? I'm getting those ugly spots?" He held up his arms, revealing a batch of budding red marks. "Oh man," he moaned. "What did you do?"

"It isn't me," Hudson insisted. And then he noticed the people sitting on his other side. Every single one of them had spots sprouting on their faces and arms.

Isabella gave Hudson a squinty-eyed glare and put her hands on her hips. "If these scar, I will kill you."

"I don't have them," Hudson insisted, "so it can't be me. It must be something . . ." Then he realized what had happened, and he felt as if he'd been kicked in the stomach. Rex had said that once Hudson owned the magic mirror, he would be the most handsome person around.

And he was. Hudson was the most handsome, because he was the only one who didn't have boils erupting on his face. This was bad. Horrible, actually.

Hudson got to his feet, gulping hard. "I, um, I think I'd better go home." He dashed away from the court and sprinted the rest of the way out of the park. Why had Rex given him the stupid mirror? It wasn't a gift. It was a curse.

Hudson needed to get rid of it. Would throwing away the mirror get rid of everyone's boils? Did he need to break it? He wanted to but didn't dare. Maybe the mirror needed to be whole to reverse the curse.

How did this sort of magic work? His only hope was that

Charlotte would know what to do. She would help him—had to help him. He couldn't go to school if he gave everyone around him boils. He couldn't go anywhere.

Hudson didn't stop running until he reached Charlotte's house.

He was out of breath and panting when he rang her doorbell. Even after she opened the door, all he could do was gulp in air and mutter, "Charlotte . . ."

Her ponytail was more lopsided than it had been during school. It looked sort of like an auburn snake leaping off her head. She watched him curiously, as though a person panting on her doorstep might be some strange custom she didn't understand. "Hi, Hudson. Do you need something?"

"Yeah," he managed, and waved vaguely in the direction he'd come from. "Everybody is breaking out in boils. I think it's because of a mirror this guy from your land gave me." Hudson reached into his pocket, tugging the mirror free. "Shouldn't this thing come with a warning label?" Without waiting for her answer, he added, "How am I supposed to get rid of everybody's boils? They're all mad at me."

Charlotte tilted her head at him. "What?"

He started again, this time from the beginning. "I pushed the knob up on your compass—"

"Wait," Charlotte interrupted. "You went to Logos instead of Bonnie?" She let out the sort of sigh you give a toddler who has dressed himself and proudly put on his pants backward. "It was nice of you to go in your sister's place, but . . ." Instead of finishing the thought, she said, "Just tell me you brought back my compass."

"I did. Look, can you help me with the boils?"

Charlotte opened the door wider and motioned him inside. "You'd better tell me everything."

Hudson hadn't expected Charlotte's home to be like anyone else's, but he still was surprised. A potted tree stood in the middle of the living room. Not a fake silk tree as he'd seen demurely decorating the corners of other people's houses. This tree was about as tall as Hudson, with a half-dozen branches holding droopy royal-blue leaves. They hung limply from the branches like raindrops waiting to fall. It needed more sunlight, or water, or a bigger pot of dirt. Maybe a tree medic.

Across the room, a battered red couch sat in front of a dresser with a TV perched on top. Four framed photographs hung on the wall—one of a forest in Logos. Hudson recognized the multi-colored trees and white jellyfish flowers. The second picture showed a murky blue sea with waves crashing into a beach. The third was a picture of a white castle full of towers and turrets. The last was a close-up of a boot.

Charlotte sat down on one side of the couch. Hudson sat on the other side and told her the entire story.

When he finished, Charlotte took the mirror from his hand, fingering it like it had sharp edges. "I bet this is a troll gift. Those are always cursed." She turned the mirror over, squinting at the glass. "But if trolls were around, the compass should have warned you."

Hudson's stomach clenched. It already knew what his mind was still denying. "The compass did say BEWARE OF TROLLS a lot."

Charlotte blinked incredulously at him. "Wait a second—the

compass warned you, and you still didn't realize that Glamora, Proval, and Rex were trolls?"

Hudson's hands rose in frustrated protest. "How could I know they were trolls? They looked like normal people."

"Of course they looked like normal people," Charlotte said. "They use magic to disguise themselves. If trolls were easy to spot, you wouldn't need a magic compass to warn you about them, would you?"

In the fairy tales and movies, trolls were always big, monstrous, thudding creatures. "I thought the compass was just warning me that trolls were somewhere in the forest."

Charlotte shook her head in disbelief. "The schools here don't teach you anything important. The first thing people should know is to stay away from the wrong side of magic."

A feeling of dread settled into Hudson's chest. "So Rex gave me the mirror just to be a trollish jerk?"

"No, he gave it to you so you would have to come back and give him my compass." She straightened. "You can't do that, by the way." She handed Hudson the mirror and then held her hand out, palm up. "Give me my compass."

Hudson didn't. "So how do I get rid of the curse? Can I just break the mirror?"

"No, that would make everything worse. You would have to keep track of all the pieces, every sliver, to get rid of the curse." She got up from the couch, went to the dresser, and took a stack of bills from the top drawer. She handed them to Hudson, then sat down and held her hand out again. "Now you've got Bonnie's money back, so you need to return my compass." Hudson put the money in his pocket.

"Tell me how to get rid of the mirror. Once it's gone, I'll give you back your compass."

Charlotte let out a squeal of protest and slapped her hand down on the couch. "You can't hold my compass hostage! I only gave it to Bonnie as a favor."

Hudson folded his arms defiantly. "Yeah, about that—Bonnie doesn't even remember to look both ways before she crosses the street. Why would you send her to a place with trolls and giants and who knows what else?"

"Bonnie would have been fine, because she's pure in heart. The unicorns would have helped her and kept her safe. It's not my fault you're not pure in heart."

Hudson's mouth dropped open. "I accidentally took a swing at the unicorn. That doesn't make me blackhearted."

"You're not pure in heart." Charlotte sounded haughty. "Don't even deny it. And you'd better give me back my compass or I'll . . ." She broke off, frustrated, and looked like she might burst into tears. Her hands clenched at her sides. "Well, I won't do something worse to you, because the pure in heart don't take revenge like you're doing right now. But I'll tell my dad about this. And *he* might do something worse to you."

The conversation was not going in the direction Hudson wanted. He had the unsettling fear that if Mr. Fantasmo got angry, he might turn Hudson into a rabbit.

Hudson cleared his throat with new nervousness. "Can't you just tell me how to get rid of the troll curse? Once it's gone, I'll give you back the compass. Besides," he added, "you should want to help me. Any second now you're going to break out into boils."

Charlotte put her hand to her face. "I can't break out. My dad will realize I've done something." With a groan, she shot off the couch, ran across the living room, and disappeared down the hallway.

Hudson stared after her, not sure whether she was returning. After a few moments, he stood up and stepped tentatively into the hallway. "Charlotte?"

"I'll be right back," she snapped from behind one of the closed doors. "I'm putting on enchanted lotion to keep my skin clear."

Hudson went back to the living room and waited, looking around the room again. If the picture on the wall was the Forest of Possibilities, then the other pictures might be places the compass mentioned. The Sea of Life, Grammaria, and Gigantica. That would explain the close-up of the boot.

He was studying the castle picture when Charlotte came back. A blue sheen covered her skin. It looked like she'd smeared a thin layer of finger paint over herself.

"Well," Hudson said, "your dad won't notice anything different about you now."

"It's less painful than boils, and the protection lasts for a day." She'd brought out a large tube of ointment. She squeezed some onto her fingers, walked over to Hudson, and applied it to his hands. "Thorn-tree scratches will make your hands swell up like balloons if you don't treat them." Her touch was light, thorough, and for some reason made him blush.

"Thanks," he said, feeling all the guiltier for not giving her the compass back. "Can this medicine get rid of everyone's boils, too?"

Charlotte put the ointment on a side table by the couch. "Everyone's boils will fade away once you're no longer around."

Well, that was good news for the rest of the eighth grade. "So how do I get rid of a troll curse?" he asked again.

Charlotte walked to the couch and gingerly sat down so as not to get lotion on it. "There are only three ways. You can give the mirror to someone else and stick them with the curse, you can get a troll to take it back, or you can give it to a member of the Logosian royal family. They're born with a magic protection that absorbs troll curses and things like that."

Hudson thought about these options and began pacing in front of the tree as he tried to figure out a solution. "If I give the mirror to someone else . . ."

"That," Charlotte said pointedly, "is something a person with a pure heart wouldn't even consider. It's cruel to whoever gets the mirror and to everyone who comes in contact with him."

She was right, but Hudson wasn't willing to give up the idea so easily. "Couldn't I give it to some recluse who never went out? That way, I'll be rid of the mirror, and no one else will get hurt."

Charlotte lifted a blue eyebrow at him. "Do you know any recluses who never go out?"

"Um, no, although maybe I could find one on the Internet. . . ."

"You can't just send the mirror someplace. You have to physically give it to someone, tell him what it does, and he has to say he accepts the gift."

Rex had tricked Hudson into taking it by not being clear about how the mirror worked. It made him mad to think about it now, but not so mad that he wanted to face an entire village of trolls and demand that Rex take the mirror back. That was a meeting that probably wouldn't go well for Hudson.

He kept pacing. "So the best thing to do is to give the mirror to Logos royalty?"

"Logosian," Charlotte corrected.

"How do I find one?"

She sent him another pointed look. "Haven't you ever paid attention to my father's stories? Only two members of the royal family are left. King Vaygran, who's a tyrant, and Princess Nomira, who's missing."

"Missing how?"

Charlotte huffed in exasperation. "It's a good thing you only ran into trolls while you were in Logos. If King Vaygran's wizards saw the compass, they would have hauled you off to a dungeon. They know it belongs to my father."

Hudson tilted his head at her. "I thought you said the compass was yours."

Charlotte flushed, turning the lotion on her cheeks light purple. Instead of commenting on who actually owned the compass, she summarized what Hudson should have already known. "A year ago, when King Arawn died, his brother, Prince Vaygran, left his estate in the country and came to the castle. He said Princess Nomira was too young to rule and made himself regent king. Then, when she wasn't expecting it, he had his top wizard kidnap her and lock her up somewhere magical.

"Vaygran told the people he'd just hidden her in order to protect her until she was old enough to reign, but he won't ever let her out. My father knows. He was King Arawn's wizard and refused to work for Vaygran. That's why we had to come here." Charlotte looked down at her hands sadly. "To the awful Land of Banishment."

Hudson felt a twinge of guilt, which was quickly joined by several others, twinging guiltily around in his chest. No one at school had been understanding of Charlotte. But in their defense, how could they have known she'd told them the truth about Logos?

Hudson wanted to apologize, to show her there were lots of nice things about Texas. But he needed to get rid of the curse first. "Is there any way I can give the mirror to King Vaygran?"

She let out a scoff. "He wouldn't care about helping you. More likely, he'd think you were a spy sent by my father."

Hudson went back to pacing, a pointless walk that was getting him nowhere. "Is there some way I could convince the trolls to take the mirror back? Is there some way to trick them?"

She shook her head. "It's almost impossible to trick a troll. They can tell the things you're trying to hide. Besides, the trolls know you'll be desperate to get rid of the mirror, and they know you've got a powerful magic object—one that's not only a portal from this world, but one that also warns people about trolls. They'll only accept the compass or something just as important. I can't give you anything like that."

Hudson let out a groan. It was easy for Charlotte to shoot down his ideas. She wasn't the cursed one. "Then the only thing I can do is go back to the troll village and give them the compass."

Charlotte's head jerked up. "No, the only thing you can do is become a recluse, because you can't give away the compass."

He stopped pacing. "Why do you need it? You don't live around trolls anymore. What's the point of having a compass that warns about them?"

She stood and walked over to him, hands on her hips. "I'm going back someday—whether my father wants me to or not. Sooner or later, someone will stand up to King Vaygran and rescue the princess. Once Logos is safe, I'll need the compass to take me home." Charlotte held out her hand to Hudson. "So give it back."

He felt sorry for her. He really did. He promised himself that after he got rid of the troll curse, he would do his best to make sure people treated Charlotte nicely. Still, he didn't take the compass out of his pocket. "Look, I hate to break it to you, but Princess Nomira is probably dead. King Vaygran wouldn't want anybody around who could challenge his power."

Charlotte kept her hand outstretched. "King Vaygran has to keep the princess alive, because she's the only one who knows where the ruling scepter is." Her gaze drifted to the picture of the castle, and her eyes filled with sadness. "The scepter is the most powerful object in Logos. It can do all sorts of magic and counteract wizards' spells. It could even raise an army out of stones."

Hudson said the obvious: "Then why didn't Princess Nomira use it to keep Vaygran from stealing the throne?"

The sadness in Charlotte's eyes switched, traffic-light fast, to defensiveness. "Princess Nomira was ill with grief. Her mother died when she was a baby, so King Arawn was all she had. After his death, she was lost. She didn't know how to deal with the army, the guilds, the laws, or the taxes. When her uncle said he would help her rule, she believed him."

Charlotte paused, and her voice grew quieter. "Or maybe she was just too young and afraid to fight him off. But at least she had the sense to refuse to give him the scepter. She hid it before he took power and wouldn't tell him where she'd put it, no matter how many times he asked her. And then one day without warning, his wizard vanished with her. No one has seen her since."

Hudson considered this. "King Vaygran is ruling fine without the scepter, isn't he? What if he decided he didn't really need it and . . ."

Charlotte bristled. "The people wouldn't support him if he killed her. They can tell she's alive because her tree is still in the castle courtyard." Seeing that Hudson didn't understand, she added, "The royalty trees were a gift from the fairy queen to the people of Logos. Whenever a new ruler reigns, a magical tree grows in the castle courtyard. That way, the people can always tell how their leaders are doing. Before my father and I left Logos, we took a branch from Princess Nomira's tree. Charlotte gestured to the droopy blue tree in the middle of the living room. We planted it once we got here. If the princess wasn't still alive, both this tree and the one in the courtyard would have died."

Hudson gave the tree a closer look. The limp leaves seemed like a bad omen. "Her tree isn't doing very well."

Charlotte walked over to the tree and gingerly lifted one of the branches. "The princess must be sad . . . locked up where she doesn't belong . . . with no friends." Charlotte prodded a leaf upward, helping it stand. As soon as she let go, the leaf sagged again.

The longer Hudson stared at the tree, the more depressed it seemed. He could relate. If he didn't get rid of this mirror, he wouldn't ever be able to go to school again. When he was older, he couldn't have a regular job or date a girl. He'd go through life as an outcast, a wanderer. Maybe that was the deal with Bigfoot— he wasn't a mythological creature, just a guy who had made a stupid deal with trolls.

A worse thought came to Hudson. He'd been counting down the days until his dad came home from overseas. He'd imagined a hundred different reunions: going to the airport and seeing his dad emerge from the crowd—tall, confident, and wearing his Marine uniform. Or being at home and having his dad walk through the front door, drop his duffel bag on the floor, and hold his arms open wide. Or Hudson and Bonnie walking home from school and seeing him waiting on the sidewalk, grinning as they raced to him.

How could Hudson be around *any* of his family if he didn't get rid of the curse? He sat back on the couch, feeling defeated. "I don't want to give the trolls your compass, but I can't keep the mirror. It will ruin my life. What else can I do?"

Softly, Charlotte said, "We could find the princess."

"What?" Hudson asked, not sure he'd heard her right.

"We could rescue the princess," she said more firmly. "And then she could retrieve her scepter and use it to defeat King Vaygran. If we rescue her, she'll help you get rid of the troll mirror."

"How could we rescue her? You said Vaygran's wizard used magic to hide her."

Charlotte gazed at the tree, a cautious excitement growing in her expression. "Most people wouldn't be able to rescue her, but I know things about magic, and my dad has stuff we could use—so that's half the battle." She paused, correcting herself. "Actually, it's probably more like a quarter of the battle." She looked upward, still calculating, "Well, depending on where Princess Nomira is hidden, an eighth of the battle . . . maybe a sixteenth."

Hudson stopped her before she could do any more fractions. "I thought you couldn't go to Logos."

"It's not that I can't go—it's that it isn't safe for me." She bit her lip again, grazing it along the edges of her teeth. "My father and I lived at the castle, so King Vaygran knows what I look like. He'd love to capture me. But I could disguise myself. . . ."

Hudson scratched the back of his neck, thinking. Earlier that day, Charlotte had asked him if he would face danger to save someone he didn't know. What had he told her? Oh yeah, that he wasn't that stupid. "Wouldn't Vaygran have soldiers guarding the princess? And wouldn't those soldiers have weapons?"

"Maybe," Charlotte conceded.

"So actually, trying to rescue the princess is a really bad idea."

Charlotte's lips pursed into a scowl. Her brown eyes took on an angry look, and even the freckles peeking out from her blue lotion seemed suddenly offended. "Having boils follow you will brand you for life. But the compass isn't yours, so if you give it to the trolls, you'll be a thief and a coward—and that's a worse brand to carry."

Hudson nearly said, *Yeah, but it's still better than an untimely death.* She was right, though. If he cut off Charlotte's way back home, he'd never be able to undo it. And that would always weigh on him.

He let out a long sigh. What other choice, really, did he have? "Okay. We'll try to rescue the princess." He didn't even want to think about how dangerous it might be. "Where do we start and what do we do?"

Charlotte smiled, her eagerness making her stand straighter. "We'll need to pack some things. Go home and get a change of clothes, some food, and all your stuffed animals. Bring a sleeping bag and pillow, too. Hurry," she added, because he hadn't moved. "We've got to leave before my dad gets home."

"Right." Hudson stood up and trudged to Charlotte's front door. "I wouldn't want to face an angry wizard."

Even as Hudson said the words, he had the sinking feeling that angry wizards were exactly what he would face when he went to Logos.

5

FORTY MINUTES LATER, Hudson was back on Charlotte's doorstep with his backpack, sleeping bag, pillow, and a sack full of trail mix, granola bars, and peanut-butter-and-jelly sandwiches. He didn't know how long he would be in Logos, so he'd explained the situation to Bonnie. Their mother wasn't going to believe one word of it. And she'd be mad at Hudson for going somewhere without her permission. That was a grounding offense. He didn't even want to think about what the punishment would be for heading off to a dangerous foreign country to overthrow a tyrant.

Bonnie believed him about the troll curse. Just as he had finished packing things into his backpack, boils flared up on her skin, polka-dotting her face. She had been sitting on his bed while he told her about his trip to Logos.

He'd checked the clock on his dresser. It had been a half hour since he'd come home. Apparently, anyone who was around him for that amount of time would break out. "Sorry," he told her. "They'll fade away as soon as I'm gone."

He had expected Bonnie to get weepy about his leaving. After all, he might never return. His sister seemed to miss this point altogether. "You got to meet unicorns, and now you get to have an adventure and rescue a princess, and I bet you'll meet fairies, too."

"I brought you catflower," he reminded her. Sunshine was completely recovered and darting around his bedroom, pouncing on his shoes. A fierce battle with his shoelaces ensued.

"Yeah," Bonnie said, "but *I* was supposed to be the one who went, and you wouldn't let me, and now I have boils." She flounced off dramatically, an action that sent Sunshine scurrying under the bed.

Pure in heart. Right. Bonnie probably would have been trampled by the unicorns after she annoyed them to death.

Hudson rang Charlotte's doorbell, and she let him in with a smile. The blue lotion had dried into an opaque film.

"I'm almost done packing," she said, and headed across the living room to the hallway. "Do you have any more room in your backpack?"

"A little." He followed her down the hall and into a room. He expected it to be her bedroom, but it wasn't. Bookcases lined the walls and stood in the middle of the room, library-style. Instead of books, odds and ends covered the shelves: bowls, jars, boxes, a ball of yarn, a candle, a pair of glasses. Charlotte had made a pile of things on the floor—clothes, a sleeping bag, a pillow, and a half-dozen stuffed animals.

He raised an eyebrow at those. He'd always thought Bonnie was silly for sleeping with a bunch of stuffed animals. Charlotte was actually going to lug toys around Logos? He hadn't planned on taking any, even though Charlotte had included them in the list of things to bring. He was in middle school. He didn't sleep with teddy bears anymore.

Right before he'd left his bedroom, he grabbed a stuffed penguin Bonnie gave him last Christmas. Since Charlotte was willing to help him get rid of the mirror, he didn't want to start out the trip by not following her instructions.

"Show me what you brought," Charlotte told him.

He took out his clothes, a toothbrush and toothpaste—his mom would be proud of him for remembering that—the stuffed penguin, a sack full of food, a flashlight, a pocketknife, and a first-aid kit.

"You only have one stuffed animal?" Charlotte asked in disbelief.

"Yeah, I gave Bonnie the ones I had when I was little." Come to think of it, this was probably the reason his sister had chosen the stuffed penguin for a present. She knew that sooner or later he'd give it back to her.

"Oh," Charlotte said in that tone of voice girls get when they think something is really sweet. "That's so self-sacrificing."

He shrugged. At the moment, Bonnie didn't think he was such a great brother.

Charlotte picked up his first-aid kit, flipped it open, then set it aside. "You don't need to bring this. I've got better stuff. Which reminds me, I still need . . ." She walked along a row of shelves until she came to a metal box of candy hearts, the kind stores sold on Valentine's Day. "These." She added the box to her pile.

Hudson noticed a black calculator sitting with her things. It had symbols he didn't recognize. Must be calculus. He picked it up for a closer look. Why would she bring a calculator on their trip?

Charlotte saw him and snatched the calculator out of his hand. "Don't play with that. It's dangerous."

"Only if your teacher catches you with it during a test."

She didn't smile, and he realized she was serious. "It's not a calculator." She put it firmly back on her pile. "It's a calcu*later*. It's used to subtract or add to a person's memories. If you push the wrong buttons, you'll end up giving yourself amnesia."

"Really?" He couldn't decide whether that was frightening or cool. He regarded it with added interest. "Why would anyone make a calculater look like a calculator? Isn't that unsafe? Don't people make mistakes?"

"Most people don't have them." Charlotte rummaged through some jars on the shelves. "My dad made that one, and he likes to make magic objects look like ordinary things from your world. That way, there's less chance anyone will steal them." She pulled two small jars from the shelf, each no bigger than a cell phone. "Do you have room for these?"

"Will they break in my backpack?"

"Probably not. They're sturdier than they look."

He unzipped the front pocket of his backpack to make room. "What's in them?"

"Hope," she said. "We're bound to need it."

Jars full of hope. Okay. He wondered if she had boxes of optimism, too.

Charlotte took an intricate silver bell from the shelf. Tiny colored crystals studded its surface in swirling patterns.

"What's that for?" Hudson asked.

"Calling fairies. Otherwise, we'll never find one when we need one. I mean, when was the last time you saw one?"

"Um, never."

"Exactly." She slipped the bell into her jacket pocket, then took a tube of toothpaste from the shelf. She fingered it tentatively. "My dad will be mad at me for taking this, but I'm going to need it."

"Your dad will be mad at you for brushing your teeth?"

"It's not toothpaste. It's disguise paste. Plenty of people know I fled with my father when King Vaygran took power. I can't let anyone recognize me."

Hudson looked closer at the tube. What he'd thought was the word COLGATE actually read CLOAKGATE. Underneath that, it said, WITH FLOHIDE.

"I should disguise myself before we go," Charlotte decided. She left the room, and he figured she was getting a hat or a wig or something. Instead, she came back with an advertisement ripped from a magazine. It showed a girl with brown curls and hazel eyes sporting cotton-candy-pink lipstick. Charlotte squeezed a tiny dab of the paste on her hand and shut her eyes. Almost immediately, her red hair darkened and twisted into short brown curls. The blue lotion on her face disappeared, and her nose and chin changed shape to match the model's. When Charlotte opened her eyes, they were hazel. The only difference between her and the picture was the color of her lips. Instead of pink, they were vivid purple.

Hudson stared at them.

"What?" she asked. It was still Charlotte's voice. "Didn't I get it right?"

"Mostly right."

Charlotte picked up a small mirror from the shelf and looked at herself. She frowned, pursed her lips, then sighed and put the mirror back. "Well, at least no one will recognize me." She handed the tube of disguise paste to Hudson. "Can you put this with your things? My pack is going to be full."

Judging from the pile of stuffed animals on the floor, she would need her backpack and a suitcase, too. He slid the tube into his backpack's side pocket.

Charlotte took an orange calculator from the shelf and pointed it at him. He nearly dropped his backpack in alarm. "What are you doing? I thought you said that was dangerous?"

"This isn't a calculater," she said. "See, it's orange. It's just a compactulator. It shrinks belongings, so they're easier to carry." She pushed a button, and his sleeping bag and pillow shrank to the point where they looked like doll accessories.

"Cool." Hudson picked up the sleeping bag. It was lighter than he'd expected. The compactulator must change the weight, too.

Charlotte shrank her pile of stuff, then went back to the shelves to rummage for more things. While Hudson packed up her backpack, she opened a jewelry box full of silver four-leaf-clover necklaces. She slipped one around her neck and gave him another. "These are for warding off wizards' spells."

He put in on, tucking it into his shirt.

Charlotte took a small metal bar from a shelf and handed it to him. "Iron to give us extra strength."

He slid that into her backpack, as well.

She grabbed a plastic bag from the floor that he'd missed. "And some hair bands," she said, handing him those, too.

"What are these for?" he asked.

She lifted one eyebrow like it was a stupid question. "For putting up my hair."

"Right," he said. "I knew that."

Finally, when they'd packed up everything, Charlotte wrote her father a note telling him where they'd gone. She placed it on one of the branches of the tree and gave the room a last look. "I'm ready. Wait until we're both touching the compass, then pull the knob."

Hudson took the compass from his pocket and held it out to Charlotte. As soon as she touched it, he flicked the knob upward. The living room vanished, replaced by a panorama of multicolored trees.

The earthy scent of plants swirled around them, and the strange pianolike call of the birds chirped overhead. A dirt path at their feet wound haphazardly through the forest like an indecisive river.

How far away were they from the troll village? "Does the compass always take you to the same place?" Hudson asked, looking around.

"No, we could be anywhere in the Forest of Possibilities. And it's a bigger place than most people realize."

They both checked the compass face. It read FOREST OF POSSIBILITIES, GRAMMARIA, MERMAID LAKE, GIGANTICA. The needle rested against FOREST OF POSSIBILITIES.

"Why did the Sea of Life turn into Mermaid Lake?" he asked.

"It didn't. The compass shows you which lands are closest. We landed in a spot that was nearer to the Mermaid Lake than to the Sea of Life."

"It's not showing the warnings," Hudson said. "Does that mean there's nothing dangerous around?"

"No, it just means there's no trolls, giants, tyrants, or drowning hazards around. The compass only warns you about the most troublesome thing in each land."

Charlotte took the compass from Hudson, tilting it to better see the face. "Show us the way to Princess Nomira."

Hudson watched the compass. Nothing happened. The needle didn't budge.

"Is it supposed to answer back?" Hudson asked.

Charlotte let out a snort of laughter. "Of course not. Compasses don't talk. The needle isn't moving because it doesn't know the answer." As though to prove her point, she asked, "Which way is Grammaria?"

The needle swung to point at the pathway in front of them.

Hudson felt a flush of heat creep into his cheeks. "Well, how am I supposed to know how the compass works? Everything is so weird here."

This made Charlotte snort again. "It's your world that's a weird shadow of mine."

"A shadow?" Hudson repeated, vaguely affronted.

Charlotte set off down the pathway toward Grammaria, and Hudson kept pace beside her.

"Our worlds have lots of similarities," she said. "But my world came first, so yours must be the copy—the nonmagical version."

"How do you know your world came first?" He kept his gaze on the trees, watching for anything out of the ordinary—which was hard to do in a world where everything seemed out of the ordinary.

"You need words to create things, and that's what Logos is based on. Words."

Hudson wasn't sure he could follow her logic, let alone refute it. How could anything be based on words?

"My dad thinks that your world was populated by people who were banished from mine. Sort of like the prison colony in Australia. It's natural for you people to want to copy Logos."

"We don't want to copy your world," Hudson said. "We don't even know about it."

"Most of you don't," she agreed. "Can you imagine the people who would pour into Logos if they knew?"

Knew about what? Hudson wondered. *The trolls? The giants? The tyrant king and his evil wizards? Yeah, there'd be a real rush.* "So how are we going to find the princess?"

"We'll need to ask one of the magical folk to help us, someone who can see through wizard spells."

"Okay." Hudson shifted his backpack to make it more comfortable. "Who would know where she is?"

Bluebirds flew across their path and disappeared into a nearby blue tree, blending in with the leaves. "The Dust Might is an expert on hidden things. He probably knows where she is."

"The dust mite?" Hudson repeated. "Aren't those tiny bugs that get into your mattress and eat dead skin?"

"In your world they're tiny," she said. "In Gigantica they're really big."

Great. The last thing he wanted was to go talk with a huge creepy bug that lived on dead skin.

"The problem with the Dust Might," Charlotte went on, "is you never know whether he'll help you. He might or he might not. He might also decide your skin is dead enough for his tastes and you look really appetizing."

"I don't think we should go to Gigantica," Hudson said. "Isn't there someone smaller and less violent who could help us? How about the mermaids?"

Charlotte rolled her eyes. "Guys always want to talk to the mermaids."

Hudson shrugged. "It's just a suggestion."

Another eye roll. "Mermaids don't know anything except how to apply lip gloss. They're incurable flirts."

Incurably flirting mermaids didn't sound like such a bad thing, but Hudson didn't say this. Charlotte obviously didn't like mermaids, and besides, he was here to find the princess and get rid of the mirror, not to socialize with new species.

Charlotte looked off into the distance, thinking. "The castle courtyard in Grammaria has magical statues that can answer questions, but King Vaygran and his wizards live in Grammaria. What if someone recognizes me?"

Hudson gestured to her brown curls. "You're disguised."

"My voice is still the same. And besides, wizards have revealing powder. It counteracts disguise paste."

Hudson looped his finger through his silver four-leaf-clover necklace. "I thought these protected us from wizard spells."

Charlotte shook her head. "Revealing powder isn't a spell. It's a magical substance. Our necklaces prevent wizards from turning us to stone, or into beetles, or levitating us so we can't escape. Things like that."

"Wizards sound like fun guys."

A wind blew through the trees, and their leaves shimmered in a rainbow of colors. Pinwheel flowers along the path whirred and spun in the breeze.

Charlotte paid no attention to them. "Sometimes the king's wizards sprinkle revealing powder on people who come into the castle courtyard, checking for enemies or criminals." Her gaze shot to his. "Hudson, you haven't committed any crimes, have you?"

He tilted his head in disbelief. "Yeah, Charlotte. Every once in a while, when the mood strikes me, I hot-wire a car and hold up a few convenience stores."

"I asked," she said pointedly, "because revealing powder not only strips away any disguises you have, it also lists any crimes you've committed on your forehead."

"How does it know what crimes you've committed?"

"It's magic," she said in a tone that indicated that the answer was obvious.

He wanted to say, *That wasn't a stupid question where I come from.*

Instead he said, "I haven't committed any crimes, so I can go to the castle courtyard alone. No one will recognize me."

"True," she said, still hesitant, "but you might mess things up." She held up a hand to ward off his protest. "Nothing personal. You're from the Land of Banishment, which means you don't think clearly."

This from Charlotte, the girl who thought you could buy happiness in a soda pop bottle. "I think clearly," he said.

"How many times did the compass tell you to beware of trolls?"

Fortunately, she didn't actually expect an answer to that question, because he didn't want to give it.

A rumble of footsteps sounded in the forest behind them, and Charlotte turned toward the noise. "Oh, good. Unicorns have come."

Hudson didn't turn to them right away. He was afraid they would be the same unicorns he'd seen before. He didn't want to face those ones, or find out if they remembered him.

Charlotte waved her hand happily. "Huzzah, noble unicorns!"

Hudson slowly turned. Two unicorns trotted toward them, manes flowing, horns glinting like crystal in the sunlight. A gray one and a tawny one, like before. Hudson shifted so he stood behind Charlotte.

The gray unicorn gave his mane a particularly dramatic swish. "Welcome to the Forest of Possibilities, fair purple-lipped maiden. What is your quest?" Both unicorns came to a halt in front of Charlotte. Up close, the unicorns' coats shone, glimmering silver on the gray unicorn and gold on the tawny one.

Charlotte curtsied. "We wish to find Princess Nomira and free her."

The gray unicorn gave a whinny that almost sounded like laughter. "A valiant, if not foolishly hazardous quest. I can tell you're pure in heart. We shall gladly carry you through the forest."

Charlotte curtsied again, making her brown curls bob up and down. "We would be so grateful for a ride to Grammaria. May I have the honor of your names?"

"I am Cecil the Silver," the gray unicorn said, and motioned his horn toward the tawny unicorn. "This is my brother, Nigel the Gold."

Definitely the same unicorns. Maybe if Hudson didn't say anything, they wouldn't remember him.

The tawny unicorn addressed him. "And what is your name and quest?"

Hudson bowed so low he nearly tipped his backpack over his shoulders. "I'm Hudson," he mumbled. "I'm helping Charlotte."

Both unicorns lowered their heads, examining him. Cecil sniffed near his shirt. "Say, aren't you that bloke we saw earlier—the one who took a swing at me?"

"Um, sorry about that." Hudson hurriedly added, "I'm a lot purer now."

The unicorns tilted their heads toward each other, conferring in quiet voices. "A person doesn't change from impure to pure so rapidly," Cecil said.

"It's possible, but not probable," Nigel agreed.

Hudson tried to catch their eye. "I've reformed. Really."

"Mark my word," Cecil said, ignoring him. "If we take the boy, he'll be nothing but trouble. Human boys are always throwing rocks and setting things on fire."

"Rude behavior will get you nowhere in life," Nigel added. "And it especially won't get you anywhere on a unicorn's back."

Cecil glanced at Hudson out of the corner of his eye. "He's with the girl, though. She must need him for something, or she wouldn't have brought him."

Hudson cleared his throat. "I won't throw anything. And we didn't even bring matches." Which, come to think of it, was probably an oversight on their part. Wouldn't they need to make a campfire at some point?

Nigel made one of the snorting noises horses make. "He probably came because he's hoping for a reward from the princess. The impure only go on quests if they've something to gain."

Hudson opened his mouth to protest, to say he'd never even thought about a reward, but it wasn't quite true. Getting rid of the troll mirror was his reward.

"Charlotte needs my help," he emphasized, and looked to her for support.

"It's true," Charlotte put in. "He's, um . . . carrying some of my things."

Neither unicorn paid attention to them. "We might as well carry him," Nigel said. "Otherwise, she'll have to wait at the edge of the forest for him. And besides, if we're attacked by a dragon, I'll buck him off. That way the dragon will be too busy devouring him to come after us."

"Hey," Hudson said, then stopped himself from protesting more. He didn't want to walk all the way to the edge of the forest.

The unicorns turned back to them. Nigel swished his tawny tail. "We agree to carry the boy, as well."

"Thanks," Hudson said stiffly.

Cecil bent down on one knee so Charlotte could take hold of his silvery mane and pull herself onto his back.

Hudson waited for Nigel to do the same. The unicorn only huffed out a breath. "I don't kneel before the impure. You'll have to take hold of my horn." Nigel lowered his head so the long horn pointed at Hudson's waist.

"Okay." Hudson took hold of the horn. It was as smooth as a polished stone and felt as solid. "How is this going to—" He didn't finish. Nigel tossed his head back, flinging Hudson upward through the air. Startled, Hudson let go of the horn. He flipped over the unicorn's neck and landed on his back, stomach down and facing the wrong way.

The breath was knocked from Hudson's lungs. For a moment he couldn't do anything except groan and lie there.

"Hmph," Nigel said. "And to think you took a swing at me. I daresay we know who would have won that fight."

Hudson didn't reply. Slowly, he pulled himself upright. Nigel didn't wait for Hudson to get situated before he started down the path, and Hudson slid one way and then the other as he turned around.

"Hold on tightly," Nigel told him.

Hudson nearly fell and grabbed onto Nigel's mane. "I'm trying."

"Trying and bothersome, but I suppose I have to put up with you."

When Hudson was finally able to get his balance, he didn't let go of Nigel's mane. He wouldn't put it past the unicorn to buck him off, even if a dragon wasn't around.

Charlotte and Cecil were trotting in front of them at a fast pace. Charlotte began singing, and the melody drifted back to Hudson, clear and strong. He didn't know the tune, but it was nice. Happy. He'd never realized she had such a pretty voice.

"Well," Nigel said. "Aren't you going to sing for me?"

"I thought unicorns only liked to hear girls sing." In fairy tales, a maiden's song could tame a unicorn.

"Girls usually have more pleasing voices," Nigel said. "However, I was giving you the benefit of the doubt. Do you know any ballads?"

Hudson didn't usually sing in front of other people, but if it would put Nigel in a better mood, he'd give it a try. "I only know rock songs and Christmas carols."

Nigel neighed disapprovingly. "Rock is so uncivilized. Carols, on the other hand, have a festive ambience to them. Let's have one of those."

Whatever it took to make the horse happy. Hudson took a deep breath and sang out, *"You know Dasher and Dancer and Prancer and Vixen—"*

"We've met," Nigel said.

"Comet and Cupid and Donner and Blitzen—"

"They cheat at cards, you know."

"But do you recall the most famous reindeer of all?"

"According to Donner, he is. And he'll tell you so, too."

This was not going how Hudson had expected. Nigel's commentary kept making him falter. Louder, Hudson sang, *"Rudolph the red-nosed reindeer had a very shiny nose, and if you ever saw it, you would even say it glowed."*

"How unfortunate. Did he see a vet? Sounds like a glowworm infection."

"All of the other reindeer used to laugh and call him names."

"Pity. Some reindeer have atrocious manners."

"They never let poor Rudolph join in any reindeer games."

Nigel let out a bray. "Who would want to? I just told you those blokes are terrible cheaters. Knaves, every single one of them."

Hudson couldn't remember the next line. The image of a bunch of reindeer sitting around a table cheating at poker was stuck in his mind. "Um . . ." he said.

"Listen," Nigel broke in. "You've given singing a go. Unfortunately, it's not where your talents lie. And aren't carols supposed to be about beautiful things? Who wants to hear about mean-spirited reindeer? If you don't mind, I'll listen to Charlotte for a bit."

Nigel galloped to catch up with his brother, then trotted beside him quietly. Hudson was only a little offended. He liked hearing Charlotte sing better, too. She matched her tune to the clomping of the unicorns' hooves so they sounded like drumbeats. Several black-and-white-striped birds fluttered over, blending their pianolike chirps with the melody.

The group traveled through the forest for hours this way. While Charlotte sang, she braided Cecil's mane. She knew songs about the beauty of the mountains in Gigantica, the perils of the waves in the Sea of Life, the mysteries of the Forest of Possibilities, and how happy the people were under King Arawn's rule. Those songs made her sad. She sang a ballad about the goodness of unicorns, and Nigel and Cecil made her repeat it a half-dozen times, singing along as she did.

Hudson learned many things about unicorn-back riding. Most of them had to do with how uncomfortable unicorn backs were. Hours of jostling up and down made his legs ache.

The unicorns didn't stop trotting. Not even when night blackened the forest into shifting shadows. Hudson was glad the unicorns could see in the dark, although he sure couldn't. More than once, Nigel went under a low-hanging branch that whipped into Hudson's face. Nigel always called out, "Sorry, young chap," afterward, but somehow Hudson doubted he was.

Really, with the way fairy tales went on and on about how awesome unicorns were, you wouldn't expect them to hold grudges.

Finally, the trees thinned, and Hudson saw a few lights glowing in the distance. Grammaria.

Charlotte looked at the lights longingly. "I'm home."

"Home, sweet home," Hudson said, to let her know he understood.

"No," she said. "Home, dangerous home."

6

HUDSON AND CHARLOTTE dismounted at the edge of the forest. Cecil and Nigel wouldn't go any farther toward the city than that. Unicorns had a policy of staying away from places where people congregate. This was why unicorns were never seen in cities, stadiums, or stores on Black Friday.

Charlotte kissed both unicorns on their noses. "We appreciate your help."

Hudson added, "Thanks for bringing us here."

Nigel eyed Hudson warily. "Take care of Charlotte. It's the least you can do."

"I will," Hudson said. "Seriously, I'm a pure-in-heart sort of guy."

The unicorn let out a disbelieving whinny. "Conduct yourself that way, then. Remember what I said before: Rude behavior will get you nowhere in life." With that, the unicorns turned and disappeared back into the tree cover.

Charlotte and Hudson left the forest and tromped in the direction of Grammaria. They still had to cross through farmland to reach the city walls; fields of crops patchworked the land in front of them. It would be at least an hour's walk before they reached the city gates. They headed down a trail that snaked through the fields, and the night seemed oddly quiet now that Charlotte wasn't singing.

A multitude of stars shone above them, and a fat, round moon slept high in the sky, full and self-satisfied. Hudson couldn't tell what sort of plants grew in the fields. They looked dark and stalky. When the wind blew through them, they made a soft hushing sound, like they didn't want anyone to disturb their rest.

Charlotte walked easily, without evident soreness, which told Hudson that she was used to riding horses, or unicorns, or whatever else people rode here. Hudson's legs ached so badly it was hard for him to walk at all. His tailbone felt like someone had kicked it.

Charlotte glanced over her shoulder and noticed he wasn't keeping up. "Do you need some painkiller?"

"Yeah, that would help."

She pulled the metal box of candy hearts from her backpack, shook one into her palm, and handed it to him. "Here you go."

He stared at the little heart in disbelief. "Valentine's candy?"

"It's a piece of love. That's the best kind of painkiller there is."

"Love," he repeated. She had told him to leave his first-aid kit, and she'd taken candy hearts instead. He made himself walk forward again, even though his legs protested.

"I gave you a pink one. That's a mother's love. It's some of the best."

He put it in his mouth, even though he didn't believe the candy would do anything. It was sweet with an edge of tanginess, like orange juice and 7-Up mixed together. Surprisingly, the pain in his legs faded.

Hudson took the candy out of his mouth and examined it the best he could in the dark. "I thought this was something from my world, but it's magic, isn't it?"

"Yeah." Charlotte picked up her pace again. "Love is always magic."

He put the candy back in his mouth. Part of him thought he should save the rest of it until later, just in case he needed more painkiller. The heart tasted so good, though. It made him think of the times his mom had tucked him into bed and kissed his forehead.

Hudson and Charlotte walked past a few darkened cottages scattered amid the farmland. Some were stone and some were wood. All of them had an abundance of bushes, flowers, and ivy growing up walls and crawling over fences. The leaves rustled in the breeze, gently patting the homes like a mother calming a child at bedtime.

When Hudson and Charlotte were almost through the fields, he realized that the dark stripe that ran in front of Grammaria's walls was a river. It wrapped around the city, keeping out invaders, robbers, and wandering eighth-grade students.

A few minutes later, Hudson and Charlotte's path joined one that led directly to the city gates. A sign there read:

WELCOME TO GRAMMARIA,
the home of
KING VAYGRAN THE MAGNIFICENT,
*the leader who brought Logos
peace, prosperity, and unity.*

Charlotte scowled at the sign, and her eyes grew hard.

"I've got a pen," Hudson said. "Do you want me to cross something out?"

"It's all true," she said, still frowning at the sign. "When King Vaygran took the throne, he decreed that war was unlawful. No one disagreed with that. No one wanted to support war. He declared that all weapons except his own were illegal and had his soldiers gather up the rest."

"Oh," Hudson said. He could already tell this story wouldn't end well.

"King Vaygran's next decree outlawed poverty. No one argued with that, either. Maybe because they didn't have weapons anymore. Since poverty was illegal, the poor were rounded up and sent away."

"And unity?" Hudson asked, with a sick feeling running through him.

Charlotte turned away from the sign and strode down the path again. "He decreed that the country must be unified, which basically means everyone has to agree with him. Anyone else is breeding disunity."

"No one stands up to him?"

She shook her head. "Some people actually think the king has given them peace, prosperity, and unity."

"What about the people who don't? Why don't they do something?"

Charlotte let out a grunt, and her speed picked up with her anger. "The Land of Scholars tried."

"What happened?"

"Now it's called the Land of Desolation."

They reached the edge of the river. Lights along the top of Grammaria's walls illuminated its crenellated outline and the towers that rose up at the corners.

"The drawbridge has already been raised," Charlotte said, "so you'll need to take a ferry over."

On the ride through the forest, when Charlotte had taken a break from singing, she'd given him instructions about what to do once he got inside. He would make his way to the castle, walk across the courtyard, then go to a walled garden on the left side of the castle. A guard stood at the garden's doorway collecting an entrance fee of one silver coin. People came from all over the kingdom to visit the garden and sample the fruit from the compliment trees there.

Hudson was supposed to ignore the trees. Very often, after someone tried one piece of fruit, they wanted another, and another, until they stayed in the garden for hours—days even—listening to compliments. "It's always flattering to find out that the trees think well of you," Charlotte had said, "but keep in mind that trees think well of everybody. Trees aren't that discerning."

Magical statues were spread throughout the garden, each one

in the shape of a different animal. If a person laid a gold coin near the animal, he could ask it a question, and it would answer.

Many people asked their questions of the owl because he was wise. Others chose the wolf because wolves, living in packs as they did, understood social issues. The deer was a favorite, too. She knew answers to questions about grace and beauty. Mostly, though, people asked their questions to the lion. He was the most powerful animal and sat regally in the center of the garden.

"Don't ask the lion," Charlotte told him. "Most of the time he doesn't know what he's talking about, but he always thinks he's right anyway. And if he doesn't know the answer, he just makes up something that sounds good."

"The lion is lying," Hudson said, committing this piece of information to memory.

"You want to find a tiny statue of a bee. She's near the lion's tail—so small most people don't notice her. If anyone knows where Princess Nomira is, the bee will, and she'll tell you the truth."

This seemed like a lot of trust to put in an insect. "Why is the bee smarter than the deer, owl, wolf, or lion?"

"Bees aren't showy," Charlotte said. "They go everywhere, getting their jobs done, without anyone really paying attention to them. My father says bees are like common sense. Everybody takes it for granted, and few people use it."

Hudson thought this over. "We should ask where the royal scepter is, too. We could use it to free the princess."

Charlotte shook her head. "We only have one gold coin. And besides, wherever Princess Nomira hid the scepter, she most likely used its magic to ensure that only she could retrieve it. Once we free her, she'll know how to find it, and she can use it to defeat King Vaygran."

Now Hudson regarded the sprawling city walls and hoped he could locate the magic bee in the darkness. Charlotte had already told him he couldn't use his flashlight. It would brand him as a stranger from the Land of Banishment, and people would ask why he was there. She had no confidence in his ability to come up with a believable alibi.

Charlotte opened her backpack and gave Hudson the silver coin he needed for the guard and the gold coin to lay by a statue. She also took out a small bottle. "Shake it when you need some light. It's full of hope."

He took the bottle. "I'd feel better if this were full of matches."

"Matches burn out after a few seconds. Hope lasts longer."

He turned the bottle one way and then the other. "It looks empty. Does that mean we're hopeless?"

"I hope not."

While he slipped the bottle into his jacket pocket, Charlotte went through her backpack again, this time taking out the silver bell and two marbles. "These are muselings for the ferry." She handed him a cloudy red one. "Use this one to return back here."

Charlotte rang the bell softly, and it made a sound like an airy laugh that tumbled through the night air. In a quiet voice, she called, "We need a ferry to cross the river!"

Or at least he thought that's what she said. He didn't see a boat on the riverbank anywhere. Instead, something small and glowing zipped past him. It flew over to Charlotte and hovered in front of her face.

Hudson gawked at the thing, not quite sure he was seeing right. The image didn't change. A girl who was smaller than his hand floated in the air, her bright white wings fluttering. She had dark blue hair that hung past her shoulders, and her dress looked like it was made from a filmy fishtail. Charlotte had called a *fairy*, not a *ferry*.

A tiny pad of paper and a pen no thicker than a piece of yarn appeared in the fairy's hands. "One passenger or two?"

"One," Charlotte said. "And he'll be returning tonight."

The fairy marked something on her paper. "First class or economy?"

"I can pay one museling each way," Charlotte said.

"Economy." The fairy made another mark on her paper. When she finished, she slid her pen behind her ear, ripped off the paper, and dropped it into Charlotte's outstretched hand. The pad of paper disappeared from the fairy's hand, replaced by a wand. She flicked it at the marble in Charlotte's palm, and the museling rose up like a soap bubble, shrinking as it flew over to the fairy. When the museling hovered in front of her, the fairy grabbed it and popped it into her mouth. She smiled and glowed brighter.

Still smiling, the fairy zipped over to Hudson. "Welcome to Fairy Riverside Travel," she chimed. "We hope you have a safe trip and enjoy your time in the city of Grammaria. Remember to watch for predators, mischief, and magic. When you're ready for your return trip, just ring the bell for assistance."

Charlotte handed Hudson the bell, and he put it in his pocket. "What was that about predators?"

Instead of answering, the fairy waved her wand at him. His vision went foggy for a moment, and he felt himself shrinking, falling. Alarmed, Hudson let out a yell. Instead of his voice, a high-pitched noise came from his throat. He flung his arms out wide to catch himself and found he had no arms. In their place, two dark wings beat against the air, propelling him upward. He was a bird now. *A bird.* No. This absolutely couldn't be happening.

He looked at Charlotte to see if she was as surprised—as outraged—by this change as he was. She calmly fluttered her hand in the direction of the castle. "You only have five minutes until you transform back. You've got to hurry."

If birds could growl, he would have. Instead, he let out an angry chirp and headed across the river.

Really, there are some things a person should be warned about. Being turned into a bird was on that list.

Below him, the river didn't seem to move at all. It was a placid, dark street. He soared higher into the air to make it over the city walls. The wind rushed around him, holding him aloft. He felt light and sleek as he sped over the city.

Flying might have been fun if he didn't have to worry about how long he'd been up in the sky. Had a minute already passed? Down below him, rows of homes and shops spread out. Roads snaked between them, made visible by the lantern posts that dotted the way. A few people were out on the streets coming and going. They looked like the troll villagers, wearing the same sort of bright medieval clothes and elaborate hats. He saw one woman who seemed to be carrying a wedding cake on her head.

Hudson zoomed downward, maneuvering himself into one

of the city's roads that headed toward the castle. The lower to the ground he was, the less his fall would hurt when he changed back to his human form.

He read the signs on the buildings he passed. One outside an armory read SHOOT THE BREEZE HERE. The words over a restaurant door read GRAMMARIA'S BEST REST-A-RANT.

Well, it was nice to know rants needed a rest, too.

A shop window displayed multiple versions of the word *good*. There were puffy goods, sleek black goods, tiny glass goods, and thick wooden goods. A sign above the shop door read THE BEST GOODS: WHEN OTHER WORDS JUST AREN'T GOOD ENOUGH.

What a peculiar place Charlotte had come from.

The castle drew closer. In another minute, he would reach the courtyard. Two old men were slowly shuffling down the middle of the street, and Hudson pushed upward and went over them. It was then that he transformed back into himself. Arms replaced wings, and he fell, tumbling to the ground right in front of the men's feet. For a moment, Hudson just lay there sprawled out, the air knocked from his lungs.

One of the old men peered down at him curiously. "That boy just fell from the sky."

The other man cocked his head. "This is exactly the sort of thing I've been talking about. Since King Vaygran took the throne, nothing's been right. Now it's raining boys." He looked up warily, holding his hand over his head as though he might be deluged by a downpour of children.

Hudson didn't say anything. By the time he'd caught his breath, the two men had ambled around him, still mumbling complaints.

With his arms still stinging from his fall, Hudson stood and brushed himself off. Nothing appeared to be broken. Besides a couple of dirty spots he'd gotten when he'd hit the ground, his clothes were exactly as they had been before he'd been turned into a bird. He felt his pocket. The bell and coins still sat there. The bottle wasn't broken.

He set off down the street, forcing himself to run. The sooner he finished this task and got away from King Vaygran's city, the better.

Finally, he reached the castle courtyard. He had never seen a real castle before, and he couldn't stop staring. Its white stone towers pierced the night sky. A large balcony ran along the front side, a place for the king to address his subjects. Underneath the balcony, two huge doors led into the castle. It should have been too dark to see much detail on the building, but the stone glowed with its own inner light. Carvings lined each arched doorway and window, swirls and letters mixing together. The inscription above them read WORDS CREATE.

The courtyard spread out in front of the castle, paved in the same white stone. A circular garden area stood in the back of the courtyard, and two trees grew there: a huge steel-colored one with crooked, grasping branches, and a smaller, droopier tree with royal-blue leaves. It was a larger version of the tree growing in Charlotte's living room: Princess Nomira's.

Hudson walked to it and ran his hand along a low branch. It felt like bumpy velvet. He petted one of the wilting leaves. Perhaps he'd been in this strange land too long, because he couldn't resist leaning closer and whispering, "Don't worry. We're coming to find you." He never would have talked to a tree back home.

He looked at the bigger tree again, at its many crowded branches. He supposed it must be King Vaygran's tree. The thought made him keep a wary distance. He was almost afraid one of its long branches would reach out and grab him.

Hudson made his way down the courtyard and around the left side of the castle until he came to a walled garden. Lantern posts lit up the area so the treetops poking over the wall were visible. Brightly colored fruit weighed down their branches. What, he wondered, did turquoise fruit taste like? While he and Charlotte had ridden through the forest, he'd eaten a couple of sandwiches, but all the walking and flying had made him hungry again.

He saw the arched gate that led into the garden and strode up to a guard sitting in a chair in the doorway. He was a big man, dressed in silver armor with a large yellow plume that stuck straight out of his helmet. His eyes were shut in sleep, his head tilted down so his bushy gray beard lay tangled against his chest. A soft snore rattled his lips.

Hudson cleared his throat. "Excuse me."

The man didn't wake, didn't even stir. His beard twitched with every snore.

"Hello?" Hudson said a bit louder.

He still didn't wake.

Hudson gently nudged the guard's shoulder. "I need to go inside the garden."

The man stayed firmly asleep.

Hudson supposed he could just walk in, but that was probably illegal. The last thing he needed was to get in trouble before he and Charlotte had even started searching for the princess. He reached into his pocket. He could leave the silver coin on the man's lap, then go through the gate.

As soon as the coin was out of Hudson's pocket, the guard jolted awake and held out his hand.

Hudson was so startled he nearly dropped his coin. "Sorry, I thought you were asleep."

"I was," the man said gruffly. "There was no point waking up, was there, until you had money to pay."

"Um, I guess not." It seemed like the polite thing to say. He dropped the coin in the man's outstretched palm.

The man slipped Hudson's coin into his pocket. "This isn't the place for guessing. If you want to throw around guesses, you can do that at the economic advisers' policy meeting tomorrow."

"Oh. Um, I just want to go to the garden." Hudson edged away from the guard and went through the gate before the guard spoke to him again.

Things were so odd in this place he wouldn't have been surprised by anything he found in the garden. Umbrellas and lollipops could have grown next to the bushes.

For the most part, the garden seemed normal enough. Pathways led through rows of trees. Bushes and flowers were planted in colorful arrangements. Some of the flowers glowed like nightlights, and dandelions kept puffing out their seeds in firework-like explosions, but the rest of the plants behaved respectably.

Hudson walked by the statue of the deer. She was a beautiful bronze statue, so lifelike that she even had sculpted eyelashes. She turned her head and blinked at him with soft eyes. He didn't stop to talk.

Farther down the path, Hudson came across a silver wolf statue the size of a Great Dane. The statue perked up its ears and barked playfully. Hudson waved at the dog and walked on. He didn't see the owl statue at first. As he walked under a tree with fruit like a popcorn ball, a voice called down, "Who?"

"What?" Hudson asked, and looked up. A statue of a white marble owl sat perched on a tree branch above him.

The owl surveyed him with large eyes. "Witch."

"Where?" Hudson asked, spinning around to check behind him. He didn't see anything. Then he realized the owl had probably meant "Which."

"When?" the owl asked, and then added, "How?" He cocked his head sideways. "I know the answer to all those questions if you have a gold coin."

"No thanks," Hudson said. "I'm looking for the bee."

The owl lifted his head haughtily. "Be that way."

Or maybe the owl meant "Bee, that way." It was hard to tell in this place. Hudson mumbled, "Thanks," in case the owl was being helpful instead of offended, and then walked down the path again.

He kept noticing the fruit hanging from the trees. Charlotte had told him not to eat any fruit from the compliment trees, because eating it might distract him, but that didn't mean he couldn't pick some to eat tomorrow. The food they'd brought with them would run out soon.

He walked under a tree with red-and-white-striped fruit. It smelled like Italian food—manicotti or spaghetti. Hudson ran his finger over one on a low-hanging branch. It was bumpy but not messy. He plucked off two pieces of fruit and put them in his jacket pockets.

The next tree had pink fruit that smelled like snow cones. He added a couple of those to his pockets. He did the same with a fruit that smelled like french fries. Even though his pockets were bulging, he had the urge to collect fruit from every single tree. He and Charlotte could have a feast when he got back. Then he remembered that Charlotte didn't want to feast; she wanted an answer about the princess. He stopped picking fruit and went and found the lion statue.

It was as large as a real lion and made from shining gold that made the beast look even more majestic. He sat on a raised platform, swishing his tail into the shrubbery that surrounded him.

When Hudson walked up, the lion lifted his head in a royal manner, and his thick mane glistened in the lantern light. "Welcome, my young adventurer," he said in a deep, rich voice. "For a gold coin, I will give you knowledge."

"Thanks," Hudson felt around his pocket for the coin. It was somewhere underneath the fruit. "But I came to talk to the bee."

The lion let out a growl, a low rumble of disapproval. "I can tell you anything that the bee knows, and many things besides. What do you seek?"

Right now, his gold coin. He still couldn't find it. He took out the fruit piece by piece, laying them on the pedestal so he could search better. "That's nice of you to offer, but I really need to talk to the bee. She's somewhere around here, right?"

The lion swished his tail angrily and then turned away, ignoring Hudson. "Bees," the lion said disdainfully, "are only good for making honey and spelling things."

Hudson pulled out the jar of hope and finally found the gold coin at the bottom of his pocket. He walked around the statue of the lion, examining the area by his tail. That's where Charlotte said the bee was. He didn't see it. Of course, since the lion could move his tail, and did often enough—he nearly smacked Hudson in the face with it once—Hudson had a large area to search.

And if the lion could move, couldn't the bee move, too? Maybe she had moved someplace completely different. If Hudson were a bee, he wouldn't stick around by the lion's tail. He'd be over in the snow-cone tree.

Hudson looked around the garden, searching. If the bee had flown off, how would he ever find it? Bees were tiny, and it was dark.

Before he became completely discouraged, he shook the bottle of hope. At first nothing happened, and Hudson wondered if he was hopeless after all, then a tiny spark of light appeared in the middle of the jar. Just a glimmer. It grew stronger and stronger until the light shone brighter than a flashlight.

He held the bottle over the surrounding flowers. A gray stone bee sat on top of a daisy, wings outstretched. Hudson bent his head to see her better, and the bee buzzed happily.

"I need to ask you a question." Hudson laid the gold coin

near the daisy. To his amazement, the coin disappeared, making a clinking sound like it had fallen into a slot. "My friend wants to find and rescue Princess Nomira. How can we do that?"

The bee tilted her head up, antennae swaying. "With bravery and perseverance."

Hudson waited for more instructions. They didn't come. The bee turned her attention back to the daisy.

"So where do we go to rescue the princess?" he asked. "Where is she?"

The bee tromped around on the surface of the flower, gathering bits of pollen. "She is closer than you think. Rescuing her, however, is a process, not an event."

What did that mean? Maybe Hudson should have gone with the lion after all. He tried to coax more information out of the insect. "We need to find Princess Nomira before we can rescue her."

"That's always a necessary step," the bee agreed.

"So where is she hidden? Where did King Vaygran lock her up?"

The bee rubbed her antennae together. "To get the correct answer, you must ask the correct question."

"I thought I was," Hudson said, frustrated. "How do we rescue the princess?"

The bee let out an angry buzz. Hudson didn't know why. She wasn't the one who had paid a piece of gold and wasn't getting any information.

Wings fluttering, the bee paced around the circumference of the flower. "The Cliff of Faces has the answers you seek."

"And where is the Cliff of Faces?"

"Past the Sea of Life. Charlotte knows where it is."

Hudson straightened in surprise. "How did you know my friend's name was Charlotte? I didn't tell you that."

Another buzz from the bee. "People pay gold for my answers because I know many things. Bees see without being seen."

For the first time, Hudson believed the bee might actually know what she was talking about.

"If Charlotte is successful in her quest," the bee continued, "she'll be called Colette. Victory for the people."

"Um, okay." Hudson wasn't sure why the bee wanted to change Charlotte's name. "So we need to go to the Cliff of Faces to find out where the princess is? Is that all you have to tell me?"

The bee flew off the daisy, circling upward. "If you succeed, your name will be Boudewijn, which means bold friend. Right now you are only named Hudson, which is a muddy river in the Land of Banishment. An unfortunate name, really."

Maybe. But Hudson still preferred it to Boudewijn. He thanked the bee, put the fruit back in his pockets, and left the garden. The evening was colder now, and the chill pressed against his jacket, looking for openings.

He ran down the street, retracing the way he'd come. He was slower now, too tired to go very fast. When he was nearly to the city wall, he pulled out the bell and rang it. "I need a fairy to cross the river."

Moments later, a glowing figure zipped in front of him. The same blue fairy held her wand aloft. "Ready for departure?"

"I guess so." He reached in his pocket to find the marblelike museling.

The fairy put her hands on her hips, bobbing up and down as she hovered in front of him. "If you want to guess about things, you need to go the other direction. The politicians and advisers work in the castle."

Hudson found the museling and held it out to the fairy. "What I meant is, yes, I'm ready to go."

"All right, then." The fairy flicked her wand, and the museling floated over to her, shrinking. She plucked it from the air, put it in her mouth, and smiled as she savored it. The light around her pulsed stronger. "Thanks for flying Fairy Riverside Travel!"

With a wave of her wand, Hudson felt himself contracting, transforming into a bird again. Instead of fingers, feathers sprouted from his hands. And then he had no hands or arms at all, only wings. He shot up into the night air.

It was more fun this time, now that he knew what to expect. He liked the feeling of sailing upward, liked the way he could glide through the air. He flew over the wall, and with a few more beats of his wings, he soared over the river. He spotted Charlotte right away. She stood by the riverbank, her jar of hope held high and bright.

He sailed over to her and hoped she would tell him that a trip to the Cliff of Faces would be quick, easy, and not dangerous.

7

WHEN HUDSON TRANSFORMED back into a boy, he stood in front of Charlotte with his arms crossed. "You know, you shouldn't go around changing people into birds without their permission."

"I didn't change you into a bird," she said, as though the technicality mattered. "The fairy did. And I don't know why you're upset about it. I'm the one who had to pay the muselings." She made an impatient rolling motion with her hand. "Did the bee tell you where to find the princess?"

"She said the Cliff of Faces has that answer."

Perhaps it was just the light from the hope jar, but Charlotte seemed to grow paler. "The Cliff of Faces?"

"Is it hard to get there?" he asked.

She took a deep breath and then sighed. "I suppose if rescuing the princess was simple, someone else would have already done it. We have to expect this quest to be hard." She picked up her backpack from the ground and slid it onto her shoulders. "We'd better set up camp for the night. Let's go back to the forest. It will be safer there." She turned and started back on the path in that direction. "Tomorrow we'll ask the unicorns to take us as close to the Sea of Life as they can. The Cliff of Faces is on an island there."

Hudson picked up his backpack and followed her. He didn't exactly look forward to spending more time with the unicorns. "Could a fairy get us there?"

"Not for muselings."

"What exactly is a museling?"

"A memory of something good happening."

Hudson looked at her to see if she was serious. "Why do fairies want memories?"

Charlotte raised an eyebrow at him, as though he should know. "What else do people have that's really valuable—that makes them happy? Fairies don't need gold or silver, but they do enjoy a good memory. Which is why if you don't guard your memories, fairies will steal them while you sleep."

"Like what—they wave their wand and suck them out of your head?"

"Pretty much."

Hudson shuddered and glanced over his shoulder to the place they'd met the river fairy. He didn't see her. He could only make out the dark shapes of trees and bushes. "I'm glad that doesn't happen in my land."

Charlotte laughed out loud, not even trying to hide her amusement for politeness' sake.

"It does?" he asked incredulously.

"It happens mostly in your land," she said, "because your people hardly guard their memories at all. Do you remember your fourth birthday party or the first time you blew bubbles?"

Hudson thought about it. "No."

"How about the first time a dog licked your face?"

"No."

She shook her head sadly. "Fairies are terrible thieves, really."

Hudson stopped for a moment and just stood there, wondering what other memories the fairies had taken from him. Was there anything important? Maybe memories with his dad? It totally ticked him off. When Hudson started walking again, he strode along beside Charlotte silently, remembering everything he could about his dad—his wide grin, his deep voice, the way he used to pick up Bonnie and twirl her around the living room. He'd volunteered as Hudson's baseball coach and used to take him to a batting cage to practice his swing. "How do you guard your memories so fairies can't take them?"

"Writing things down is the best way. That's why people keep journals. Taking pictures helps, too."

Journal writing. It sounded sort of like schoolwork. Then again, Hudson didn't want to forget anything else, at least not the important stuff. When he got back home, he would get a journal. "So what memories did you give the fairies?"

"Ones I don't care about anymore."

"How do you know that if you don't remember them anymore?"

Charlotte reached into the side pocket of her backpack and took out a small notebook. She flipped it open and held her hope jar over it so she could read the page. "The red museling was the first time I met Isabella and Macy. They smiled and told me they hoped I liked school. It made me happy, but . . ."

Hudson knew what Charlotte didn't say. But it didn't stay that way. As soon as Charlotte started saying weird things, Isabella and Macy made fun of her just like everybody else. No wonder she didn't care about losing that memory.

Charlotte must have mistaken Hudson's dismay for worry. "I still have ten more muselings to use when we need fairy help again. That's what I was doing with the calculater while you were packing up your supplies from home—making muselings."

"Oh," he said. "That's good." Only it didn't feel good. What happened to a person if they lost their happy memories?

For a long while, neither of them spoke again. They just hiked past fields of shushing grain and listened to its soft murmur. Finally, they made it to the forest. Charlotte cast one last look over her shoulder at the farms and their cottages. "People used to open up their homes to needy travelers. Not anymore, though. No one trusts anyone else. You don't know who might report you to the king's men." She turned back to the forest, holding her jar high so she could make her way around the trees. "King Arawn and Princess Nomira never paid spies to find out who disagreed with them. Everything will be better when she comes back."

Arawn and Nomira. Such odd names. Which reminded Hudson that he hadn't finished telling Charlotte everything the bee had said. He relayed the rest, including the bee's proposed name changes. "Do you think Boudewijn fits me?" he finished with a laugh.

"I hope so," she said. "Logosians need a bold friend."

"I'll stick with Hudson."

Charlotte slipped off her backpack and walked to a spot on the ground that was mostly clear of plants and rocks. "We have many names during our lives. When my father and I came to the Land of Banishment, he gave me the name Charlotte and took the name Lysander. Both names mean freedom—because my father and I are free from King Vaygran's grasp."

Hudson tilted his head at her. "Charlotte isn't your real name?"

"Yes, it's my real name. I'm still free."

"What was your name before that?"

She unzipped her backpack and rifled through it. "Erica. So now I'm Erica Charlotte Colette. Or at least I'll be Colette once we're successful."

Hudson set down his backpack and pulled out his miniature sleeping bag and pillow. "Your dad's name is Lysander? I thought it was Fantasmo."

"It is. Lysander Fantasmo, because he's fantastically free. Before we came here, he was Aziz Fantasmo—fantastically powerful."

Charlotte set her things in a row, including her stuffed animals: an eagle, a falcon, a tiger, a wolf, a squirrel, and a polar bear. She took out the compactulator and pushed a button, and her possessions grew back to normal size—except for her stuffed animals. Those grew bigger. Life-size.

They moved around, stretched their legs, and swished their tails. The eagle and falcon flew from the ground and landed on nearby tree branches. The tiger sauntered over to Charlotte, purring as she rubbed her face against Charlotte's arm. The wolf scratched his ear, and the squirrel scurried up a tree trunk. The polar bear loped around the area, sniffing at the foliage on the ground.

Hudson eyed the animals with his mouth hanging open in surprise. "How did you do that?" He took a step backward from the polar bear as it lumbered by. "Are those things safe?"

"Of course they're safe. They're my shabtis." Charlotte pointed the compactulator at Hudson's things. His pillow and sleeping bag immediately grew to their original size.

"Shabtis?" he asked, still keeping his eye on the bear.

"Figurines in one realm that become magical helpers when you go to another realm." She pointed the compactulator at his backpack, pushed a button, then put the device away. "That's the whole point of stuffed animals, isn't it?"

Hudson didn't answer. He was too busy gaping at his pack. His penguin, the one Bonnie had given him for Christmas, had grown full size. It crawled out of his backpack and brushed itself off. Well, brushed itself off as well as it could with stubby little wings.

Charlotte clapped her hands to get her animals' attention. "We need to set up our camp for the night. Blaze, Flash, and Meko"—the tiger, wolf, and squirrel perked up their ears—"I want you to stand guard while we sleep.

"Bolt and Striker"—Charlotte looked up at the eagle and falcon—"watch from the treetops. When it's almost morning, fly around and find some food for breakfast.

"Chancellor," she said, petting the polar bear's furry white neck, "it's cold, but if I could sleep next to you, I'm sure I'll be warm enough."

The polar bear nudged Charlotte's hand affectionately. "The ground is too hard for you," he said in a deep, growly voice. "I'll lie on my back so you can sleep snugly on my stomach."

She leaned toward the polar bear and gave his nose a kiss. "Thank you. You're so sweet."

The bear lay down and stretched out his arms to make room for Charlotte.

Hudson's penguin waddled over to his side. "Don't look at me," the bird said. "I don't do snuggling."

Hudson didn't reply to that comment. He was transfixed watching Charlotte's animals disappear into the forest to do their tasks. "If you already had birds who could run errands for you, why didn't you send one of them to talk to the bee?"

Charlotte laid her sleeping bag onto the polar bear's waiting stomach. "Shabtis can help and protect you, but for magic to work, you've got to do the important stuff yourself." She laid her pillow under the bear's chin. He stretched happily, nearly purring with the attention. "My father says the first thing a wizard learns is that anything worth doing takes a sacrifice of some sort."

Hudson unrolled his sleeping bag. "We're not wizards. We're two kids who should take all the help we can get. I say we send your birds to find answers at the Cliff of Faces. They'll be faster, and we'll be safer."

Charlotte kicked off her shoes and climbed into her sleeping bag. The polar bear draped his paws across her sleeping bag so it didn't slide around. "It doesn't work that way. An acorn gets help from the sun and rain, but it's the one who has to break its shell and push to the sky. The sun and rain can't do that for the acorn."

"We're not acorns, either," Hudson said, even though he knew it was no use. Charlotte wasn't going to see reason. She shut her eyes and turned her face away from him.

He sighed and wondered how long it would take them to get to the Cliff of Faces. His mom was probably already worried because Hudson had disappeared. Could he and Charlotte possibly find the princess before Thanksgiving? His dad would be home by then. Hudson kicked off his shoes and climbed into his sleeping bag.

On the bright side, they had some cool animals to help them. Or at least Charlotte did. He had a penguin. It stood at Hudson's feet, absentmindedly grooming its feathers.

"So, penguin—" Hudson started.

"My name is Pokey," the penguin said.

Pokey? All of Charlotte's animals had cool names. Hudson shook his head. "I never named you that. You need a better name. Something like Phantom or Freeze."

The penguin let out an offended sniff. "Bonnie already named me. When you're not around, she comes into your room and plays with me. And by the way, she also knows about the candy you hide in your underwear drawer."

"You're *my* penguin," Hudson insisted. "And I never named you Pokey."

"Speaking of underwear," the penguin went on, "some of yours is pretty raggedy."

Hudson made shushing motions with his hands and checked over his shoulder to see if Charlotte had heard any of this. Her back was to him, her hair barely visible over the top of her sleeping bag.

"We're not speaking about my underwear," Hudson hissed. "That subject is definitely off limits." He regarded the penguin again, looking him over. "So what can you do to help with our quest?"

Pokey shrugged. "I swim and catch fish. If there's ice around, I can also slide."

"Great. That's . . ." *Completely useless.* Only Hudson didn't say the words out loud. He didn't want to hurt the penguin's feelings. Hudson gestured in the direction the wolf had gone. "Why don't you help the other animals stand guard until morning?"

"All right." Pokey took slow, waddling steps in that direction—steps that crackled every time his webbed feet crunched across the dead leaves on the ground. Which was probably why no one ever used the phrase. "As stealthy as a penguin."

Hudson settled into his sleeping bag, trying to get comfortable on the hard ground. He wished he'd brought a polar bear with him. Or a cot.

Strange sounds echoed in the forest. Something whirred. Something else chimed. The faint notes of a song drifted through the night.

"Charlotte," he whispered, "where's that music coming from?"

"That's tree sprites singing lullabies to the forest. The trees sleep better that way."

Tree sprites? They sounded harmless enough. Hudson shut his eyes again and thought about his father so he wouldn't wonder what else roamed around in the dark. When Hudson's dad was younger, he wanted to travel to new and different places. Couldn't get enough of it. That's why he joined the Marines—so he could see the world.

What would his dad make of this place?

"Hudson?" Charlotte whispered.

"Yeah?"

"What are you thinking about right now?"

"Nothing. I'm just missing my family."

"Me, too," she said.

WHEN HUDSON AWOKE THE NEXT MORNING, HIS HEAD LAY ON the ground, and Pokey was sleeping in the middle of his pillow. "Hey," Hudson said, nudging the penguin awake. "You were supposed to guard the camp."

Pokey clacked his beak open in a yawn. "The wolf wouldn't let me. He said I kept getting in the way."

Charlotte was already up, sitting cross-legged on her sleeping bag. She still looked like the girl from the magazine with curly brown hair, hazel eyes, and purple lips. Hudson wondered how long it would take him to get used to seeing her like that.

The tiger sat behind Charlotte and ran her paw over Charlotte's hair, using her claws as a comb. The squirrel was perched on Charlotte's shoulder, rubbing blue protective lotion onto her neck with his tail.

Hudson pulled himself out of his sleeping bag and stretched. A caw cut through the morning air, and the falcon glided down from the sky holding an apple in his talons. He dropped it into Charlotte's lap and flew off to an overhead branch. Using his teeth, the wolf pulled a tin plate out of Charlotte's backpack, trotted over, and placed it on the ground in front of her. A few moments later, the eagle swooped down holding a large muffin. He dropped it onto her plate.

"Where did you get this?" she asked.

"The inn will never miss it," the eagle replied, landing on the ground in front of her. "Do you need anything else?"

She pulled the lid off her water bottle. "Can you find some fresh water and fill this up?"

The eagle bobbed his head, clutched the water bottle in his talons, and took to the air. As he flew away, his large wings flapped in graceful arcs.

Hudson looked over at the penguin. "So are you going to get me some breakfast?"

Pokey bit at a loose feather on his chest. "I can waddle to the river and catch some fish. Of course, it will take me a few hours to get there."

"Never mind," Hudson said. "I don't like fish that much." He remembered the fruit he had picked from the garden last night, and he rifled through his jacket for it. "Hey, Charlotte," he said, showing her the fruit that smelled like manicotti. "It's okay to eat fruit from the compliment trees now, isn't it?"

She took a bite of her muffin. "You can eat it, but it's not very filling. Bolt can get you something after he comes back with my water."

Hudson bit into the fruit. As he ate, he heard a small, friendly voice that came from the vicinity of the fruit. "You have a great sense of humor."

Cool. The fruit complimented you while you ate it. And it tasted pretty good, too, like spicy melted cheese. Hudson took another bite.

"You could easily be a straight-A student," the voice murmured.

His mother had said the same thing, although not as nicely. Another bite.

"You're the best baseball player in your grade."

Well, when your family didn't have cable or a lot of electronic games, you played sports.

"Charlotte," he called, "is what the compliment fruit says true, or is it just flattery?"

"Tell me what it's saying," she said, "and I'll let you know."

He took another bite.

"She digs you," the fruit said. "All girls do."

"Never mind," Hudson called to her.

"It's true," the fruit insisted. "You're a hottie."

Hudson ate several more pieces of fruit, enjoying it so much that he turned down Charlotte's offer to have her eagle get more food for him. Her animals helped pack up—Pokey wasn't much assistance in that regard—and then Charlotte used her compact-ulator to minimize things so they fit in their backpacks again. When she minimized Pokey, he got all huffy, insisting that Hudson's backpack smelled like moldy school lunches. Even after Charlotte shrank him back into a stuffed animal, he had a sort of angry look on his face.

Charlotte left her birds full size. While Hudson and she set out through the forest, the eagle flew overhead, scanning for signs of danger. The falcon headed back to Grammaria to—as he put it—procure something for them to eat at lunchtime. Hudson didn't know what the word *procure* meant, but he hoped dessert would be involved.

The sun lit up the forest, making the trees shine, their glossy leaves fluttering in the wind. Brightly colored birds hopped around the branches like gems shaken loose from a royal treasury. They called to each other with flutelike chirps and sprang away from Charlotte and Hudson's path.

Flowers grew in patches here and there across the forest floor. Every once in a while one glowed neon. When Hudson asked Charlotte why they kept doing that, she said, "Oh, they're just happy. You know how flowers are."

Apparently not. He'd never considered flower moods before.

After a few minutes of walking, Cecil and Nigel appeared through the trees and trotted over to them. Cecil tossed his silver mane so it glistened like Christmas-tree tinsel. "Greetings, Charlotte and Son of Hud. We've come to see how you fare."

Charlotte curtsied, managing to look regal and proper, even though she still had a blue film of lotion covering her face. "We're traveling to the Sea of Life."

Hudson gave a short bow, too. "Um, actually, my name is Hudson."

"We shall carry you on your quest, fair lady," Cecil said, then both unicorns eyed Hudson.

Nigel let out a resigned huff. "I suppose if we must, we'll also carry Son of Hud."

Charlotte stroked Nigel's velvety nose. "You're most gracious."

Hudson could think of some other adjectives that described the unicorns, too. He didn't say them.

Charlotte mounted Cecil, and Hudson got on Nigel—this time, the unicorn didn't fling him quite so hard—and the group set out at a gallop through the forest. Charlotte sang as she had yesterday, doing multiple renditions of the unicorn song. Cecil and Nigel never got tired of that one.

Hudson's stomach felt empty, so he ate more compliment fruit. It put him in a better mood. "You're strong and brave," the fruit murmured. "You'll be a hero. The unicorns are completely wrong about you."

He hoped so.

During one of Charlotte's refrains, Nigel glanced back at him. "What did you bring from the Land of Banishment to help you accomplish your quest?"

Clothes and food, mostly. Only that seemed lame. "Um, I brought a magic penguin." Pokey, after all, could talk.

Nigel let out an unimpressed whinny. "Haven't you any useful skills? What did you do with your time in the Land of Banishment?"

"I went to school and played baseball."

"Baseball?" Nigel asked. "What sort of thing is that?"

Hudson spent several minutes explaining the sport. After he finished, Nigel said, "So you're good at hitting a ball with a skinny stick?"

"Yep," Hudson said. "I'm really good at it."

"Are there a lot of rogue balls in the Land of Banishment that need this treatment?"

"It's a game," Hudson said.

"Skilled at games." Nigel flicked his tail. "What you need is skill at living."

Hudson wasn't quite sure what the unicorn meant. How did you get skilled at living? So far, his life hadn't needed that much skill.

Overhead, Charlotte's falcon let out a caw and swooped down from the sky, gliding toward her with outstretched wings. He didn't carry any food in his talons.

Charlotte stopped singing and held her arm out to him. "Is something wrong?"

The falcon landed on her wrist in a flurry of feathers. "Maybe it's wrong or maybe it's right." The falcon folded his wings and adjusted his grip on her arm. "At Grammaria, a crowd was gathered around the princess's tree. I flew into the branches so I could hear them.

"The tree bloomed last night—yellow flowers everywhere. The townsfolk said it hasn't happened since King Vaygran hid the princess away." The bird ruffled his wings. "King Vaygran came out on his balcony to see what the commotion was. Several people pointed to me and said a falcon in the tree was a sign Princess Nomira would return, because she had a pet falcon."

Charlotte tilted her head, perplexed. "Did she? I don't remember that."

"King Vaygran must have remembered. He told one of his advisers to catch me." The bird momentarily spread his wings, as though to emphasize that they were free. "I flew to a perch on the castle and waited to see what the king would do next. He told the people the yellow flowers meant nothing. But not much later, a dozen of his soldiers prepared horses for a trip."

Nigel had increased his pace as the falcon told his story so that he trotted side by side with Cecil.

Soldiers. That couldn't be good news. "What do you think is happening?" Hudson asked Charlotte.

Her brows furrowed as she thought. "Yellow is the color of hope."

Cecil nickered. "It's also the color of warning."

Hudson had been talking about the soldiers, not the flowers. He hadn't realized hope and warning had their own colors. "Weren't the blossoms on the tree always yellow?" he asked.

"They were usually purple or pink," Charlotte said, "for generosity and happiness. The tree stopped flowering and the leaves turned deep blue when her father died." She didn't add why. He supposed that must be the color of sorrow.

"What about the soldiers?" Hudson asked. "If they're going to check on Princess Nomira, we should have your falcon follow them."

Charlotte considered this. "King Vaygran wouldn't send soldiers to check on her, not when he's keeping her location a secret. Still, it wouldn't hurt to watch and see where they go." She lifted her hand, a motion indicating she was sending the bird off again. "Striker, follow the soldiers. When they get to their destination, come back and tell us where it is."

The falcon bobbed his head, then took flight, quickly disappearing back the way he'd come.

The group moved on, but Charlotte didn't start singing again. "Yellow," she said, tasting the word.

It was then that Hudson remembered he had spoken to the

tree. "Charlotte, could the princess have heard me if I said something to her tree?"

Nigel and Cecil both erupted into braying laughs at the question. Hudson supposed that meant no.

Charlotte answered more gently. "In Logos, people can't hear through trees. Logos is sort of like your land that way."

"I only asked," Hudson said, feeling defensive, "because last night I stopped at Princess Nomira's tree and told it we were coming for her."

Charlotte's eyebrows drew together. "That's curious."

Cecil neighed. "That's foolish—to go announcing your plans where anyone might hear them."

Instead of growing worried, Charlotte brightened at the thought. "Perhaps one of Princess Nomira's servants was hidden in the tree—some moth or sparrow. Perhaps it flew to her and told her what you said."

"That could be it," Nigel conceded. "But if it is, were the yellow flowers a sign of hope or a sign of warning?"

No one had an answer to that.

8

AFTER SEVERAL HOURS of riding, the group reached the outskirts of Scriptoria, a town near the Sea of Life. By then Hudson had eaten all his fruit and felt hungrier than ever. Charlotte was right about the compliment fruit. It tasted great, but it wasn't filling.

Charlotte and Hudson dismounted from the unicorns, gave them their thanks, and headed toward the town. As they walked, Charlotte took Hudson's backpack from his shoulders and sifted through his things. "I need the disguise paste so I can change my appearance and hide this blue lotion. I'm too conspicuous with it showing." She pulled out the tube from a pocket. "And you'll need to alter yourself, too, so you blend in better."

Hudson held up his hand. "The last time you changed me, I was turned into a bird."

"Oh, don't be a baby." Charlotte unscrewed the lid off the

tube. "Being a bird wasn't that bad. Lots of species are birds full time. You never see flamingos complaining."

How could Hudson argue with that logic?

Charlotte held up the tube. "Disguise paste is rare and expensive, so we've got to be careful with this. Smear a dab on your skin and then picture what you want to look like—and make sure you give yourself Logosian clothes. It works best if you think of someone you know. If you only have a vague idea in your mind, you're likely to end up with a fuzzy nose or an incomplete mouth."

She squeezed the tube until a pea-size blob sat on the end, then she put it on her chin. "You have to close your eyes for it to work." She shut her eyes for a couple of seconds, then opened them. She hadn't changed. "Now you try it."

"You look the same," he told her. "Well, the same, except I think you have a blob of toothpaste on your chin."

"What?" She checked the tube in her hand. COLGATE, not CLOAKGATE. "Oh. I grabbed the wrong one." She wiped the toothpaste from her face, then went to Hudson's pack and pulled out the other tube, checking the label more carefully this time. "This is the problem with making things look alike. Well, anyway, now you know how to do it." She opened the tube and squeezed out another small dab.

He took it from her finger. "How long does the disguise last?"

"Until you use another dab to change yourself back or until someone sprinkles revealing powder on you. That probably won't happen outside Grammaria. It takes a powerful wizard to make revealing powder."

Hudson began thinking of guys he knew well enough that he could transform into them and laughed at the irony of it.

"What?" Charlotte asked.

"I took the troll mirror because I wanted to look more like Andy or Caidan. I should have just come over to your house and asked for a dab of Cloakgate."

Charlotte tilted her head. "Why would you want to look like either of them?"

Hudson shrugged. "Everybody likes them."

"I don't."

Yeah, well, the idea of popularity was completely lost on Charlotte. Still, Hudson decided not to transform into Andy or Caidan. He didn't want to change into someone Charlotte disliked. He kept mulling over faces. Who did he want to become?

Charlotte got tired of waiting. She took the dab from Hudson's finger and wiped it onto his cheek. "Never mind. I'll do it for you." With her hand still on his cheek, she shut her eyes for a second, then opened them. "There. Now you'll be Andy, but better dressed."

Hudson's clothes wavered like the reflection on the lake. He held up his hand and watched as it grew larger. He felt himself getting taller, too. He now wore baggy blue pants, a red shirt with puffy sleeves, and yellow shoes with ski-slope points at the end. They looked vaguely like bananas. His backpack had become a large leather bag.

Hudson touched his face to see if he could feel a difference. "You didn't tell me other people could change you."

"I didn't think I needed to. Isn't it obvious that other people can change you?"

He felt his chin and nose. "Do I really look like Andy?"

"See for yourself," she said proudly. "I think I did a pretty good job. And you've got the clothes of a nobleman."

Hudson reached into his pocket for his mirror. "Yeah, about these clothes. Next time, I'd like to be a little less . . . noble."

When Hudson held up the mirror, Andy's face stared back at him. Well, Andy's face, if he wore a dorky cone-shaped hat with a tassel on the top. Hudson pulled off the hat. "You don't expect me to actually wear this. It looks like a triangle is attacking my head."

Charlotte took the hat, offended, and plunked it back on his head. "It isn't nearly as silly as that baseball cap you wear."

Hudson ran his fingers across his cheek. "I feel kinda weird about having this face."

"Just think about poor Andy. He has to wear it all the time."

"That's not what I meant." Hudson held the mirror down and turned to Charlotte. Only it wasn't Charlotte anymore. Isabella stood in her place. She wore a burgundy dress with sleeves so long they looked like flags waving around her wrists.

The surprise made Hudson let out a startled "Arp!"

"What?" Charlotte asked in alarm. She took the mirror from his hand and checked her face, examining one side and then the other. "I got it right," she said defensively. "I bet I could fool Isabella's mother."

"Right," Hudson agreed. "That's why it's so freaky."

Charlotte rolled her eyes. Or Isabella's eyes, anyway. "The

Land of Banishment puts way too much emphasis on the way people look."

Hudson flicked the tassel on his hat. "Which is why you never see us wearing these."

Charlotte handed Hudson the mirror, and they set off along a dirt path. As they walked, she concocted a story to use if anyone asked why they'd come to town without parents. They were orphans going to consult the Cliff of Faces in order to find relatives.

Hudson kept stealing glances at her, reminding himself that she was still Charlotte. Nice, friendly Charlotte. She wasn't going to start saying judgmental things like Isabella, or act bored so he'd feel like he was somehow failing as a person.

When they got close to Scriptoria, the path widened, and the dirt became cobblestone. Rows of squatting wooden buildings with brightly painted shutters and mossy shingles stretched out in front of them. Several people walked through the streets, and a few rode animals. Not horses. One man rode a multicolor-striped zebra. Another trotted by on a miniature giraffe. A stout woman with an enormous feathered hat and a decided air of dignity passed by on an ostrich. Hudson couldn't stop staring at them.

"They don't ride horses here?" he asked Charlotte.

"They used to." She sidestepped a woman who was ambling the other way. "King Vaygran made it illegal. He doesn't want anyone to have something that could outrun his soldiers' horses. That's why he outlawed unicorns."

"He outlawed unicorns?" Hudson repeated. "We just rode here on criminals?"

Charlotte nodded. "Vaygran put a bounty on their heads. Although few people would try to kill one. Unicorns have a magic all their own that not even wizards understand."

The longer Charlotte and Hudson walked through the town, the better he felt about his clothes. Charlotte was right. Everyone wore outlandish clothing here: puffy shirts, baggy pants, and hats that looked like wandering traffic cones.

Several guards in red uniforms also strolled around the town. Charlotte eyed them with distaste. "King Vaygran said he sent guards to keep the peace. They're nothing but spies, though. We'll have to avoid them."

Hudson and Charlotte walked past a bustling post office with a sign that read POSTSCRIPTORIA. A dozen bluebirds flew from windows carrying letters in their beaks. One zoomed near Hudson's head. "Watch out for the airmail," Charlotte said.

It suddenly occurred to Hudson what Scriptoria, Grammaria, and Logos had in common. They were words about words. Or at least *script, grammar,* and *logo* were. "Grammaria is the capital of Logos," he said, figuring it out, "because grammar rules."

"Of course," Charlotte said. "You wouldn't be able to read without grammar rules. Can you imagine how horrible that would be?"

He shrugged. He'd never been much of a reader. "Why do the people here love words so much?"

Isabella's expression had never looked so earnest, as though what she was saying deeply mattered. "Words have power. People who know how to use them wield that power."

The road reached the main marketplace, where dozens of

people browsed at the stalls. Smells of baked goods drifted toward them. Scents that reminded him it had been a while since they'd eaten. "Words are just words in my land," Hudson said.

Charlotte snorted, a familiar Isabella sound. "Words have power in all lands, even yours."

Hudson cocked his head. "No, they don't. Nobody casts spells in my land."

"Haven't you ever read a book? What do you call that?"

"Homework."

Charlotte and Hudson went around a group of people congregated at one of the busier stalls. "Books can take you to new lands," she said. "And words can hurt or heal. They also can solve all sorts of problems. That makes them completely magical in any place."

A few moments later, they came to a plump woman standing by a food cart. The warm-honeyed aroma drifted toward them, making his stomach feel even emptier. "Do we have enough money to buy something?" he asked, walking closer. A sign tacked to the cart read MADAM LOLA'S SUMPTUOUS WORDS. In smaller print underneath this title was written BAKED GOODS THAT ARE RENOUNED COUNTRYWIDE.

Hudson reread the sign. "I think you've got a spelling mistake. Shouldn't it say renowned?"

"Not at all." The woman gestured to her cart. "Verbs and adjectives become nouns when they're made into tasty pastries." She held up something that looked like a doughnut, but instead of being shaped like an O, it spelled out the word *luscious*. "A half a copper a word. They're well worth the price."

Charlotte gazed at the doughnut hungrily and pulled a coin from her pocket. "I guess we can afford to split one."

She and Hudson stepped closer to the spread of food on the cart. A pile of pastry-shaped words lay together on a tray. There was a steaming *succulent,* a golden-brown *epic,* and an iced *lackadaisical.* Hudson didn't know what *lackadaisical* meant, but it smelled delicious. "Let's get a long word." He eyed a crisp *ostentatious.* "There will be more to split."

Charlotte surveyed the words at the other side of the cart. "You can't break words any way you like. *Succulent* might be good, but trust me, *succu* is going to taste nasty, and *lent* won't be much better."

That wouldn't have made any sense back in Texas, but Hudson didn't question the logic here. He just looked for something that could be split into two reasonably good words. He pointed to a pretzel that spelled out *to enjoy.* "How about this one?"

The plump woman made a tsking sound. "Everyone knows you shouldn't split an infinitive."

"Oh, right." Hudson went back to searching. He needed a compound word. Something like *supernatural* or *honeymoon.*

He noticed that the woman had a picture of a pretty girl taped on the underside of the awning. She looked about twelve years old, with long black hair and large brown eyes. She was smiling, or at least her lips were turned up in an attempt. Her eyes seemed sad and wistful.

The woman saw Hudson staring at the picture and frowned.

"Is that your daughter?" he asked, hoping his interest wasn't rude.

The woman laughed and relaxed again. "You must be a stranger if you don't know who Princess Nomira is."

The woman leaned toward Hudson, keeping her voice low. "Her name means unseeing, and none of us have seen her for the past year." The woman touched the picture tenderly. "Some say it's dangerous to keep a picture of the princess with me, but it reminds me of better times."

"Before she left?" Hudson supplied.

"No." The woman stroked the edge of the picture again. "When she comes back. Those will be better times." She dropped her hand and wiped it on her apron. "But it isn't wise to talk of such things. Have you decided on a word you want?"

Charlotte picked up a glazed *readjust*. "We'll take this one." She handed the woman a coin, thanked her, and she and Hudson headed down the street. As she walked, Charlotte broke the word down the middle. "Just read," she said. "Good words and good advice." She handed him the half that said *read* and took a bite out of *just*.

Hudson sunk his teeth into *read*. It tasted buttery, sweet, and a bit mysterious. He had to admit reading had never been so good.

They walked on through the center of town, past more people standing at carts or in front of stalls, selling their wares. One man waved people over to his stall, yelling, "Get your rare words here! We've got *lugubrious*, *tenacity*, and *petulant*. Impress your friends with a saucy *persnickety*." Those words smelled spicy and exotic.

A little farther off, a crowd of people watched a woman do a demonstration. She held up something that was curved and black. "Never be without the right punctuation again. Some people think an apostrophe is only a comma that's putting on airs. Others think a comma is an apostrophe that's feeling down. Not so, friends. This beauty is an all-purpose punctuation.

"Need quotation marks? Buy two! Don't let your *she'd* turn into a *shed* or your *she'll* become a *shell*. And trust me, folks, you don't want to be out of apostrophes when you need one for *he'll*. Buy a supply now!"

Charlotte and Hudson ambled by another stall, and a mustached man asked where they were headed. When Charlotte told them they were going to the Sea of Life, the man tried to sell them a bottle of acceleration for their boat. Only the word was spelled *excelleration*. Whatever it was, the price was too high, and Charlotte didn't want to pay it. They walked on.

Hudson wished he could stay longer and explore Scriptoria. He would have liked to see what other odd things were in the shops or go to a café and eat a real meal. He couldn't, though. He couldn't stay anywhere for more than a half hour without making the people around him break into boils.

At the end of town, one lone stall stood beside the road to the sea. The sign read LAST WORDS, which seemed kind of creepy and perhaps a bad omen. Hudson sincerely hoped he wouldn't be saying his last words for a long time.

A man with a double-coned hat waved for Hudson and Charlotte to come over. "Take a look at these beauties!" he called. "Everybody wants the last word. For five coppers, it can be yours!"

Charlotte pointedly ignored the man and walked on. "People who have to have the last word are so annoying."

"Um, yeah," Hudson said, and wondered if Charlotte had felt as confused in his world as he did in hers.

They walked until the village of Scriptoria lay far behind them, keeping on the road that led to the sea. After an hour, the ground became rocky, the trees grew sparser, and a dark blue sea came into sight on the trail below them. Sunshine glinted off the water like swords flashing in a fight, and waves rippled, racing one another to crash on the shore. An island sat only a mile or so away from the shore, close enough that Hudson could make out a ragged cliff wall. Tall, grayish brown, and imposing. The Cliff of Faces.

He and Charlotte headed down the trail and went across the sand toward a marina, where three rows of docks stretched into the water. Hudson had gone to the ocean before and expected the beach to have the fishy smell that always loitered around wharfs. It didn't. This place smelled of salt, danger, and things lurking at the bottom of the sea.

A sign near the docks read CHOOSE YOUR OARS, CHOOSE YOUR BOAT. CHOOSE WISELY TO STAY AFLOAT. THE SEA GIVES BUT ONE GUARANTEE. YOU'LL MEET WITH WAVES APLENTY. Smaller words underneath continued WARNING TO STRANGERS: THIS SEA IS CALLED THE SEA OF LIFE BECAUSE SO MANY PEOPLE DIE AT THE END OF IT.

Not the most comforting inscription.

No one was around to offer any other instructions. Hudson pointed out the smaller print to Charlotte. "Are you sure it's a good idea to cross to the island?"

"Oh, that," she said, dismissing the phrase with a wave of her hand. "The writer was probably joking around. You know what comedians signmakers are."

He didn't. In his world, signmakers just made signs that said things like SPEED LIMIT 55 and RIGHT TURN ONLY. Those weren't jokes, although his father often claimed speed-limit signs were only suggestions.

Hudson turned his attention to the docks that lay in front of them. Each was surrounded by a half-dozen wooden rowboats that bobbed up and down in the waves. He and Charlotte made their way to the closest dock and walked down it, their footsteps thunking across the wooden beams. "Have you ever done this before?" Hudson asked.

"No." Charlotte peered over the edge of the dock at a weatherworn rowboat with the word *valor* painted on the side. "My father told me how the Cliff of Faces works, but he never said anything about these boats." She hurriedly added, "It can't be that hard to row one to the island. They all seem sturdy."

No, they didn't. They seemed old, battered, and cracked. Each had a word painted on its side. He passed *hope* and *strength* and saw *love* and *gratitude* rocking in the water on the other side of the dock. The paint on the boats looked as though one good wave would completely wash it off.

"You think these are sturdy?" Hudson asked. The wind had picked up, and the tassel from his hat kept blowing in his face.

Charlotte stepped carefully into the *valor* boat and sat on the bench. "*Valor* should get us where we want to go." She picked up an oar from the side of the boat. The paddle was shaped into the word *talent*. "Should I use this?" she asked, putting it down and picking up a second oar. "Or *intelligence*?" She didn't wait for an answer. "Never mind. I found the right one." She held up a third oar. This paddle spelled out the word *work*.

Hudson stepped into the boat, steadied himself against the motion of the waves, and sat on the bench beside her. His side of the boat had an identical trio of oars.

Charlotte threaded the *work* oar into the oarlock and tested the paddle in the water. "My dad is always saying that talent and intelligence will only take you so far. You need work to get the rest of the way."

"That sounds like something adults would say." And since adults had obviously built the marina, the *work* oar was the best choice. Hudson untied the boat from the dock, pushed off, and picked up his *work* oar.

At first, he and Charlotte didn't time their strokes right, and the boat veered to the left, went forward for a bit, then veered to the left again as though chasing its tail.

"We have to work together," Hudson said, feeling it must be doubly true, considering the oars. "On the count of three." He was looking at Charlotte, which is why he didn't notice the water leaking into the boat until it soaked through his shoes. The boat had a hole, and judging by the amount of water pooling around their feet, it wasn't a small one.

Hudson let out a stream of words—none of which would have made tasty pastries—while he and Charlotte searched for something to bail out the boat. They had nothing, and even if they'd brought a bucket with them, the water was now rushing in too quickly. The lapping cold surrounded their ankles and was gurgling upward to their calves.

Hudson looked helplessly around at the waves. "What should we do?"

"Swim," Charlotte said, and then the boat sank completely, leaving the two of them flailing in the sea.

The frigid temperature made Hudson gasp, and the weight of his leather bag pulled him downward. He slipped it off without letting it go. He didn't want to lose his things.

The Cliff of Faces was too far away to swim to. They would have to go back to the shore they'd come from. As Hudson turned in that direction, a wave slapped into his face. The water tasted salty and bitter.

Not far from him, Charlotte treaded water while she unzipped her bag. She pulled out the compactulator, and the next moment her animals bobbed in the sea next to her. The polar bear swam up beside her, and she grabbed hold of his neck, relaxing into him so he could tow her along. The tiger took hold of Charlotte's bag with her teeth and headed to shore with it. The wolf paddled along behind her, with the squirrel riding atop his head, shaking the water out of his bushy tail.

Charlotte pointed the compactulator in Hudson's direction. "Get your penguin out."

He opened his bag, felt through the soggy remains of a sandwich, and pulled out the penguin. Seconds later, Pokey was full size and gazing around. "This is more like it," he said happily. "We're finally doing something fun."

"This isn't fun," Hudson spit out. Another wave hit him in the face. "Here, carry my pack."

"I would if I had opposable thumbs." Pokey held up one wing. "These are only good for swimming."

"Use your beak," Hudson snapped. By this point, Charlotte's animals were almost to the shore.

Pokey sighed, took hold of one of Hudson's bag straps, and dove into the water. Once Hudson was no longer weighed down by his bag, he swam without problem to the shore. Well, mostly without problem. As he reached the beach, an especially large wave crashed into him, pushing him face-first into the sand. Which was probably another reason this place was called the Sea of Life. It was cold and gritty, and just when you thought you were okay, you got knocked down again.

Pokey made it to the shore ahead of Hudson. The penguin pulled the bag onto the sand, said, "I'll check and see if anything fell out," and without waiting for Hudson's reply, slid back into the water and disappeared into the waves. Pokey obviously just wanted to swim.

"If you find my hat," Hudson called, "don't bring it back!"

He picked up his soggy bag, noticing that the *valor* boat had resurfaced near the dock. It propelled water from its insides with a gush, coughed a few more streams of water over one side, then shuffled back to its spot at the dock.

Hudson slung his dripping bag over his shoulder and headed up the beach to Charlotte.

She was pulling everything out of her pack and spreading things out in the sunshine to dry. It didn't look like the sleeping bag or pillow would be usable anytime soon. Hudson emptied his bag and laid his things beside hers.

"On the bright side," Charlotte said, "we've learned a valuable lesson. Valor alone won't get you through life."

Hudson checked his pocket to make sure the troll mirror hadn't fallen out. It was still there, a hard, cold disk. "We should have gone with *strength*."

"Blaze and Flash are checking all the docks in the marina to see what the other boats say."

Hudson considered the boats at the nearest dock again. *Valor, love, hope, strength*, and *gratitude*. "On second thought," he said. "I bet the right boat is *love*."

Charlotte shook water out of her museling bag and set it on the sand. "Why love?"

"Love is always the answer. That's why people are always writing songs about it."

The tiger and wolf trotted up to Charlotte. Panting, the wolf said, "We found *duty, endurance, humor, patience*, and *sympathy*."

The tiger sat on her haunches, flicking her tail. "We also saw *greed, resentment, luck, materialism, sloth*, and *indulgence*, but those won't get you anywhere. They didn't look seaworthy."

Water dripped from Charlotte's long sleeves. She wrung them out the best she could. "Duty and endurance must be good. And you need humor to get through life. . . . There are so many boats to choose from."

"It's going to be love," Hudson said. "Trust me on this one."

"Trust," the tiger said pointedly, "wasn't on the list." It was clear the tiger didn't like Hudson telling Charlotte what to do.

Charlotte gave up on her sleeves. "Hudson is probably right. Love is the most important thing in life, so that's what will get us over the sea." She brushed sand from her clothes and addressed her animals. "I want you to stay here and guard our things. We'll be back as soon as we're done at the Cliff of Faces."

A birdcall sounded overhead, and Hudson looked up, expecting to see a seagull. Instead, the falcon sped toward Charlotte, calling out, "Beware! Beware!"

9

THE BIRD SWOOPED down onto Charlotte's outstretched arm. "What's wrong?" she asked.

"Soldiers," the bird cried, high-pitched with alarm. "They're on the way to Scriptoria."

Charlotte's gaze swung to the road they'd come from. "Why?"

The falcon fluttered his wings in agitation. "I heard the general and the wizard talking. They're coming for Hudson."

"Me?" Hudson asked. A cold feeling washed over him, a feeling that had nothing to do with his soaking clothes.

The falcon's head bobbed up and down. "When Princess Nomira's tree bloomed, King Vaygran asked the lion statue if he'd heard any news about the princess. The lion told him a boy had asked the bee how to rescue her. They know you're going to the Cliff of Faces." The falcon flicked his tail feathers. "The king was so furious he tried to smash the bee. She flew off vowing never to return to the king's courtyard until Princess Nomira reigns."

Charlotte stared at the road again and gulped. "How far away are the soldiers?"

"Two hours," the falcon said. "Maybe three."

The tiger prowled in circles around Charlotte, kicking up spurts of sand. "They're only searching for the boy. He should head off in a different direction to lead the soldiers away from you."

"No," Charlotte said with a reprimand in her voice. "That's not how to treat friends."

Hudson gestured to his clothes, now wet and sticking to his legs. "I'm in disguise. How will they know who I am?"

The falcon hopped from Charlotte's arm to her shoulder. "They've a wizard with them and a pack of dogs following your scent. They took it from the silver coin you gave the guard."

Charlotte surveyed the things they'd left drying on the ground. "When you see us sailing back to shore," she told her animals, "pack up our bags." She set out for the dock, motioning for Hudson to follow her. "If we hurry, it will only take us half an hour to row to the island, half an hour to hike to the cliff and back, then another half an hour to row back to the beach. We'll be gone before the soldiers reach here."

Neither she nor Hudson said anything else until they sat down inside the boat marked *love*. "Are we still rowing with the *work* paddles?" he asked. "You don't want to use *intelligence*?"

She laughed, and he realized how that sounded. "We probably ought to use some intelligence once in a while," she said.

"You use *work*," he told her, "I'll use *intelligence*. That way we're working smart."

They pushed off from the dock. The wind gusted around

the boat, making Hudson's wet clothes feel colder. The waves seemed higher now, choppier. He and Charlotte concentrated and timed their strokes, pushing through the water as quickly as they could. No water leaked inside.

Pokey popped up next to Hudson's side of the boat and backstroked along with them. "Taking the *love* boat, I see."

Hudson dug his oar into the water. "You're supposed to be onshore so you can help repack our stuff."

"But instead, I'm helping by showing you the way to the Cliff of Faces." Pokey pointed a wing in the direction of the island. "There it is."

"Thanks." Hudson looked at the floor again. Still dry. Love was good. It totally deserved Valentine's Day.

Pokey kept pace with the boat. "Love will keep you together. Love conquers all. You and Charlotte are definitely in love."

Hudson shot Pokey a sharp look and swiped at him with his paddle.

Pokey darted out of the way. "Missed me. Love is blind."

"Yeah, but I can still smack you with all of the intelligence I've got."

Pokey flipped onto his back again. "Which isn't much."

Hudson glared at the penguin. "The tiger insulted me earlier. I should make you fight her to defend my honor."

Hudson didn't hear Pokey's response to that because Charlotte nudged him. "You shouldn't threaten your shabti. Honestly, Hudson, don't you know how to treat your magical helpers?"

"*You've* got magical helpers," he said. "I've got a taunting, worthless penguin."

Charlotte pulled on her oar. "Well, maybe he'd be better if you treated him kindly."

This sentence seemed completely out of place coming from Isabella's mouth. Which made Hudson realize again how different Charlotte was from her. He could have told them apart even if the real Isabella was sitting in the boat with them. Charlotte was more caring. And braver.

It made him wonder why he had ever liked Isabella to begin with.

He wanted to tell Charlotte that, to tell her that everyone at school had been stupid to judge her. He didn't know how to say it, though. Then he felt water lapping against his shoes. The boat was leaking, and this time they were farther away from shore.

Charlotte noticed the leak at the same time he did. "Oh no!" She looked around the boat for something, anything, that might help.

Hudson searched, too, even though he knew he wouldn't find anything. "Not again," he said. "Not now."

The water rushed in faster until it swirled around their legs, chilling them. They were still too far away from the island, so they let the boat sink and swam for the beach again.

Pokey popped up alongside Hudson. "Sometimes love lets you down."

Yeah, obviously.

Charlotte's polar bear had seen what happened and swam toward them to help tow them back to shore. When Hudson and

Charlotte were halfway there, the sunken boat resurfaced near the dock. It sprayed water from its middle, twirling streams into the air like a fountain, then it glided serenely into the empty space near the dock.

Stupid boat.

By the time Charlotte and Hudson reached the beach, his muscles ached and his hands and feet felt numb. He shivered and wished he had something to dry himself off with. Charlotte sat down on the sand, shaking with cold. The wolf loped up to her and wrapped himself around her to warm her up.

The tiger glared at Hudson with accusing eyes. "So love wasn't all you expected it to be."

"Love sucks," Hudson admitted.

The squirrel gave a sympathetic chitter. "He can't help it if he was unlucky in love."

Hudson hadn't noticed that Charlotte had taken the iron bar from his pack until she handed it to him. "Here, we need some of this."

Iron for strength. As Hudson gripped the bar, it grew smaller, and he no longer felt as tired.

The road that led to Scriptoria was empty, but how much time had they wasted? How far away were Vaygran's soldiers now? "Maybe we should use the *talent* oars," Hudson said. "People with talent glide through life, right?"

Charlotte shook her head. "We chose the wrong boat. We need to figure out the right one."

Hudson pushed strands of wet hair away from his face. "I wish we'd bought some excelleration."

"Then we would have been farther away when we sank."

"Maybe we should use *strength*," he said. "It's got to be the strongest boat, right?"

Charlotte glanced at the dock uncertainly. "We don't have time for another mistake."

"What else could it be?" he asked.

Charlotte shut her eyes. "I'll see what my inner compass says."

Inner compass? "What's that?" he asked.

She didn't open her eyes or answer. She sat perfectly still on the sand.

Probably to keep him from bothering her again, the falcon flew over and landed on Hudson's shoulder. "An inner compass," the bird said, "is the part inside Charlotte that tells her what she should do."

Oh. It must be another one of those magical Logosian things.

The falcon cocked his head at Hudson. "Don't you have an inner compass?"

"No," Hudson mumbled. "The only thing that tells me what to do is my mother. Or if I'm at school, my teachers."

"Pity." The bird kept his dark eyes on Hudson. "How will you find the roads you should travel in life?"

"GPS, I guess."

With her eyes closed, Charlotte listed the names of the boats. "*Duty, endurance, humor, patience, sympathy, hope, strength, gratitude.*" She repeated the names again and again.

Hudson couldn't help noticing that Charlotte's notebook lay drying nearby. It was open to a page with two columns. One listed museling colors. The other listed memories. The brown color was "Eating chocolate ice cream on July Fourth while I watched the fireworks." The speckled blue was "When Mrs. Clark said in front of the class that I was creative." The green striped description read, "When I couldn't understand an algebra problem and Hudson showed me how to do it."

That one surprised him. He remembered the day. She had been trying to do the last problem of their math homework while she walked to school. She was concentrating on the example in the book so intently she nearly ran into him. He explained how to do the equation, walking beside her so she didn't step off the sidewalk and get hit by a car.

Why had she chosen to give that memory away? Was he like Isabella and Macy to her, and she didn't care about remembering him? The thought made him feel like he'd swallowed more than bitter salt water.

Charlotte's eyes fluttered open. "I know which boat we need." She stood up without bothering to wipe the sand off her clothes. She just headed, fast-paced, to the first dock. Hudson followed her.

"*Gratitude* will keep us afloat," she said.

Hudson didn't question her. His choice had already sunk. They climbed into the rickety *gratitude* boat, untied it from the dock, and pushed off. Hudson dug his *intelligence* oar into the water, glad for the shot of strength the iron had given him.

Charlotte timed her strokes with his, and they made their way slowly, steadily into the waves. A few minutes went by. No water came through the bottom. "I'm grateful this boat is working," she said, which in Hudson's opinion was tempting fate. An odd thing happened, though: The boat pushed forward with an oomph it hadn't had before. Charlotte noticed it, too. "I'm grateful to be back home," she added.

The boat picked up a little more speed. "I'm grateful Bonnie's cat is better," Hudson said, and the oars seemed to slice through the water.

After that, Charlotte and Hudson took turns saying what they were grateful for. They covered birthday parties, sunsets, indoor plumbing, soft beds, candy bars, friends, family, books, computers, and Hudson's favorite one: "I'm grateful that my dad will be home soon."

Charlotte smiled. "I'm grateful that my dad will be home soon, too."

Neither of them mentioned that this would only be true if things went well. They were busy being grateful. The boat kept skimming along the water. Waves knocked into it, but the boat went faster than Hudson ever would have hoped. He hadn't even run out of things to be grateful for when they landed on the island's shore.

He and Charlotte dragged the boat up the beach, then hurried along a dirt path toward a sheer rock cliff. It towered above the vegetation like a craggy, grayish-brown skyscraper. When Hudson first heard the term *Cliff of Faces,* he'd envisioned something that looked like Mount Rushmore. As far as he could tell, the Cliff of Faces was a normal cliff. Rocks jutted here and there with bits of moss growing in patches.

Charlotte stepped around some overgrown brush blocking the path. "I think we'll only need to ask two questions: Where did King Vaygran put the princess, and how do we get her out? Will you ask one?"

"Sure," Hudson said. "Will the cliff just tell us the answers?" He hoped—but didn't think—it could be that easy.

"Um, more or less," Charlotte said.

"Which part is more and which part is less?"

"Each of the faces on the cliff gives truthful answers," she explained. "The problem is that only one is answering your question. The rest are answering questions asked by someone else in some other place. You've got to figure out which face has your answer. It changes every time you ask a question, so the face that gives you the right answer the first time will probably answer someone else's question the next time."

Hudson and Charlotte had reached the base of the cliff. He still didn't see any faces, unless you counted the odd assortment of bugs that were sunning themselves on the rock wall. He reached out and touched one that resembled a toothbrush with legs. It bristled, shot him a suspicious look, then scurried away.

"The more important the question," Charlotte went on, "the more faces speak. You could have hundreds of answers."

Hudson suppressed a groan. He and Charlotte didn't have time to waste. By the time they figured out the correct answer, the soldiers would not only have arrived at the Sea of Life, but they also would have had time to build their own ships to sail to the island. Hudson ran a hand through his hair in aggravation. "How did I get myself into this?"

He'd barely finished speaking when patches in the cliff wall changed and moved. The lines on the rocks formed into sets of eyes, noses, and mouths until three old men were outlined in the rock.

The first said, "By being vain and wanting through magic what wasn't yours."

The second exclaimed, "She ends up with Edward."

"Forty-two," the third pronounced.

Hudson nodded. "Okay. This doesn't seem too hard."

Charlotte let out a sigh. "That's because you asked something really easy."

"Then how do we find the right answer?"

He had been asking Charlotte the question, but two more rock faces appeared on the wall next to the others, all of them looking like stern old men. They didn't wait before they spoke, and their answers ran into each other.

"Bake at three hundred and fifty degrees for sixteen minutes."

"Be. It is much better than not being."

"Years of practice."

"Put others before yourself."

"By paying with a life coin."

Hudson narrowed his eyes, searching each face. "Which was the right answer?" he asked.

"Mine," all the faces said at once.

Charlotte shifted her feet. "I already know how it works. Those piles over there are our life coins." She pointed to a spot, not far off, where two piles of colored coins sat on the ground. Some were silver-, gold-, and copper-colored, but others were blue, green, red, and purple, making them look like Mardi Gras favors.

They hadn't been there a minute ago. It wasn't this fact that bothered him, though. His name hovered above one pile and Charlotte's name above the other—floating there like a neon sign.

"Each coin represents a year of your life you haven't lived yet," Charlotte said. "In order to have only one face answer, we have to agree to come back here after our quest and pay the faces one of our coins."

"Wait," Hudson said, sure he misunderstood. "We don't literally have to pay them a *year* of our lives, do we?"

He ignored the jumble of answers that came from the cliff.

Charlotte nodded solemnly. "Actually, we do."

Hudson's mouth dropped open. "Are you crazy?"

"Yes," a rock face chimed.

"No," another insisted.

"Multiply the base times the height, then divide by two," a third declared.

Hudson turned his back on the cliff so he could concentrate on Charlotte. "You never told me that asking a question would cost a year of my life."

Charlotte straightened and lifted her chin. "Knowledge has a price. You should know that. In your land, people spend thirteen years in school before they can even start college. That's much longer than a year."

"Yes," he said, "but you only have to sit in class for that, not die earlier."

She folded her arms. "The troll mirror isn't my curse. I'm not the one that has to find the princess and give it to her."

She had him there. It was worth a year of his life to get rid of the troll gift. Still, he hesitated. "Isn't there another way? What about your inner compass? Can't that help us instead?"

The faces had multiple opinions on that, all of which Hudson ignored.

Charlotte held up her hands. "My inner compass isn't telling me where the princess is. Is yours?"

"I don't have an inner compass," Hudson said.

"Of course you do. If you can't hear it, that means you stopped listening to it."

Many of the rock faces—who had been throwing out random answers during Charlotte and Hudson's conversation—now mumbled in agreement and nodded their heads.

Hudson turned to Charlotte in frustration. "I've never heard anything from an inner compass. What would it have told me?"

Again the rock faces offered a volley of answers. Most sounded like nonsense, but he recognized the right answer. It pierced through the other noise: "It told you to stick up for someone, but you didn't."

He did have an inner compass, he realized, and he had ignored it that day when Andy and Caidan had made fun of Charlotte. Now she'd come to Logos to help him and was even willing to give up a year of her life.

He hadn't spoken. Charlotte took it for reluctance. "We can ask about the princess without paying. I doubt we'll be able to pick out the right answer, though." She turned to the cliff. "Where is Princess Nomira?"

The rock wall seemed to shift outward, swelling. Faces grew

faster on the wall than Hudson could keep track of. Instead of a dozen faces, over a thousand appeared.

"She is here."

"Under the sea."

"On a grassy knoll."

"She ran from the ball on the stroke of midnight."

He couldn't even hear them all; their answers bled into a rumble of words, echoing around them. Finally, the cliff fell silent.

"See?" Charlotte said.

"Okay," Hudson said, resigned. "I'll give up a year of my life for the right answer." He wasn't just doing it to get rid of the curse. He was doing it for Charlotte, so she could have the home she wanted. He was also doing it to help Princess Nomira, the girl with the sad brown eyes, whose tree had finally bloomed again.

Phrasing the question carefully, he asked, "Where did King Vaygran imprison Princess Nomira?"

Only one voice spoke this time, a face high above Hudson. "He put her in the gray tower, beyond the Land of Desolation in the Land of Backwords."

Charlotte took a step toward the cliff. "I give a year of my life for your answer. How do we get Princess Nomira out of the tower?"

A voice far off to the side answered, "The key is the right sword—the most powerful defender, enforcer, convincer, and educator. Depending on how it's wielded, it will right wrongs or inflict them. Put the beginning at the end and you will wield it well. Once the key gets you into the tower, the princess can simply walk out."

Charlotte repeated the instruction to herself, smiling. Excited. "That's not nearly as difficult as I thought it would be."

It wasn't a question, so the faces didn't reply.

Hudson turned toward his pile of coins. He wasn't about to leave them here where anyone could pick up the years of his life and walk off with them. But the piles had vanished; the space where they'd sat was empty.

One of the craggy faces saw him staring and said, "We'll keep your coins safe until you return to pay your debt." The face gave him a stern look, its mossy eyebrows dipping together. "And don't try to get out of payment by getting yourself killed beforehand."

"We won't," Charlotte replied happily, and set off down the path that led to the boat. She seemed to think all of this was good news. Hudson hadn't even understood most of it. The key was a sword? Put the end at the beginning? What did that even mean?

On the trip back across the Sea of Life, Charlotte spouted off things she was grateful for. She was thankful the princess wasn't being held in the land of the giants, or under the sea, or being guarded by trolls.

"We don't know she isn't guarded by trolls," Hudson pointed out. "The face never said she wasn't guarded."

"He didn't say we had to defeat anything to rescue the princess." Charlotte pulled on the work oar. "He just said we needed the right key to get in."

"He said we need the right *sword* to get in, and we should wield it well. That sounds like we've got to fight something."

"Maybe," she conceded, "but if we have the right sword, we'll be successful."

The boat slowed, and Charlotte quickly said, "I'm grateful the soldiers haven't made it to the beach yet."

"I'm glad about that, too." Hudson glanced at the beach nervously. "So what is the most powerful sword in the land? What did the rock face mean about it being an educator? How can a sword do that?"

Charlotte rowed silently for a minute, thinking. Hudson listed foods he was thankful for to keep the boat speeding along. Cheeseburgers were high on the list.

"It's got to be King Vaygran's sword," she finally said. "He not only leads the country; he can dub men knights. I suppose his sword could be called an educator, because King Vaygran keeps the peace, and peace makes it possible for children to be educated."

"Are you sure?" Hudson asked. "We chose the wrong boats and had to swim to shore. What will happen if we choose the wrong sword?"

"It's the only sword that fits the description," Charlotte said, but she didn't sound positive. "We'll have to head back to Grammaria."

The boat had slowed again, so she added, "I'm grateful Hudson is helping me rescue the princess."

Hudson smiled. "I'm grateful you're helping me get rid of the troll mirror." His oar felt lighter, stronger. "How are we going to get the sword from King Vaygran?"

"I'm grateful my father taught me about magic," Charlotte

said, "because that's the only way we'll be able to break into the castle and steal the sword. We'll need fairy help, too. I'm grateful I have a way to contact and pay them."

Hudson thought about the green striped museling, the good memory she had of him, and wasn't grateful she wanted to sell it. He didn't say it, though. It might stop the boat dead in the water.

When Hudson and Charlotte reached the beach, their things were packed up. Still wet, but packed up. Charlotte shrank their animals so they would fit in their packs—Pokey complained about this quite a bit—then she and Hudson got back into the *gratitude* boat. They rowed it down the shore. Dogs couldn't track people over water, so they would row a long way down the beach, then jump out of the boat, wade to shore, and make their way back through the forest to Grammaria.

It was a good plan. Unfortunately, they weren't quite out of sight when the soldiers reached the beach.

10

A PACK OF bright red dogs loped off the trail from Scriptoria—big dogs with wolfish faces and hard black eyes. They bounded down the beach and sniffed around the sand, circling the spot where Hudson and Charlotte had laid out their things to dry.

Charlotte saw them and gasped. "Bloodhounds."

She and Hudson both rowed faster, plunging their oars into the water. "I'm grateful we left already," she said.

"I'm grateful for, um, telephones," he said. "And microwaves and french fries."

A man on a black horse was the next to arrive on the beach. It was hard to tell where the horse ended and the man began, because he wore a long black cloak that draped over the animal. His stringy black beard twisted off the end of his chin like a trailing shadow.

"It's Nepharo," Charlotte whispered, and her voice caught with fear. "He became King Vaygran's top wizard after . . ." her words broke off. "King Vaygran used to have another top wizard. I can't remember what happened to him."

Hudson didn't care. Two dozen men on horses joined the wizard. They wore red uniforms and hats with horns growing out of them. The sunlight glinted off the hilts of the swords hanging at their sides. The men hadn't seen the boat yet, but it wouldn't take long for them to look down the shore. Even going at a fast pace, the boat couldn't outrace horses.

Hudson pulled on his oar extra hard to turn the boat to the beach. "We've got to reach land and get out of sight before they spot us."

Charlotte turned her oar in the same direction. She was still spouting off bits of gratitude, panic creeping into her voice.

The dogs sniffed along the sand, making their way to the first dock. That's when the wizard saw them. The man lifted his wand and shouted something. The soldiers all turned to look in Hudson and Charlotte's direction.

Almost immediately, Hudson felt the boat lifting. The oars dangled uselessly at the side, no longer touching the water. He grabbed the edge of the boat in disbelief. A huge wave had formed underneath them and was lifting them upward. "I thought the clovers protected us from wizards' spells!"

"They do." Charlotte grabbed her bag and scrambled to the front of the boat. "But the water underneath us isn't protected."

Hudson took hold of his bag and joined Charlotte at the front of the boat. With their weight there, the boat slid off the wave, riding it like a sled down a snowy hill. Water sprayed everywhere, shooting white streams away from them. In seconds, the boat skidded onto the shore, nearly capsizing. Hudson and Charlotte jumped out and tore up the beach. Sand spit from beneath their shoes as they ran.

"What do we do now?" he asked.

"Keep running," she yelled. She was behind him, struggling to keep up with his pace.

"Yeah, I figured out that part. We can't outrun dogs, though." He glanced down the beach at the bounding bloodhounds and charging soldiers. They would catch up to them in a minute, maybe two. "Get the iron bar! We need extra strength!"

Charlotte reached into her bag, took out the iron rod, and grasped it tightly. As it shrank in her grip, her speed picked up. She overtook Hudson and, like a relay racer passing the baton, handed him what was left of the iron.

He took hold of the iron and squeezed it hard. New energy infused his muscles. He was already a fast runner. Years of running laps in baseball practice had seen to that. Now he sprinted at an Olympic speed, but it still wouldn't be enough to lose their pursuers.

In moments, he and Charlotte reached the edge of the forest. They rushed through the trees, trampling a patch of neon-pink ferns in the process. Charlotte yelled, "Nigel! Cecil! Help us!"

As they ran, Hudson searched the woods for a glimpse of the unicorns. They were nowhere around. It had always taken a few minutes of walking before they showed up to help.

The trees grew far apart from one another near the beach, but farther into the forest they became thicker. Hudson dodged around scrubby purple bushes that looked like the plant versions of porcupines. He raced through a patch of red tulips, and their petals drew together like pursed lips.

How long did he and Charlotte have until the dogs reached them? A minute? Seconds?

The barks of the bloodhounds cut through the woods. The dogs were closing in. Even with the extra strength the iron provided, Hudson was growing tired.

Charlotte took panting breaths, pushing low-hanging branches out of the way. "Cecil! Nigel!" she yelled. "We need you!"

No flash of gold or streak of silver passed through the trees around them. The unicorns still hadn't come, and the bloodhounds were nearly to them. Hudson heard the dogs thrashing through the underbrush, growling.

Charlotte slowed. She slid her bag off her shoulders, took out the compactulator, and dumped out the tiger, wolf, and polar bear. Moments later, the animals sprang from the ground full size. They bounded toward the bloodhounds, teeth bared and snarling.

Charlotte didn't stop to see how the fight turned out. She kept running. Hudson did, too. Behind them, a dog yelped. The tiger roared. A man yelled, "They went that way!"

Hudson's lungs burned. He didn't dare slow down. Charlotte stumbled over a tree root. He paused to help her up, and they ran on. She sang a few words of the unicorns' favorite song. The singing made her go slower, or perhaps she was just exhausted.

Hudson glanced over his shoulder. One of the dogs had gotten past Charlotte's animals. It streaked forward, barking. It was so vibrantly red it seemed like a flame racing toward them. In another moment, it would reach Charlotte. Hudson stopped, pulled his bag off his shoulder, and put himself between the dog and Charlotte.

"Go!" he told her. He was the only one who'd spoken to the stone bee. Maybe the soldiers would let her escape.

The bloodhound opened its mouth in a growl, showing rows of crimson teeth as it sprang at Hudson. He swung his bag into the hurtling dog, smacking it in the head.

The impact knocked the dog on its side, but seconds later it jumped back to its feet. With ears pressed back and fur bristling, it snarled and paced toward Hudson. He aimed, ready to swing again, and wished his bag held something more dangerous than a damp sleeping bag and a stuffed penguin.

The dog took slow steps, circling, growling, and waiting for the right moment to lunge.

"Hudson!" Charlotte called from a few yards behind him.

He didn't take his eyes off the dog. "Run!" he yelled. "They're only looking for me."

"A noble sentiment," Nigel said. And the next moment, the golden unicorn charged the bloodhound.

The dog leaped away from the unicorn's horn but wasn't fast enough. Nigel's horn pierced the dog's side, and the dog popped like a water balloon. Or, more accurately, a blood balloon. A large red spot oozed on the ground where the hound had stood.

More dogs were coming, though. Their barks echoed through the forest. The thundering sound of the soldiers' horses wasn't far behind.

Nigel bent down so Hudson could grab hold of his mane. "Hurry," the unicorn said. "We've no time to spare."

Hudson pulled himself onto Nigel's back, then held on, panting, while the unicorn raced through the forest. Trees flashed by in a jumble of colors. Every once in a while, Hudson caught sight of Cecil and Charlotte dashing through the forest ahead of them. The dogs' barks grew fainter and fainter until they disappeared altogether.

Hudson laid his head on Nigel's mane and wondered what had become of the tiger, wolf, and polar bear. Had the soldiers killed them? Was it possible to kill something that had started out as a stuffed animal? If they were alive, would they be able to find Charlotte again?

Charlotte must have told Cecil where they needed to go next. The unicorns kept galloping long after they left the soldiers behind. Hudson held on to Nigel's neck, breathing out deep sighs of relief. He and Charlotte were safe. At least for now.

Hours passed. Nigel and Cecil didn't lessen their speed until darkening shadows replaced the sunlight. Then they slowed to a walk. By that time, Hudson's legs ached from all the jostling. Charlotte must have noticed him wincing, because she pulled the candy-heart painkillers from her bag and tossed him a yellow one. "Yellow is a father's love," she said. "It works really well."

It did. It was as smooth and rich as chocolate. It not only took the pain away, but it made him feel like he could accomplish anything.

At last, the unicorns reached the end of the forest. Hudson recognized the place this time. They were by the farmlands and cottages that lay outside Grammaria.

"The soldiers won't pursue you at night," Nigel told Hudson as he dismounted. "Their steeds can't see in the dark. But they'll start their search again in the morning. Be wary and quick in everything you do."

"We will," Hudson said. "Thanks again for saving us."

Nigel let out an approving whinny. "Sacrificing yourself for Charlotte was an act of one who is pure in heart. Perhaps there is hope for you yet."

CHARLOTTE AND HUDSON HAD EATEN THE LAST OF THE GRANOLA bars while they rode the unicorns. It was the only food that their dunk into the Sea of Life hadn't ruined. The few packages hadn't been enough to fill them, so the eagle and falcon flew to the city to get more food. While they were gone, Hudson and Charlotte built a fire to dry out their things. Instead of using matches, she found some romantic-love candy hearts. Those made sparks and surprisingly hot flames.

Pokey and Charlotte's squirrel, Meko, helped spread things out around the fire. It seemed odd not to have the tiger, wolf, and polar bear helping, too. Charlotte kept sniffling back tears. She missed them.

"If your animals escaped from the bloodhounds," Hudson said, holding his pillow as close to the flames as he dared, "your wolf will able to find us. Wolves are good at that."

She shook her head sadly. "They wouldn't have tried to escape. They stayed and fought."

"I bet the bloodhounds didn't hurt them," he said. "Those dogs pop pretty easily, and your animals all had fangs."

Charlotte laid her extra clothes around the fire, barely looking at them. "The unicorns pierced the dog's skin so easily because their horns are made of strong magic. Shabtis only have weak magic. And the soldiers had swords. . . ." Her voice broke, and she bit her lip.

"If you want, I'll give you Pokey."

More sad headshaking. "He's your only shabti. I couldn't take him from you."

Hudson didn't press the point. Pokey wouldn't be much help to Charlotte, anyway.

The eagle returned with a cluster of plums grasped in his talons, and a few minutes later, the falcon brought a small loaf of bread. Charlotte shared them with Hudson.

When it was late enough that King Vaygran had most likely gone to bed, Charlotte and Hudson put out the fire and set off for Grammaria. She left Meko and her birds to guard their things. Hudson left Pokey to help guard, too, mostly so he didn't have to lug the penguin around in his bag.

He and Charlotte didn't speak much as they walked to the city. They were both tired. Hudson's confidence seemed to fade with every step they took. When they had nearly arrived at the river, he asked, "Are you sure there isn't a better way to get King Vaygran's sword? Isn't there some way the shabtis could do it? Squirrels are good at finding things, aren't they?"

"Stop worrying," Charlotte said. "The castle is the last place King Vaygran will expect us to be."

"Yeah, because only crazy people would break into a castle."

"Crazy people and people with magic," she clarified. "I used to live at the castle. I know every room, floor, and secret passageway. The king's bedroom is in the highest tower. The armory is on the first floor. His sword has to be in one of those two places."

"Where was your bedroom?" Hudson asked.

"It was . . ." Her brows drew together, perplexed. "That's funny, I don't remember."

This did not inspire confidence in her ability to navigate their way through the castle. "What do you mean, you don't remember? Didn't you sleep there every night?"

"I remember I had to climb up stairs to get there—the stairs in the highest tower. And it had a fireplace. . . . Why can't I remember more about my bedroom?"

"Did you give away those memories?" Hudson asked.

"I would have written them down, if I had."

"Maybe you misplaced the notebook where you wrote those memories."

"Maybe," she said, still not happy with that explanation. "I suppose I wouldn't realize I lost a notebook, if I don't remember the memories I wrote in it."

Charlotte didn't ponder the mystery any longer. They'd reached the river's edge. The drawbridge was raised, the city gates shut, and only faint lights glowed over the city walls. She took the silver bell from her bag and rang it. "We need a fairy to cross the river."

A speck of light flew out of the river and made lazy loops over to them. The river fairy wore a different dress this time. The gown was as dark as the river at night, with lace that glowed like moonlight on the waves. She hovered in the air in front of them, wand at the ready.

Charlotte dug her muselings out of her bag and counted out four. "We both need passage to the city. We also need some magical assistance." A flicker of nervousness passed over her expression, and her voice dropped to a whisper. "We need a way to take King Vaygran's sword without getting caught. What do you have that can help us?"

The fairy tapped her wand against her hand, thinking. "Something like that will be expensive. Much more than muselings. It will cost you a powerful remembrance. What are you offering?"

Charlotte hesitated, then looked down. "I have the memory of three friends who probably gave their life for mine."

"Perhaps," the fairy said, gliding closer to Charlotte. "I want to see what else you've got." With the flick of her hand, her wand became a flashlight that she shone into one of Charlotte's eyes.

Hudson had thought his internal compass had stopped working, but he heard it this time and spoke up. "Take one of mine instead," he told the fairy. "I've got lots of good memories." It was true. He hadn't realized how many good memories he had until he listed them in the *gratitude* boat. Family, friends, a country without kings who set wizards on innocent people.

The fairy glided over to Hudson, wings fluttering. "Let's hope your memories are in better shape than your friend's. Hers have already been cut to ribbons." The fairy swung her wand at Hudson, and the beam of light went into his right eye. It didn't hurt like a normal light would have. It just felt uncomfortable, sort of like something warm pinging off the walls of his brain.

"Ahh," the fairy chimed. "There's a delicious one." She didn't have to tell him which one she meant. It unfolded in his mind in perfect detail.

Hudson was in his front yard, saying good-bye to his dad before he deployed. His mom stood a little ways away, telling Bonnie she didn't need to cry, but was crying herself. "Six months isn't so long," she said, trying to sound brave. "It takes me longer than that to make it through my to-do list. How much do you want to bet that none of the clutter on our dressers is even cleared away by the time your dad steps back through the door?"

Hudson knew then that, while their dad was gone, their mother wouldn't bother telling him and Bonnie to straighten their dressers. It was her way of denying that he'd be gone for too long.

Hudson saw his father's face clearly, his broad smile and dark brown eyes, the same ones Hudson had. His dad wrapped him in a hug. "You take care of your mom and sister, you hear?"

"I will," Hudson said.

His father didn't let him go. Hudson leaned against his dad's shirt, breathing in the smell of his aftershave.

"You take care of yourself, too," his father said, "and remember I'm thinking of you every day." He gave Hudson's shoulder a squeeze. "I love you, and I'm proud you're my son."

That was the memory the fairy wanted.

Hudson shook his head. "I can't give you that one."

The fairy lifted her chin, and her pale wings beat faster. "Then you'll have to get King Vaygran's sword by yourself."

Charlotte's gaze bounced between Hudson and the fairy. "I must have a memory you'd like. Take one of mine."

"No," Hudson said. If Charlotte's memories really were cut into ribbons, he didn't want anything else taken from her mind. "Just let me write the memory down first so I know what I'm forgetting."

Charlotte gave him a thankful look, one tinged with sadness, then she got out a pen and her notebook. She handed them to him.

He wrote down the memory as thoroughly as he could, trying to capture every second of the good-bye so he could preserve it. He wished he were better with words, that he could find a way to describe all the things that were in his father's smile. His confidence, his humor, his trust. When Hudson finished, he handed the pen and paper back to Charlotte. "I'm ready now."

The fairy flicked her wand, moving it in strokes like a maestro conducting an orchestra. Something sparkled in front of Hudson's eyes. At first, he thought the sparkles were coming out of the fairy's wand. Then he realized they were coming from his mind and traveling into the wand.

Hudson searched his memory for his father's good-bye. It was a blank spot in his mind now. He only remembered the words he'd just written down about it.

The fairy glowed as brightly as a miniature firework and smiled at him happily. "I'll treasure that one."

"What about the magic you owe us?" he asked stiffly.

"Oh, right." She pulled a small, dark object out of her bag. "I've programmed this magnet to guide you to wherever the king's sword is." She tossed it to him, and the thing grew in midair to the size of a cell phone. Hudson caught it and turned it over in his hand. He held a horseshoe-shaped magnet that had a tiny map in the middle. It showed the streets of Grammaria with a star on the castle. Words on top of the map read *Fly straight for 6.5 miles.*

The fairy zipped closer to Hudson, hovering near his hand. "Once the magnet touches the sword, the sword will shrink until it's travel size. You can just put it in your pocket after that. Then ring your bell, and you'll automatically be turned into birds again so you can escape out of one of the castle's windows."

Charlotte glanced at the map on the magnet. "We'll need to be birds longer than five minutes each way. Otherwise, we'll end up trapped in Grammaria."

The fairy considered this. "I'll make it ten minutes, and I'll turn you into falcons." She waved her wand in a swooping motion at Charlotte and Hudson. "Peregrine falcons can fly up to sixty miles an hour horizontally and over two hundred miles an hour when they dive. That should be fast enough for you to span the distance."

As the fairy spoke, Charlotte transformed, shrinking into a sleek brown falcon with a white throat and black eyes. The next moment, Hudson felt the familiar contracting sensation. His fingers flattened into feathers, his arms stretched into wings. He flapped his wings and flew upward, shooting out over the river in easy, swift strokes. He was light and swift, and flying made him feel like he had conquered gravity. He wanted to glide for a bit, but Charlotte was zooming ahead of him so quickly he had to push himself to keep up with her.

They sailed over the walls and sped across the city, past winding roads and boxy shops. He barely glanced down at them. He kept his eye on the castle, watching it grow closer with every stroke of his wings. He enjoyed the rush of air, the feeling of speed and freedom. Minutes later, they arrived.

Charlotte headed straight toward the highest tower. She circled the tower once, then twice, searching for an open window. The height worried Hudson. How long had they been falcons? Eight minutes? Closer to ten? If they switched back to their human form now, they'd fall to their deaths.

Charlotte found some shutters ajar and slipped through the opening. Hudson followed her. The room was dark, but with his falcon eyes, he could make out shapes. It was an empty bedroom. Maybe a guest room. He flew over to the headboard, perched there, and tried to catch his breath. A moment later, he nearly fell face-first onto the bed. He was human again.

Charlotte stood on the floor in front of him, still looking like Isabella—a slightly worried, jumpy Isabella. She took the jar of hope from her pocket and shook it softly, just enough to create a dull glow.

Hudson pulled the magnet from his pocket and looked at the map. It showed a diagram of the castle, indicating with a star that the sword was in the top of the highest tower.

Charlotte glanced over his shoulder, checked the map, and let out a small whimper. "The sword is in the king's room. I was hoping it would be in the armory." She swallowed hard. "I really don't want to see King Vaygran again, even if he is sleeping."

"We'll make sure we don't accidentally wake him up."

Hudson expected Charlotte to go to the door and lead the way. She stayed where she was.

"We can do this," she said. "Once we touch the sword to the magnet, it will shrink. Then all we have to do is find an open window and ring the fairy bell. We'll automatically be turned back into birds." She still didn't move to the door.

"Are you trying to convince me, or yourself?" he asked.

She glanced at the door nervously. "We've come this far—we have to do it."

"We don't have to do it," he said. "We could go back to our camp and send your birds to do it instead."

She shook her head. "I already explained this. For magic to work, you have to do the important things yourself."

Hudson raised his hand in protest. "This isn't magic. This is stealing. Your birds steal food all the time."

She took a deep breath and slowly let it out again. "I have to do this for the princess, and for all the people of Logos who need her."

Hudson let out a sigh. He supposed he hadn't really expected Charlotte to back out now. "Okay, then. Let's do this." The faster they got the sword, the sooner they could get away from King Vaygran's city.

Charlotte carefully opened the door and peered outside. "The way is clear," she whispered.

Hudson followed her into the hallway. The magnet shifted in his hand so its ends pointed to the left, the same direction the map showed they needed to go. "Follow the hallway for two hundred and fifty feet," the magnet said in a quiet, automated voice.

He and Charlotte tiptoed in that direction. When they came to a staircase, the magnet's ends pointed up. "Follow the—"

"We know," Hudson said, cutting off the magnet, and started up the stairs.

Charlotte took hold of his arm, stopping him. "If we go that way, we'll run into guards posted in the hallway. I know a passageway through the fireplaces. Come this way."

Hudson turned and went with her, shoving the magnet into his jacket pocket when it said, "Make a U-turn . . . or an R-turn. An M-turn would also point you in the right direction. . . ." The last thing Hudson needed was a bossy magnet alerting people that he was sneaking around the castle.

Charlotte padded down the hallway until they reached an ornately carved door. She carefully pushed it open.

From the glow of the hope jar, Hudson could tell it was a large bedroom. An elaborate chandelier hung from the ceiling over a golden four-poster bed. A pink lace canopy draped across the bed, and flowering vines twined along the posts. The dresser, desk, and an assortment of chairs were each intricately carved, proclaiming their cost.

Charlotte gazed around the room with puzzlement. "They've changed the princess's room. Nothing looks familiar." She shook her head, as though to clear her mind of such mundane facts, and walked over to a large fireplace. It was made of white stone with leaf carvings around the sides and across the mantel. Two stone falcons sat atop each corner. "The passageway will still be the same," Charlotte said. "No one knew about this but me and . . ." She stopped, and her eyebrows drew together as she tried to retrieve the memory. "Someone else knew. I can't remember who."

"The princess?" Hudson guessed. "Were you friends with the princess?"

Charlotte's eyebrows remained pinched together. "Yes," she said vaguely, still puzzled. "We must have been."

She pulled the falcon on the left side of the mantel, tilting it downward. Without making a sound, the blackened back of the fireplace slid open to reveal a hidden stone staircase.

Charlotte had to dip her head to go under the mantel but was able to stand straight when she reached the stairwell. She beckoned to him, holding the hope jar toward him so he could see his way.

Hudson crouched through the fireplace and joined her on the steps. The stairwell was dark with soot and smelled of smoke, and the layer of ashy dust told him no one had come this way for a while.

They climbed slowly up the circular stairs, doing their best to muffle their footsteps in a place that seemed ready to echo. Shadows flickered on the gray wall next to them, dissolving into darkness after they passed by. Hudson didn't like the feeling that the darkness was somehow following them up the stairs, creeping along behind them.

Finally, they came to a small landing where another stone-panel door waited. This one had a crown-shaped knob on one side.

Charlotte placed her hand gingerly on the panel. "It's cool," she said in a hushed voice. "He doesn't have a fire going." She leaned forward, listening at the door. After a minute, she whispered, "I don't hear anything. He must be asleep." She shut her eyes as though saying a prayer. "He must be."

Charlotte reached over and twisted the crown knob. The stone door noiselessly slid open into a bedroom that was four times the size of the princess's.

Hudson could see it all because several of the room's chandeliers were lit. King Vaygran wasn't sleeping in his large, velvet-draped bed. He sat in an armchair across from the fireplace reading a letter. He glanced up when the fireplace panel opened, and he looked straight at them.

11

KING VAYGRAN WAS a tall man with thick shoulders and black hair that shone like it had been rubbed with oil. His black beard came to such a sharp point, it might have been cut by a pencil sharpener. The beard would have looked odd on most people, but it made him seem tough, like a pro wrestler. Except a wrestler wouldn't wear a gold-trimmed purple tunic or jeweled rings on every single finger. King Vaygran looked so downright royal Hudson could only gawk at him and wonder if he should kneel.

The king's sword scabbard was leaning up against his chair. He'd probably taken it off to sit down.

King Vaygran stood up, a cloud of indignation gathering across his features. "Who are you?"

Hudson didn't know whether to run into the room and grab the sword or to retreat backward and close the door in the fireplace. Retreating would be smarter. He took a step backward.

Charlotte dashed toward the scabbard.

King Vaygran stepped forward to intercept her, his height making her look wispy by comparison. "Guards!"

Charlotte darted around him. She wasn't fast enough. King Vaygran grabbed hold of her arm, twisting it as he pulled her closer. "What have we here?" he asked.

Hudson rushed into the room to help Charlotte. She writhed and wriggled, unable to free herself. "The window!" she called to him.

Hudson understood what she meant. All the shutters in the room were closed. He needed to open one so once they changed into birds, they could escape. He ran to the closest window.

"Guards!" King Vaygran shouted again.

The king's bedroom door rattled. "Your Highness," a man on the other side called back. "The door is locked."

The latch on the shutters was shaped like a small silver cat. Hudson fiddled with it, unsure how to open it. He pushed and pulled. Nothing worked. The silver cat just peered back at him condescendingly.

King Vaygran was dragging Charlotte toward the door so he could unlock it and let his guards in. She flailed, hitting him and struggling with every step. She only managed to slow his progress. Once the guards came inside, he and Charlotte would be captured.

"How do I open the shutters?" Hudson yelled. He wasn't sure Charlotte heard him.

At the same time he spoke, King Vaygran boomed out, "Who are you, bratling? Who sent you to sneak in here to slay me?"

Charlotte planted her feet and tugged at his grip. "Let me go! You're a tyrant and a bully!"

Hudson tried sliding, yanking, turning, and prying the cat off the shutters altogether. It only hissed at him with disdain.

King Vaygran peered at Charlotte more closely. "Your voice is familiar. I know you, don't I?" He stopped pulling her toward the door and began pulling her toward some shelves in the wall. "Revealing powder will tell me who you are. Then we'll find out what sort of treachery you're up to."

There had to be a way to open the cat latch on the window. How come nothing in this place made sense? It was then that Hudson realized he was going about things the wrong way, expecting the rules of his world to apply here. He scratched the cat under its chin, and it lifted its paws, letting the shutters swing open.

King Vaygran had managed to drag Charlotte over to his shelves. He was holding on to her arm so tightly she winced in pain. To the guards outside, he shouted, "Break down the door!"

He took a drawstring bag off one of his shelves. Probably the revealing powder. He would sprinkle it on Charlotte and find out she was Fantasmo's daughter.

Hudson ran to Charlotte. Normally, he wouldn't be able to take anything from a man as big as King Vaygran. This time, however, the king was busy struggling with Charlotte. Hudson wrenched the bag from his hand and threw it across the room. It sailed directly out the window. Baseball, it turned out, was not such a useless skill.

King Vaygran cursed, and his face contorted with rage. He

let go of Charlotte and lunged at Hudson, grabbing him so his arms were pinned to his sides. Hudson felt as though he were being squeezed by a boa constrictor.

He kicked at the king's legs as hard as he could. "Get the sword!" he yelled to Charlotte.

His kicks didn't do any good. The king wore thick boots, and Hudson had on the stupid banana shoes.

"Where are my guards?" King Vaygran shouted.

Something heavy thunked against the door. It shook, but held. The door had obviously been built to keep the king safe from intruders.

Charlotte reached the chair and the scabbard lying there. She picked it up and turned back to Hudson with an expression of horror. The scabbard was empty. The sword hadn't been in it at all.

Where was it? The sword had to be somewhere in the room. The magnet had told them it was here. If Hudson could get the magnet out of his jacket pocket, it would be able to point them to the sword.

King Vaygran pulled Hudson toward his bed, threatening him with various painful deaths along the way. Hudson couldn't reach his pocket, let alone get to the magnet.

Charlotte headed back across the room toward them, the scabbard still in her hand. Hudson didn't know what she planned to do with it and didn't get to find out. In one fast move, King Vaygran reached beside his bed and pulled out his sword. Before Hudson could break the man's grasp on him, King Vaygran brought the sword to Hudson's neck, pressing the edge into his throat. Hudson stopped struggling. One wrong move, and the sword would cut him.

"Halt!" King Vaygran yelled at Charlotte.

She did. Her eyes went wide, staring at the sword.

Hudson's heart beat like a basketball team full of panicked dribblers. It was hard to breathe.

He had wanted to find the sword, but this was not how he had envisioned locating it.

"You will tell me everything," the king said through gritted teeth. "Or your friend will be dead before you can cross the room."

King Vaygran held on to Hudson's left arm, but his other hand was on his sword. This meant Hudson's right arm was free. Carefully, slowly, he reached into his pocket.

Charlotte saw what he was doing but kept her gaze on King Vaygran's eyes so as not to draw attention to Hudson. "Don't hurt him," she pleaded. "I'll tell you the truth. I promise."

The door banged. The castle guards were still fighting against the lock. Splinters flew across the floor. The men would break in soon.

"Who are you?" the king demanded.

"A student," Charlotte stalled. "A daughter. A friend—"

Hudson carefully fingered through his pocket, feeling for the magnet.

King Vaygran pressed his sword farther into Hudson's neck, sending a sharp pain into his throat. "Don't play games with me," the king spat out. "What's your name?"

"Charlotte," she said. This was true, although it wasn't the name King Vaygran would recognize.

"Where did you come from?"

"The fireplace."

King Vaygran let out an impatient grunt. "Before that."

"Before that, I was downstairs, and then in the forest."

Hudson tugged the magnet free from his pocket. The time for moving slowly was over. He slid the magnet onto the sword blade. The move startled the king, and he pushed his sword into Hudson's neck. Fortunately, the sword shrank as quickly as the king pushed. Soon he held nothing at all.

The disappearance of the sword so surprised King Vaygran that, for a moment, he just stared at his hand. Hudson broke away from the king's grasp and headed toward the window, putting both the magnet and the sword into his pocket.

Charlotte pulled out the bell and rang it fiercely.

The king gasped. Perhaps he recognized the bell, or perhaps he'd finally placed Charlotte's voice. He pointed at her. "I know who you are!"

Immediately, Hudson felt himself shrinking. His arms stretched into wings, already flapping before the transformation was complete.

King Vaygran grabbed at him, managing to pull out a couple of tail feathers before Hudson sped across the room. Charlotte, already in her bird form, chirped angrily at the king, then dove out the window. She zoomed downward, going so fast she seemed hardly more than a blur. At first, Hudson had no idea what she was doing, and he hovered in the air, uncertain whether to follow. Then he saw the bag of revealing powder lying on the ground. She snatched it in her talons, pushed upward, and headed toward the city wall.

From the window, the king yelled, "Shoot those birds! Bring

them down from the sky!" King Vaygran's guards must have finally managed to come into his room.

Hudson heard the twang of bows, and arrows whizzed by, piercing the air around them. None hit them. It was hard to hit a small moving target in the dark.

He and Charlotte flew over the city, skimming through the air as they raced against time. He felt a growing relief with each flap of his wings. They were free and cloaked by the night. The king's men couldn't catch them now.

As they flew over the city walls, a feeling of wild elation filled him. They'd done it. They'd stolen King Vaygran's sword—not while he slept, but while he was awake and fighting them. Now they had the key to the princess's tower. After they freed her, everything would be set right in Logos, and Hudson could return to Texas. He could go back to his normal life.

He and Charlotte soared over the river, then flew low to the ground as they made their way over the farmland. They were nearly to their campsite when the transformation overtook them. They tumbled to the ground, human again.

Hudson got to his feet, brushed himself off, and grinned. As Charlotte stood up, she took the jar of hope from her jacket. She jiggled it to produce a glow so they could see their way to the campsite. Hudson walked beside her, pulling the magnet and miniature sword from his pocket. He showed them to Charlotte. "We've got the key. We're on our way."

"We need to be," she agreed. "The farther we go tonight, the better. You heard King Vaygran—he recognized my voice. He knows who I am." As she said the last words, she shuddered.

Charlotte had never said what sort of relationship she'd had with the king when she'd lived here before, but Hudson could tell it wasn't good.

THEY MADE SLOW PROGRESS THROUGH THE FOREST. HOPE, AFTER all, can only cast away so much darkness. The trees that had been so colorful in the daytime seemed gray and tangled now. Hudson couldn't see farther than a step or two away and kept running into bushes. Before long, they grew too tired to keep going, and they set up a quick camp—quick in this case meaning laying out damp sleeping bags and falling asleep on them.

Hudson awakened a few hours later with Pokey pecking at his hair. Hudson swatted at him. "What are you doing?" he grumbled, and turned over. It wasn't even dawn yet.

"The other birds said I should wake you with a welcoming birdcall. Penguins don't do that, so I decided to root around in your hair for bugs. I found one."

The morning didn't get much better after that.

Hudson and Charlotte packed up their things, checked the compass, and set off walking through the undergrowth toward the Land of Desolation. The Skittles-colored forest wasn't nearly as charming when you had to keep pushing branches out of your face. He knocked into an oak branch and was promptly pelted by acorns, bcorns, and even a few ccorns.

He hoped the unicorns would pick them up soon. He didn't know how far away the soldiers were, or if King Vaygran would send a new group of bloodhounds from the city after them.

"We should change our appearances again," Hudson said,

shooing away some dragonflies that buzzed by his head. They shot tiny flames at him before darting off. "King Vaygran's men will be on the lookout for Isabella and Andy now."

"You're right." Charlotte rifled through her bag for the disguise paste. "I'm sorry Isabella will have to go."

"Why?"

"Well, I know how much you like looking at her."

"What?" Hudson asked, flushing. "What are you talking about?"

Charlotte sent him a meaningful gaze. "Back in school, you stared at her a lot."

"That was only because"—Hudson made an airy, pointless gesture—"I was sort of suffering from . . ." He had meant to say something along the lines of vision problems, but Charlotte was staring at him in a way that didn't allow for flagrant excuses.

"Stupidity," he finished.

His answer made her smile. That was another thing that wasn't very Isabella-like—Charlotte's easy smile. It was genuine, not like Isabella's precise and perfected smiles.

Charlotte found the disguise paste and pulled it out of the bag.

"Will you be sorry to see Andy go?" he asked.

"No," she said. "Every once in a while, I expect you to sneer at me and say something horrible."

"Andy and Caidan were jerks to you." More quietly, Hudson added, "Sorry I didn't stick up for you."

"It's okay," she said, and smiled again. He wouldn't have traded that smile for ten from the real Isabella.

After a few minutes of discussion, Hudson decided to change into Trevor, and Charlotte became Macy. She got Macy's light brown hair and hazel eyes right but somehow missed the air of judgment Macy always had. They both wore less flamboyant clothes this time, and Hudson insisted upon wearing regular boots instead of the stupid banana shoes.

While they walked, he took King Vaygran's sword from his bag. Last night, it had been too dark to get a good look at it. Now he turned it over in the palm of his hand, examining it. The blade wasn't much bigger than a car key. It was straight, silver, and shone in the sunlight. Besides the fancy markings on the hilt, it seemed like a normal sword.

He gave it to Charlotte and then considered ditching the magnet. The entire time Charlotte held the sword, the magnet announced directions to it, calling out things like, "Turn right in ten inches."

When Hudson ignored these directions, the magnet's voice became snottier. "Just reach out and take it," the magnet insisted. "It's right there. Can't you see it? Right there."

Finally, for the sake of quiet, he put the sword back on the end of the magnet. It hummed happily like a child who'd been given a favorite teddy bear. "My destination," it murmured.

Yeah, magic could take some weird turns.

He tucked both sword and magnet back into his bag. Charlotte kept checking her compass to make sure they were headed in the right direction. While they hiked through the forest, she told him the story behind the Land of Desolation. "Two cities used to be there: the City of Rhyme and the City of Reason.

One was supposed to teach and study all things factual and the other to study and teach all things beautiful. However, there's too much fact in beauty and too much beauty in fact, and the cities never did stop arguing about where history should be. So finally, King Arawn decided they should combine their efforts, and he united both places into the Land of Scholars."

"Oh," Hudson said, not quite sure he followed the part about beauty being in facts.

"Rhyme and Reason were growing together a bit in the middle lands anyway, which meant the Land of Scholars was shaped like an hourglass. Everyone in Logos thought it was fitting, because there should always be time for learning."

"Right," Hudson said, still wondering if there were indeed facts in beauty.

"After King Vaygran took the throne, some of the scholars criticized his policies. They knew if enough people realized what the king was doing, they would oppose him. They told stories about the plight of the banished poor, and of citizens who were imprisoned for having wrong opinions. They wrote poems about freedom and songs that asked for the princess's return."

"So King Vaygran attacked them?"

"He had some of his wizards cast a spell on the Land of the Scholars. Everything disappeared. The people, the cities, the land. And worst of all—the memories of them."

"If he took your memories of them," Hudson asked, "then how do you remember what happened to them?"

"He took the memory of people, not the place," she said.

"None of us remember the people. I could have had friends or brothers and sisters who went to study in the Land of Scholars, but as soon as the spell came over the land, I forgot them. We all did. And nothing will bring back those memories while King Vaygran rules."

"That's horrible." Hudson's hands tightened around the straps of his bag. He wanted to take out the sword and hold it, to reassure himself that he had the key that would bring the princess back.

"As retaliation for the way the scholars used words against King Vaygran, his wizards created a border around the land that sucks words away. It's dangerous to cross it."

"Why?"

"It's *wordless*," she emphasized, as though that explained everything.

"So?"

"People get hopelessly lost there."

He still didn't understand what she meant. "You mean because there aren't any signs?"

"It's not just signs. You can't speak, and thinking is almost impossible. Without words, you're reduced to reactions, wants, and fears. Who you are," she said slowly, "depends a lot on the words you have."

Hudson didn't quite believe her. Who he was didn't have to do with words. It had to do with the choices he made. It had to do with his Hudsonness.

He and Charlotte didn't talk about it more. Nigel and Cecil trotted through some trees in front of them.

"Greetings, good unicorns." Charlotte gave a curtsy, and Hudson remembered to bow.

Cecil let out a happy whinnying sound. "See," he said to Nigel, "I told you they were still alive. I win the bet. King Vaygran doesn't kill *everyone* who crosses him."

Nigel pawed at the ground with one hoof. "I said he *tried* to kill everyone who crossed him." He turned to Charlotte. "Did King Vaygran try to kill you?"

"He nearly stabbed Hudson, and then his guards shot arrows at us."

"Ha," Nigel said. "You didn't win. And besides, the day is still young."

It is never a good sign when unicorns are wagering on your death. Still, in a perfectly cheerful voice, Charlotte asked, "Could we trouble you for a ride to the isthmus of the Land of Desolation?" To Hudson, she explained, "The isthmus is what we call the narrow strip of land that connected Rhyme to Reason. It's only a couple of miles long, so it is the easiest place to cross."

Cecil raised his horn, and it glistened silver in the sunlight. "We'll take you as far as the forest allows." He knelt before Charlotte to allow her to get on his back. Nigel did the same for Hudson.

He was glad the unicorns had finally stopped questioning whether he was pure enough to haul around.

They trotted through the forest at a good pace. The unicorns seemed to know every secret path and hidden way. They went through a bower of trees that bent together to make a tunnel and swam across a river with a current so strong that swirling hands seemed to grab at them.

Charlotte sang for most of the time, although every once in a while Hudson sang to give her a break. The unicorns were polite enough about his singing, but as soon as he finished, they always requested another song from Charlotte. Hudson didn't blame them. She sounded happy when she sang. Well, except for when she sang songs about good King Arawn; then she always sounded wistfully sad.

Charlotte and Hudson ate fruit that the birds brought them for lunch, and then more fruit for dinner. Hudson was tired of fruit and wished they could buy some real food. He thought longingly of the warm and buttery *read* he'd eaten in Scriptoria. He would have done anything to have a good read again.

Nightfall came, and they'd only traveled two-thirds of the way to the Land of Desolation. They needed to get some sleep, so the unicorns dropped them off in a safe spot and promised to return in the morning.

That night, as they lay in their sleeping bags, Charlotte asked, "What are you thinking about?"

He'd been wondering how dangerous tomorrow would be. What was waiting for them at the tower in the Land of Backwords? "Nothing," he said, because he didn't want to worry Charlotte. "What are you thinking about?"

"Nothing," she answered.

Apparently, she didn't want to worry him, either.

12

THE NEXT MORNING, while Hudson and Charlotte repacked their things, the unicorns trotted up. Nigel ambled over to Hudson, swishing his golden tail.

Hudson shoved his pillow into his bag. "Hey, what's up?"

Nigel nickered. "The sun, the moon, and the constellations." He turned to Charlotte and lowered his voice. "He's a rather simple boy, isn't he?"

"The people from the Land of Banishment are very concerned with things that are up," she said confidentially. "Some of them are also curious about what's going down."

Hudson slipped his bag over his shoulders. "Those are just sayings. They mean, 'How's it going?'"

Nigel knelt to allow Hudson to mount. "That depends on what you mean when you say *it*. *It* generally refers to the last noun a speaker used. So when the first thing you say is 'How's it going?' you could be referring to any of the hundred thousand nouns in the language. Wouldn't it be helpful to narrow your subject down a bit?"

Charlotte had already mounted Cecil, and the two unicorns headed out through the trees. "Are there only a hundred thousand nouns?" Cecil asked. "I would have put it closer to two hundred thousand."

"Actually, I think a hundred thousand is a generous number," Nigel replied. "I was rounding up."

"That can't be right," Cecil said. "Did you count flothbartens, shimshorns, merritongs—"

"Okay," Hudson said, breaking into their conversation. " 'How's it going?' is just another way of saying, 'Hello. How are you?' "

The unicorns considered this as they went past a strand of cotton-candy-pink trees. "People from your land should learn to express themselves without confusion."

Charlotte nodded in agreement. "You have no idea how right you are about that."

Hudson didn't bother explaining any more of his expressions.

Four hours later, the trees thinned out, and the sky changed from light blue to nearly white. Even the dirt on the ground ahead was bleached to a salty tan. Where the forest ended, the ground turned pale and desertlike and spread out in a long band, both left and right, as far as Hudson could see.

"We're here," Charlotte said.

The unicorns slowed to a stop. "We are indeed," Cecil said. "And we wish you a merry isthmus." Both unicorns let out whinnies of laughter at the joke.

On the other side of the Land of Desolation, sloping hills

with forests of white trees were visible. Charlotte pointed to them. "That's the Land of Backwords."

The forests there seemed as thick as the ones on this side. In the middle, though, only a few spindly bushes grew here and there. Spots of yellow grass dotted the landscape. Mostly it looked like a huge bulldozer had scraped everything away.

A sign of some sort stuck out of the ground a few yards into the Land of Desolation. Probably a warning sign. Its words were too small to read.

Nigel knelt to make it easier for Hudson to get down. "This is where we say adieu, cheerio, and all other words of parting."

Hudson slid from Nigel's back. "Thanks for taking us."

Charlotte dismounted from Cecil and gave his neck an affectionate hug. "If all goes well, we'll return in a few hours with Princess Nomira." She looked from one unicorn to the other. "Will you be able to carry all of us?"

Cecil lowered his head so his eyes met Charlotte's. "Your confidence is your best weapon. Wield it well, but don't let it be wielded against you."

She stroked Cecil's silver nose. "Was that a yes or a no?"

Cecil and Nigel exchanged a look that indicated they weren't nearly as confident about Hudson and Charlotte's chances as she was. "Should you manage to free the princess," Cecil said, "we'll gladly carry her."

Hudson couldn't resist petting Nigel's nose, as well. It felt as soft as a new blanket. "Thanks again."

"Remember to use your words well," Nigel said. "Sometimes that's what marks the difference between failure and success."

"I'll try." Hudson gave the unicorns a last wave, then headed out with Charlotte.

They hadn't walked far before the sign became legible. It read WELCOME TO THE LAND OF DESOLATION. THERE ARE NO WORDS TO DESCRIBE THIS PLACE.

Hudson didn't know about that. *Barren* came to mind. So did *empty, dead,* and *depressing.*

Charlotte didn't go beyond the sign. She took out her silver bell and called, "We need a fairy to guide us to the Land of Backwords."

After a few moments, a fairy flickered out from behind one of the bushes. Her hair and dress were tan, making her blend into everything else, but as she flew toward them, the sunlight glimmered off her wings like tiny sparks. She hovered in front of Charlotte and lifted her wand. "To guide you across the desolation, I charge three muselings. Each way." She smiled and added, "And you'll need to pay in advance for the trip back."

"Six muselings?" Hudson protested. "It's not that far. We can see the other side from where we're standing."

"We'll pay." Charlotte dug through her leather bag.

Hudson let out a grunt and folded his arms. "The river fairy could have turned us into birds so we could fly across for less."

The sand fairy lifted her chin haughtily. "Six muselings is my price for being your guide. If you want to be a bird, that will be extra."

"We want to stay human." Charlotte pulled out her bag of muselings and opened it. "But why do we have to pay in advance for the trip back?"

The fairy hovered in the air, wings fluttering. "That way if you get lost, forget everything, and wander around aimlessly, I still get paid."

It wasn't the most encouraging thing Hudson had heard.

Charlotte dumped all the muselings into her hand. She only had six left, the price of the trip.

Hudson eyed the green striped one sitting in her palm. It was the memory of the time he'd helped her with algebra. "You can't give her all your muselings."

Charlotte held them out to the fairy. "We need her assistance."

The fairy pointed her wand at a blue one, and it lifted from Charlotte's palm, shrinking as it flew to the fairy. She slipped the museling into a purse that seemed to be made of bits of broken glass, then pointed her wand at a spotted purple one and took it, as well. Hudson picked the green striped museling from Charlotte's hand. He would let the fairy take a museling from him instead. "I know what memory this is," he told Charlotte. "I saw the descriptions while you were drying your stuff out."

"Oh," she said, and blushed.

"Why did you decide to change that memory into a museling? Was it because you wanted to forget me?"

"No," she said softly. "I knew we would make good memories here. And we have—riding unicorns, rowing boats, stealing King Vaygran's sword. That's much better than a walk to school."

He hadn't thought of that, and it made him feel better. "I still don't want you to lose this one. You can use one of my memories to make a museling."

Charlotte took the museling from Hudson's hand. "You've

already lost a remembrance. I don't want you to lose anything else." She held the museling out to the fairy. "Besides, now I have the memory of your offer, and that's even nicer."

The fairy flicked her wand, and the green striped museling floated toward her. She snatched it out of the air and turned it over in her hand. "This must be a really good one." She popped it into her mouth and immediately glowed like a night-light with wings. Tilting her head, she grinned at him and Charlotte. "Ah, how sweet. The two of you are so cute."

Great. Wonderful. She was eating a memory about him and calling him cute.

The fairy hummed as she took the rest of muselings, then said, "I'm ready to go when you are." Her wings caught the sun's light and held on to it, making them two small beacons.

Charlotte took hold of Hudson's arm to get his attention. She'd given him instructions about crossing the Land of Desolation while they'd ridden here, but she repeated them now anyway. "Keep telling yourself that you're following the fairy. Don't look at anything else. Follow her light. Say it over and over again."

"I know," he said.

Charlotte dropped his arm. "We're ready."

The fairy headed out into the desert, and they both followed after her with long, quick steps.

"I still think it would be faster to go as birds," he said.

"Magic in this part of the land is a peculiar thing. If we lose our way as birds, we might forget altogether that we're humans."

With that happy thought, they walked into the Land of Desolation.

It reminded him of stepping into the sea. Not because it was wet or cold. Without the shade of the trees, everything felt hot and dry. But this place had the same undercurrent, the same feeling of being pulled into something deep and powerful.

The fairy bobbed ahead of them, her light glowing like a flare.

He needed to follow her light. It wasn't that far. Only two miles. He could walk that in half an hour, easy. It would be over soon. It would . . .

Hudson couldn't have said when the words disappeared from his mind. Everything was just gone. Empty. He was doing something important, he remembered that much. And he knew in some corner of his mind that he needed to follow the light in front of him, but he couldn't remember why.

He didn't recognize this place, couldn't recall whether he had ever known it. A friend walked next to him. Although he didn't know why either of them was here. They had been doing something. He had memories of them being together before this, and yet none of it made sense. They seemed like scenes in a movie that had been randomly thrown together.

The longer he walked, the blurrier and more uncertain his mind got.

Maybe he should stop. A light glowed in front of him. He had a feeling it was important. He walked toward it. As quickly as he followed it, it sped onward. He couldn't catch up. Frustrating.

Maybe he should go back the way he came. It was hot here, and things felt funny.

The light bobbed ahead of him.

The light. He needed to follow it.

The farther he walked, the more fragmented he felt, like something was slicing up his mind, taking parts of it away. He couldn't make sense of what was happening. He could only see, not think.

This wasn't a good place.

Should go somewhere else.

Maybe another direction.

But

Light.

Light.

Light.

And then, as though he'd pushed through a searing fog, everything came back to him. Thoughts poured into his mind until he brimmed with memories, words, sense, and order.

He had been walking through the Land of Desolation with Charlotte, and they must have reached the other side, because he could think again. "We made it," he breathed out.

Charlotte put a shaking hand to her chest. "That was horrible. It felt like my mind was ripped away."

Now that they had passed through the Land of Desolation, even the air felt different—fuller somehow, not as parched. The forest of pale white trees spread out in front of them, their leaves rustling like pages of books. The fairy, without bothering to say good-bye, disappeared somewhere into the air.

A large dotted line ran across the ground in front of a sign that read WELCOME TO THE LAND OF BACKWORDS.

In smaller lettering underneath this sentence was the phrase BACKWORDS OF LAND THE TO WELCOME.

And underneath it, in smaller lettering still: EMOCLEW OT EHT DNAL FO SDROWKCAB

More phrases were written under these three, so small that Hudson couldn't read them. Apparently there were a lot of ways to be backward.

He and Charlotte crossed the line. Some of the trees in the forest were shaped like pine trees and had pointy tops. They looked like someone had made them out of book covers that had been turned upside down—or more likely backward—and stacked on top of each other.

A sign on the path ahead of them read WATCH WHAT YOU SAY.

He looked at Charlotte for explanation.

"I should warn you," she said, "things are sort of odd here."

Right away, he saw what she meant. He didn't just hear her words. He saw them, too. They sprang from her mouth in a stream of pale yellow letters that fell to the ground, lying in a tangled heap. *Here* had slid off the pile to the ground, leaving *odd* on top.

"You can say that again," he muttered, and light green words tumbled from his mouth. "Except don't say it again, because we've already made a big enough mess."

Mess spun to the ground dramatically. He couldn't stop staring at it.

"Wow," Hudson said. The single word popped out of his mouth in puffy white letters that reminded him of marshmallows. His *wow* bounced when it hit the ground and tumbled over so it read *mom*.

He wondered what his mom would think of this place. If she

were here, she would probably only let him say nice, safe words. And definitely no back talk in the Land of Backwords.

Charlotte consulted her compass, then headed down a fork in the path. "The poor princess," she said, hardly noticing the trail of words plunking to the ground at her feet. "Kept in a tower alone in a colorless place like this. No wonder her tree droops."

The place wasn't really colorless. Underneath the white trees, bushes and flowers painted the ground in bits of color: vibrant reds, rich greens, and cheerful yellows. Orange bees shaped in the letter *B* bobbed among the blossoms, gathering pollen.

While Hudson had been gazing around, Charlotte had gotten ahead of him. "Are we going to spill words the whole time we're here?" he called to her. It was a mistake to speak loudly. The words came out bigger, and *here* landed on his foot.

"Ouch!" he yelped, which only made it worse. He had to step out of the way so the bright red *ouch* didn't land on his other foot.

He ran the rest of the way to catch up to Charlotte. "Hey, shouldn't we hide our words? What if the soldiers come and see them?"

Charlotte kept walking. "Words only stay permanent if you write them down. Otherwise, they only last for as long as you remember them, and that's usually just a few seconds. Besides, even if King Vaygran knew where we'd gone, I doubt he'd send a large group of soldiers across the Land of Desolation to chase us. Magic was sucked out of the land when the words were taken. Most spells won't work there. He'd end up losing half his men."

"Couldn't they pay the fairy the way we did?"

"Fairies don't reveal themselves to big groups. Too many people to keep track of. They're afraid someone will try to catch them."

The path turned, and Hudson caught sight of a gray tower peeking over the treetops. It didn't look that far away. Maybe a few miles.

Birds flew overhead, but they weren't the type of birds Hudson had seen before. They looked like novels, flapping their pages as they flew across the sky. A few birds were pecking at the ground in front of them. Their heads looked like bookmarks sticking out of closed books. As Hudson and Charlotte came closer, the birds flew off in an angry ruffle of pages and showered them with indignant *caws*. The words dropped to the path and shattered.

Hudson put his hand over his head. "I think they were aiming for us. What's their problem?"

"Don't mind the birds here," she said. "They're just upset because they're looking for bookworms, and those are getting harder and harder to find."

He and Charlotte kept walking down the path, eating lunch from their packs, and talking as they went. If he spoke with a lilt to his voice, the words swayed to the ground like leaves in a breeze. If he sang them, they floated upward and popped. Loud words came out heavily, and sharp words nearly cut his tongue when he said them.

Along the path, signs popped up as though they were wildflowers. Some had direction arrows. THIS WAY TO THE BACKWOODS. THIS WAY TO THE OUTBACK. THIS WAY TO THE BACKGROUND.

One read HAPPINESS IS AS CLOSE AS YOUR BACKYARD.

Another said BACKFIRES PROHIBITED BY THE FIRE MARSHAL.

Hudson didn't know whether to be glad or not that the sign actually made sense to him.

When he came to one that said DO NOT FEED THE THESAURUS, it made him glance around cautiously.

Another sign read SLOW, WORDS AT PLAY. It made him smile. He supposed all of this was wordplay, and he wished he was faster at it.

When they finally got closer to the tower, Charlotte pulled the eagle and the falcon from her bag and brought them to life. "Go see if anything is guarding the tower."

The birds stretched their wings, took to the air, and flew toward the building. She watched them disappear and slowed her pace. "If they do find something, how should we fight it?"

Hudson shrugged. "With the sword. Besides that, all I've got is a penguin and a needy magnet."

Charlotte glanced around at the forest floor. "You're good at throwing, and there are plenty of rocks here. That will help." She paused. "Unless it's a thesaurus."

He scanned the trees nervously, looking for anything out of the ordinary. "Uh, isn't a thesaurus like a dictionary?"

"Right," she said. "And books can be dangerous."

"Dangerous how?"

Charlotte rolled her eyes to let him know it was a ridiculous question. "Don't you ever read? Books can change people. You don't want to be changed into the wrong thing."

Hudson didn't know how to answer that. "How big are thesauruses?"

"Big," she said. "The only thing worse to run into in this part of Logos is a herd of encyclopedias. Sometimes they stampede."

She went on telling him about several other books and their dangers until the eagle and falcon returned.

The falcon landed on her shoulder. "We couldn't see anything guarding the tower." The bird's words floated to the ground, swishing back and forth like feathers.

"I even landed on the ground," the eagle added, "to see if it would trigger something. It didn't. No one is around."

"Good," Charlotte said, but she didn't sound entirely convinced.

Was it possible that King Vaygran would go to the trouble of hiding the princess away and then not leave anything to guard her? Someone or something must be around to feed her and make sure she didn't escape. Then again, in a land full of magic, maybe the tower did that sort of thing itself.

Hudson and Charlotte picked up some rocks anyway. Neither of them spoke as they walked the rest of the way to the tower. They were too busy looking and listening for danger.

They didn't find any. They only saw book-birds sitting in trees preening their pages.

As they approached the tower, a couple of rats ran by. They had tails and noses with whiskers, but their bodies spelled the word *rats*. Charlotte's falcon swooped toward them. With squeaks of protest, they flipped around until the word *rats* became *star*, then with a poof of light they floated up to the sky.

Charlotte shook her head at them. "That's just showing off."

After the stars had left, everything around the tower was

quiet. It stood about six stories high and was made of uneven gray stones that circled the building in a jigsaw pattern. It didn't have any windows that Hudson could see, and with its pointy roof, it reminded him of a rocket that hadn't taken off. The tower had two doors, each on opposite sides of the ground level.

Still clutching her rocks, Charlotte whispered, "We'll need to go through the back door." Her words came out as puffy cotton balls that dissolved before they hit the ground.

"Why?" Hudson whispered so softly the word was only smoke.

"Because this is the Land of Backwords."

Hudson looked at one door and then the other. "Which one is the back door?"

"Um," she said, looking at one and then the other. "I think it's that one. It doesn't have a doorbell."

She was right. One door did and one didn't. What was the point of putting a doorbell on a prison? Although in a place like this, the doorbell was probably there just to show which was the back door.

"Keep watch," she told her birds. "And warn us if anything comes near the tower."

They both flew into neighboring trees, their gazes sweeping around the forest.

Hudson and Charlotte hurried to the back door. She tried the knob. It was locked, but they'd expected that.

Hudson pulled the sword from his bag. "We're on the backstretch," he said, ignoring the magnet's protests that it needed to recalculate.

With shaking hands, Charlotte took the sword and fit it into the slot on the doorknob. "Do you think the princess would hear if we called to her?" She twisted the sword to the right. When it didn't move, she twisted the other way. "I want to let her know we're here, but I'm afraid someone else will hear us. Someone bad."

Hudson glanced over his shoulder. "Your birds will warn us if anything comes near the doors."

The sword didn't turn far enough to unlock the door. Charlotte pulled it out and tried to put it in hilt first. It didn't even fit into the lock that way.

Her voice rose in frustration. "This sword has to be the key." She tried it blade again. The door still wouldn't open.

"That sword had better be the key," he agreed. "We paid the Cliff of Faces a year of our lives to find out how to free Princess Nomira."

"Let's try the other door."

They went there, but it was not only locked; the knob didn't even have a slot for a key. The first door had to be the right one. They strode back to it.

"Maybe the sword has to be full size," Charlotte said. "I'll change it back to normal."

"The sword won't fit in the lock if it's full size," Hudson pointed out.

She took the compactulator from her pack and used it on the sword anyway. It didn't fit in the doorknob. The door stayed locked.

"Maybe we're supposed to use the sword to hack through the door," he suggested. He took several swings at the door and a few at the doorknob. Each swipe jarred his hands and arms, but that was all it accomplished. The sword didn't even leave a mark on the door.

Hudson squeezed the hilt angrily. "I'm still glad we have this sword. I can use it to hack apart the Cliff of Faces."

With an aggravated huff, Charlotte sank down on a pile of their used words. "We came all this way. We fought King Vaygran." Tears filled her eyes. "It has to be the right sword. The face said to use the most powerful defender, enforcer, convincer, and educator. Depending on how it's wielded, it is the righter or inflictor of wrongs. What other sword could it be?"

Hudson pushed aside the words *inflictor of wrongs* and sat beside Charlotte. "The face said something about the beginning and the end. What did that part mean?"

Charlotte shrugged. "He said, put the beginning at the end and you'll wield it well. Once the key gets you into the tower, the princess can simply walk out."

"The beginning at the end . . ." Hudson repeated, watching the words tumble onto his lap.

"That's a backward thing to do, which makes sense, seeing where we are." Charlotte laid her head on her knees with a despairing thunk. "We already tried to put the hilt in first. It didn't work."

Hudson was no good at comforting girls. When Bonnie was in a bad mood, he always cracked jokes to make her smile, but that wouldn't work this time. Soldiers were searching for them, an evil king had already tried to kill them, and they'd given a year of their lives for a useless answer.

The princess was so close. Hudson needed to figure out how to make the sword work. He turned the hilt over in his hand. Was this the most powerful defender, enforcer, convincer, and educator? If it wasn't, what sword was?

"What sword . . ." he said softly, and two tiny words dropped into his lap.

He looked at them, lying silver and glittery against his pants, and knew the answer.

13

"A SWORD," HUDSON said, louder this time. "We need a sword."

Charlotte lifted her head, tears still moist in her eyes. "We have a sword. You gave your father's good-bye in order to get it. It doesn't work."

"Not that sword," he said so happily his words came out puffed up like bubbles. "One of these swords."

He leaned over and picked up the word *sword* that Charlotte had just said. It was steely gray, hard with frustration.

"The word *sword*?" she asked. "You think that's the key?"

"Nope. That's not the most powerful defender, enforcer, convincer, and educator. But this is . . ." He snapped the *s* off the word *sword,* turning it into *word.* "Now I'll put the beginning at the end. . . ." He held the *s* next to the end of the word so it read *words.*

"Words!" Charlotte exclaimed, and a golden *words* fell onto her lap, shining with excitement. She threw her arms around

Hudson and gave him a quick hug. Before he could think of how to respond to that, she let go, grabbed the *words* from her lap, and got to her feet. She slipped *words* into the lock.

The knob turned, and the door swung open.

Hudson had been right.

The room was empty except for a twisting stone staircase in the back that led upward. They stepped inside. The whole place was dark and smelled like stale, forgotten things. Without hesitation, Charlotte crossed the room and climbed the first few steps. "Princess Nomira?"

The question echoed up the stairs, hit the walls, and pinged the words *Princess Nomira* back onto the floor.

No one answered.

Charlotte took out her bottle of hope and shook it until light spilled around her. The two of them headed up the stairs, Hudson gripping King Vaygran's sword.

The second floor, like the bottom floor, was only a vacant room. A few torn sacks and empty crates sat in a corner. Perhaps it had been a storage room once.

They kept climbing the stairs. "Is anybody there?" Hudson called. His words reverberated off the wall and plunked down several stairs.

Only silence answered, and silence is rarely informative.

"Where could she be?" Charlotte asked.

He didn't have to see the light of her hope jar growing dimmer to know she was losing hope. He could hear it in her voice.

The third floor was also empty. The fourth held a table and two chairs—perhaps a dining room. The fifth floor had been someone's bedroom once. A simple dresser, bed, desk, chair, and wardrobe stood in the dim shadows. But no princess.

They made their way up to the last floor. It was another bedroom, also empty. This one was easier to see because a patchwork of light drifted inside from several small holes in the wall. The holes were grouped in the middle of shutters, taking the place of windows. They were too little to crawl out of, but they let in light, air, and—judging from the layer covering everything—dust.

The bed against the far wall had golden posts and a pink lace canopy, just like the princess's bedroom in the castle. Well, not exactly identical. The flowers twining across the bed had long since withered. Everything in the room looked wilted and dirty. Cobwebs hung from the ceiling. He knew they were cobwebs, because each was spun in the shape of corn on the cob. By the looks of things, no one had lived in this place for months.

Charlotte turned in a circle, gazing around the room in dismay. "Where is she?"

"Not here," he said. Only their footprints were visible across the dusty floor.

Charlotte kept turning, searching. "The Cliff of Faces said she was here. I paid a year of my life for that answer. I lost three animals getting here! Where is she?"

Hudson didn't answer. Charlotte went back down the stairs, calling the princess's name, each time with more anger.

Had they missed something, forgotten some important clue? He leaned the sword against a chair and sat down, causing a small cloud of dust to poof around him. He coughed and waved it away.

A few moments later, Charlotte returned and then paced across the room with hands planted on her hips. "It must be a riddle. What exactly did the Cliff of Faces say?"

He had been going over it in his mind. If it was a riddle, it was one he couldn't figure out.

"We asked where King Vaygran sent the princess. They told us he sent her to the gray tower in the Land of Backwords. We asked how to get her out of the tower. They said once we had the key to go inside, she could walk outside."

"We got the key," Charlotte said. Her anger broke, turning into a sob. "So where is Princess Nomira?" She was crying, and Hudson had no idea how to make her feel better.

"Maybe the king moved her before we came." He ran his finger across the dust on the chair's arm. "And then put a spell on the tower so it looked like no one had been here in a while." Although Hudson couldn't fathom why the king would have done all that.

Charlotte wiped at the tears on her face. More tears replaced them. She kicked the words of his last sentence, sending several of them thudding into the wall.

"It will be all right," he said. "We'll go back to Texas, tell your father what we learned, and maybe he'll be able to figure out where the princess is and how to rescue her."

This sentence only made Charlotte cry harder. She apparently thought it was hopeless. Maybe it was. Maybe whatever magic gripped the princess was too strong to break.

"Texas isn't such a bad place to live," he offered. "I'll help you fit in."

She shook her head. "I can't return to your world. It takes a really powerful wizard to work that sort of magic. You can leave through an exit, but I can't go back that way. I'm from here." She stopped bothering to wipe away her tears. They flowed unchecked down her cheeks.

"What?" Hudson stood up, the weight of her words still sinking in. "Why would you come here if you knew you couldn't go back?"

"Because," she said in a small voice, "if we rescued the princess, I wouldn't need to go back. My father could come here, and our lives would go back to the way they were before Vaygran stole the throne."

Hudson didn't know what to say. He couldn't believe Charlotte had taken that risk—that she'd been so sure they could free Princess Nomira that she'd strand herself here.

"You can still go back," Charlotte told him. "I'll understand."

"I'm not going back without you."

She walked to the bed and let herself collapse onto it. Dust poofed upward, and something underneath the bed squeaked in protest.

Charlotte stopped crying. She looked first at Hudson and then back at the bed. "Did you hear that?"

Hudson stepped closer to the bed and mouthed, "Something is under there." He hoped it was the princess, although he couldn't imagine what she would be doing hiding under a bed in a dusty room. It was probably something else. The squeak hadn't sounded human.

Charlotte slipped off the bed and lifted the dust ruffle. "Who's under here?"

The sound of muffled whispers came from under the bed, then something said, "No one. Nothing's here at all."

Another voice whispered, "You can't go saying, 'No one.' 'Cause no ones don't answer."

"We're not *people*," the first voice whispered back. "So technically I'm not even lying."

Charlotte took the hope jar and held it under the bed, trying to see what hid below. "What are you if you're not people?"

"Shhh," the second voice said. "I'll bet she has a broom."

Hudson bent down, peering under the bed, too. He couldn't spot what had made the noise. "Come out of there so we can see you."

Charlotte moved her hope jar farther under the edge of the bed, and something scuttled back against the wall, away from the light.

"Do you know what happened to the princess?" Hudson demanded. "Did you make her disappear?"

This question caused one of the things to snicker. "Did ya hear that? He thinks we can make people disappear."

There was a little rumble of laughter. One of the things deepened his voice. "Yes, we made the princess disappear, and you'll meet the same fate if you don't leave right quick!"

More laughter came from underneath the bed. Charlotte glared at the dark space. With one fast motion, she reached under the bed and swept her hand along the floor.

Two shrieks sounded, and the things scuffled out of reach.

"She tried to kill me!" one of the things squealed.

"Come out from under the bed right now," Hudson said, "or I'll send my penguin in after you."

A moment of silence followed, then one of the things replied,

"How do we know you've really got a penguin? You might be bluffing."

He pulled Pokey out of his bag and set him on the floor. Charlotte turned him into his normal size. The penguin blinked around sleepily and stretched his wings.

Hudson pointed to the bed. "Pokey, go under the bed and drag out whatever is there."

Pokey took a waddling step backward and looked at the darkness with alarm. "Bonnie says monsters live under beds."

"No, they don't," Hudson said. "Monsters aren't real."

One of the things under the bed deepened its voice. "Yes, they are. We're monsters and we eat penguins."

Pokey let out a squawk and nearly fell over in his attempt to hide behind Hudson. Hudson grabbed hold of one of Pokey's wings and pushed him forward. "Dude, can't you tell they're lying? Go in there and get them."

"I'm afraid of the dark," Pokey squeaked.

"They're not monsters."

"What if they're sea lions?" Pokey's webbed feet kept moving backward. "Sea lions have sharp teeth!"

Hudson pushed the penguin forward again. "Have you ever heard of sea lions living under someone's bed? No, you haven't. That's just a ridiculous idea."

By this time, Charlotte had pulled her squirrel out of her pack and zapped him to his normal size. "Meko, flush out whatever is hiding under the bed."

The squirrel nodded and sped underneath the bed.

The things shrieked, "Squirrel! Squirrel!" and moments later scampered out into the light. Two little rabbitlike creatures huddled together in fear, ears trembling. Instead of proper fur, they looked as if they'd been made out of brown cotton candy. The squirrel followed them out and stood guard at the edge of the bed, teeth bared.

Hudson cocked his head at the two rabbits. "What are you?"

Charlotte sighed. "They're only dust bunnies."

"You don't have to clean us up," the smaller one said. Her ears drooped, and her whiskers twitched. "Please don't get a broom."

The bigger bunny wiggled his nose, then turned to the other bunny. "Don't worry. They're children. Children never clean up."

Pokey waddled up to the bunnies, chest puffed up. "I knew you weren't sea lions." He turned back to Hudson. "Do you want me to peck them?"

"No," Hudson said, still disappointed. "You don't have to rough up the dust bunnies."

"Unless," Charlotte added, crossing her arms, "they don't immediately tell us everything they know about Princess Nomira."

The dust bunnies shrank together, eyeing Pokey suspiciously. "You used to be nicer," the smaller bunny said.

"What?" Charlotte asked.

The bigger bunny gave the smaller one a quieting nudge. "Don't mind us. In the Land of Backwords, you get a lot of backhanded compliments." He perked an ear in Charlotte's direction. "So no matter what everyone else says about you, I think you're very brave." The bunny turned to Hudson next. "And you're actually a lot smarter than you look."

"Stop that," Charlotte snapped. "Tell us about Princess Nomira."

The bigger bunny sniffed and looked oppressed. "That's the problem with living in the Land of Backwords. People always want backstory."

The smaller bunny took a cautious hop forward. "The wizard brought Princess Nomira here about a year ago, king's orders. He locked her in the tower and stayed to guard her and take care of her. She was miserable—always sighing and crying."

"Or moping and sniffling," the bigger bunny added, hopping at each *ing* word.

"Or sulking and weeping," the smaller put in and hopped even higher.

Which started the two of them hopping around like popcorn popping. "Or languishing and sobbing."

"And that was only the first week."

"On the second week, she was pining and mourning."

"Or brooding and pouting."

Hudson put his hands up to stop them from continuing. "We get the idea. She hated it here."

The bunnies settled down. "The wizard tried to cheer her up," the smaller one said. "He magicked her room to look like the one in the castle. He brought her books, made her favorite food, and told her stories of his travels."

Now Charlotte held up her hands to stop the story. "Wait, King Vaygran's wizard tried to cheer her up?"

The smaller bunny nodded. "Every day."

Charlotte cocked her head in disbelief. "Why?"

The bigger bunny wiggled his nose. "He wasn't the bad sort of wizard, the kind that yells and hurts people and cleans under the bed. He liked the princess and wanted to protect her from the king."

The smaller bunny nodded. "He realized that what King Vaygran was doing to Logos was wrong. He and Princess Nomira talked about it sometimes."

Charlotte narrowed her eyes in disbelief. "If he wasn't the bad sort of wizard, why did he work for King Vaygran in the first place?"

The bigger bunny took a hop forward. "I don't know. Maybe King Vaygran didn't start out as the bad sort. Maybe it built up on him gradually—like snow and dust and piles of unmatched socks."

Charlotte ran her hand across her forehead, taking in this information. "If the wizard realized King Vaygran was wrong, why didn't he let the princess go?"

The bigger bunny's ears straightened in alarm. "King Vaygran would have killed him if he'd done that. And besides, he had to take care of her until she was ready to rule. She didn't have the confidence."

"Or courage," the smaller bunny added with a hop.

"Or the know-how," the bigger bunny said, hopping even higher.

Which set them both off bouncing again. "She was stuck in the Land of Backwords without the backbone for payback."

Hudson held his hands up to settle the dust bunnies down. Honestly, for creatures who hadn't wanted to talk, they certainly did a lot of it. "So what happened after that?"

"The wizard brought in more things to entertain her," the

bigger bunny said. "Once, he turned the whole bottom of the tower into a pool so she could swim with mermaids. Another time, he made it snow in the dining room."

The smaller bunny nudged the bigger bunny. "Don't forget Talent Show Fridays. We always did tap dancing." At this mention, the bunny did a hopping tap move.

"And?" Hudson prodded.

"For a few months, she was almost happy, but . . ." The bigger bunny twitched his whiskers. "The sadness always came back. She was sick with it. She knew King Vaygran would never let her out of the tower."

"She didn't appreciate the beauty of a lovely, dark corner," the smaller bunny said with evident dismay. "She wanted to walk around, be with people, and have friends. The sadder she became, the more angry the wizard got at King Vaygran for ordering her to be locked up in the first place." The bunny dropped his voice to a secretive whisper. "A few months back, the wizard took her away. Just up and left with her."

The bigger bunny nudged the smaller. "We promised not to tell anyone that."

The smaller bunny twitched her tail. "Well, this doesn't count. They're threatening us with a squirrel."

Impatient, Charlotte said, "Where did they go?"

The smaller dust bunny made a shrugging motion. "The wizard told her he would take her someplace safe from King Vaygran so she could live a normal life."

Charlotte blinked in confusion. "What do you mean live a normal life? Why isn't she fighting for her kingdom?"

The bunnies both shrugged. "We don't know. We've been living under the bed."

"Maybe she can't fight," Hudson said.

Charlotte didn't seem to hear him. Her breathing got faster as her indignation grew. "King Vaygran is punishing anyone who speaks out against him, and Princess Nomira is off somewhere living a safe, normal life? She's supposed to stand up to him!" Charlotte said the last words so loud the dust bunnies scurried back under the bed to avoid being hit by irate, falling words.

Hudson wiped the dust from his hands. "Well, wherever the princess went, she must not be too happy about it. Her tree is wilted."

Charlotte's mouth pressed into a hard, angry line. "She probably just feels guilty because she's safe while everyone else has to deal with King Vaygran." She pointed the compactulator first at Pokey, then at Meko, shrinking them.

Hudson put Pokey back into his bag. "I'm definitely not going back to the Cliff of Faces and giving a year of my life for this. Okay, they got the location right—well, sort of right—but they were wrong about us being able to rescue her. At most, we should only have to give them two months—and no weekends."

Charlotte picked up the squirrel and put him in her bag, her anger evident in every motion. She stomped off down the stairs. "Everyone is waiting for the princess's return, and she's off hiding like a coward."

Hudson followed after her. "Sometimes people let you down, even when they're royalty."

Charlotte stopped going down the stairs. For several moments, she stared at the steps in front of her. "We don't have to be that sort of people."

"Royalty?"

She didn't smile. She didn't even seem to be listening. "Maybe we went about this the wrong way. We wanted to rescue the princess so she could get rid of King Vaygran. That isn't going to happen. Apparently, we've got to get rid of King Vaygran so the princess will come back."

14

AS THEY HIKED back through the white forest toward the Land of Desolation, Charlotte told Hudson her plan. It was risky, could go wrong in a lot of ways, and would most likely get them both killed. He knew he ought to shake Charlotte's hand, wish her the best of luck, and find the nearest exit back to his world. He could be crawling through his cupboards by the end of the day. After all, the whole reason he came to Logos was to get rid of the troll curse—so he could be with his family and friends again. What was the point of throwing his life away in a fruitless attempt to depose a tyrant king? Logos wasn't his home, and this wasn't his battle.

Granted, if Hudson returned home, he would have to live the life of a recluse, but at least it would be a long, safe life.

He didn't veto Charlotte's plan, though. If Princess Nomira couldn't live happily as a recluse, what chance did he have? After all, she'd had a wizard and mermaids to entertain her.

Besides, he wanted to help Charlotte. This was her battle, and she was his friend. He couldn't leave and let her down.

"The king addresses people at the end of each week," Charlotte said as they walked. "That's tomorrow. We'll sneak into Grammaria, wait in the crowd, and when the king comes out on his balcony, you'll throw the bag of revealing powder at him. Any spells and charms he has that make people think he's a good leader will disappear, and everyone will see him for what he really is: a tyrant and a bully—someone who has tricked them. He's broken the law in so many ways his entire face will be covered in accusations. The people will be outraged. They'll overthrow him."

"Won't they still be afraid of him?"

"Individually, yes, but crowds have power. Trust me, you don't want to cross a group of angry Grammarians."

A few book-birds flew overhead, flapping their pages in a hurried rustle. Charlotte had put her own birds back in her pack so she wouldn't lose them when they went across the Land of Desolation.

"The king is looking for us," Hudson reminded Charlotte. He still held the king's sword, although Charlotte had shrunk it to dagger size to make it easier to carry. "Do you really think it's a good idea to go to his city and get close enough to him that we can throw a bag of revealing powder? Won't he have guards around the city with bloodhounds who know our scent?"

"Probably not," she said, though she didn't sound convinced herself. "He knows that *we know* he's after us. He won't expect us to show up in Grammaria again."

"Yeah, because only crazy people would do that. But see, the thing is, we've already gone to the castle while he was looking for us, so we've established a certain pattern of craziness."

"We'll work out the details while we travel."

The biggest detail Hudson wanted to work out involved coming up with another plan. "What if we found the ruling scepter," he suggested. "You said it was the most powerful object in Logos. Could we use it?"

Charlotte didn't answer for a moment. He could tell she was trying to think of a way that, yes, they could use it. "I would love to be able to raise an army from the stones and bat away his wizards' spells like they were annoying mosquitoes, but . . ." She sighed and let out a breath. "But it's only supposed to work for the royal family, and I bet Princess Nomira used its magic to ensure that wherever she put it, only she could retrieve it."

Hudson liked the idea of a stone army fighting in their defense and didn't want to let it go that easily. "You don't know for sure that Princess Nomira made it impossible for anyone else to use it." He kicked at some words that had fallen in his way. "It doesn't sound like she cares all that much about it, or she would have retrieved it after she left the tower."

"It's not the scepter she doesn't care about," Charlotte said bitterly. "It's Logos."

A sign popped up on the side of the path. It read FALLBACK!

He pointed it out to Charlotte. "Should we worry about that?"

He stopped and scanned the forest around them. Was the sign telling them to retreat? In a place like this, the word *fallback* could mean autumn was coming around again. Charlotte slipped her bag from her shoulders and pulled out her compass.

Another sign popped up near Hudson's feet. It read THE SIGNS ARE ALWAYS WRITE.

Warnings had appeared on the compass face. The needle pointed to BEWARE OF WIZARD!

"Oh no." Charlotte's gaze darted around the trees on either side of them, searching for danger. Hudson didn't see anything. Was the wizard ahead of them or behind them? They'd nearly reached the Land of Desolation. Hudson could see it through the trees, spreading out before them, just a few minutes away.

Another sign popped up. RUN FOR COVER!

"Nothing is ahead of us," he said. "The wizard must be behind us." Without another word, they both ran forward. They had only gone a few steps when another sign popped up on the side of the path. It read CAUTION, BACKSTABBERS AHEAD.

Not a good sign.

Hudson and Charlotte both skidded to a stop. Before they could turn, a deep, crackling voice in front of them said, "Ah, my dear, you should have seen the signs long before now." The black wizard they'd seen at the sea—Nepharo—stepped onto the path directly in front of them. He seemed to materialize out of nothingness. His black beard twisted off his chin as though it was trying to go down a drain, and his cloak brushed against the ground as he walked. He held his wand loosely, almost casually.

Hudson held the king's sword up, wishing now that it was bigger than a dagger. "Don't come near us!"

Nepharo shook his head, unworried. "Or what? You'll spread some butter on my bread?"

A rumble of laughter came from behind Nepharo—from the air. It sounded like dozens of men, but no one was there.

The wizard flicked his wand to his side, and what had been a perfect landscape, complete with wind rustling through the leaves and birds flying overhead, folded together like a piece of paper growing smaller.

Hudson stared, not understanding how it was possible, and then realized they had walked toward a giant picture of the land-scape. A giant picture that—he now could see—hid a dozen soldiers, their horses, and several leashed bloodhounds.

"Run!" Hudson shouted to Charlotte, and he turned to flee from Nepharo. Around them, the tree trunks turned red. No, it wasn't the trees—another set of soldiers had come out from their hiding places behind the trees. They created a circle that quickly closed in on Charlotte and Hudson. He sprinted forward any-way, dagger raised, hoping to break their circle.

He didn't hear the bloodhound come after him. One moment he was running, the next he slammed into the ground with a stinging impact. The dagger dropped from his grip, and he felt the dog crouching on his back. It growled, sending its hot breath down Hudson's neck.

"I wouldn't advise moving," Nepharo called, and then chuckled.

Hudson didn't move. He listened to the dog's low growl until a soldier pulled the beast off. Then another soldier grabbed Hudson by his shirt and pulled him to his feet. Someone yanked his arms behind his back and tied them tight with rope.

Hudson hoped Charlotte had managed to get away. But a look over his shoulder told him she hadn't. A soldier had her in his grip, arms around her waist, holding her off the ground while she kicked at his legs. Another soldier stood nearby with a snarling bloodhound that looked like he'd happily eat her.

Nepharo strolled up to her, smiling. He dipped his wand into the neck of her shirt, fishing out her four-leaf-clover necklace. It dangled from his wand for a moment, then he yanked so hard that the chain broke and the clover tumbled to the ground.

Charlotte's protection against wizard spells—it was gone now. Hudson felt a cold pit of dread form in his stomach.

Charlotte grew pale.

Nepharo flicked his wand, and a piece of cloth appeared in the air and tied itself over Charlotte's mouth, preventing her from speaking. "I don't know what you're playing at," he said in a low voice, "but your game is over."

Nepharo signaled to a nearby soldier to retrieve the clover from the ground and give it to him. Apparently, wizards were too good to bend down themselves. The soldier did as he was told. With one last wink of silver, the clover disappeared into Nepharo's billowing black cloak.

"Take her things," Nepharo told the soldier. "Tie her with the silver rope and carry her on your horse. I'll deal with her once we get past the Land of Desolation."

The wizard then strode over to Hudson, dark eyes glittering with triumph. He jabbed his wand down Hudson's neckline and, with one quick motion, broke his chain and sent the clover flying to the ground.

While a nearby soldier retrieved it, the wizard leaned so close to Hudson his twisted black beard rubbed against Hudson's face. "And who are you?" With a sneer, the wizard reached into his pocket and pulled out a tiny drawstring bag. "You couldn't be Aziz Fantasmo. Not unless you've lost all your magic. Wouldn't that be a delicious irony?"

Nepharo flicked a pinch of white glittery powder into Hudson's face. He felt the tingling of a disguise change. The colors in Hudson's clothes ran down his arms and legs, washing away to reveal his old clothes, the ones he'd come to Logos in. He looked like himself again.

Nepharo wrinkled his nose in distaste, taking in Hudson's dirty jeans and tennis shoes. "Just a boy. Someone from the Land of Banishment, no doubt. Is that where she ran?"

Hudson didn't answer.

The wizard closed his drawstring pouch and tucked it back into his robe. He gestured to the soldier who held on to Hudson's jacket. "Take him on your horse."

The soldier marched Hudson down the path, holding on to the rope that tied his hands like it was a leash. He had a long, thin mustache and fierce eyes, and if Hudson walked too slowly, the man poked his sword into Hudson's back.

"How did you get across the desolation?" Hudson asked. It wasn't an idle question, although he tried to make it sound like it was. If the soldiers had a way to avoid the mental draining that happened while crossing the isthmus, he wanted to know it.

"You'll see soon enough. We've got magic that can outwit the likes of you."

A minute later, the forest cleared, and Hudson saw what he meant. A couple of dozen horses were tethered to a long metal pole that ran perpendicular to the edge of the forest. One end of the pole rested on a metal T with huge wheels on the bottom. The other side of the pole was impossible to see. It stretched out over the Land of Desolation, disappearing to some point near the Forest of Possibilities.

The soldiers had obviously used the pole to keep themselves from getting lost on the way here, but how had they gotten hold of a pole that long in the first place? How did the men know beforehand that they would need it? Did they have some way of figuring out Charlotte and Hudson's plans?

He kept his voice unconcerned. "It looks like you used a pole to outwit us, not magic."

The soldier prodded Hudson in the back again. "Sir Nepharo tethered us to the pole and enchanted it to grow steadily for two miles. That was the magic part. The clever part was that the pole is only enchanted in the Forest of Possibilities, so the Land of Desolation couldn't suck the magic away."

Hudson had to admit that a magically growing pole was a good idea. Why hadn't he and Charlotte realized the king's wizard would know a way to cross the Land of Desolation? They should have been on their guard. They should have cut through the Land of Backwords and crossed the Land of Desolation in a different place.

"For the trip back," the soldier went on, marching Hudson toward a horse, "the pole will shrink and lead us back. Nepharo has thought of everything."

When they reached the horse, the soldier picked Hudson up, tossed him over the front of the saddle, then mounted behind him. "Don't try to escape, or I'll be forced to kill you."

Try? Hudson couldn't even think of a way to attempt it. He was tied up, facedown on a horse next to a man who was a little too eager to use his sword. At this point, his options were severely limited.

He noticed Charlotte draped over a horse three ahead of him in the line. She'd been tied up in silver rope, and an armed soldier sat behind her, guarding her.

Hudson wanted to catch her eye, but she was looking forward. All he could see were the packhorses in between them. They were weighed down by sacks—provisions for the soldiers while they pursued Hudson and Charlotte. The men had apparently planned on the chase lasting a few days longer.

Hudson felt the insult of those sacks. He and Charlotte had been too easy to catch.

A horn sounded from the front of the line, and the pole began to move, pulling the line of soldiers toward the Land of Desolation. With every step the horse took, the saddle bit into Hudson's stomach.

The first horses in the caravan reached the Land of Desolation, and their hooves sent back clouds of dust. The sand fairy was out there somewhere. Could she cut through their ropes? She'd already been paid three muselings to take them back across the land. She owed them some help.

He didn't see her anywhere, but the horses in front of him were throwing up enough dust to hide a mob of magical creatures. She might be within earshot. "Hey, fairy," he whispered, trying not catch the soldier's attention. "Psst, over here. I need your . . ."

The word was gone. He searched for it, but his mind felt like an empty bowl. Part of him knew he was in danger. Something bad was happening. He sifted through flashes of memory, not understanding any of it. Red dogs. A dark wizard. He had the vague thought that he was supposed to follow a light. He couldn't see one anywhere.

He tried to sit up but couldn't move his hands or legs.

This was bad.

Bad.

Bad.

Fortunately, the stupor didn't last long. The horses moved at a fast pace, and before long they'd reached the Forest of Possibilities.

Hudson's thoughts rushed back, and he happily remembered who he was and not so happily remembered what was happening. Nepharo had found them.

The soldiers in the front of the line had already dismounted from their horses and were untethering them from the pole. His horse came to a stop.

The sand fairy couldn't help now, but the unicorns might. "Cecil! Nigel!" Hudson yelled. "Help!"

The soldier with the long mustache dismounted and shot Hudson an angry glare. "Quiet! We'll have none of your begging for mercy, or for whatever a nigel is."

Hudson saw no sign of the unicorns, and he wasn't sure what

they would be able to do against so many armed soldiers, anyway. Still, he called their names again. Loudly. Uselessly.

Nepharo strode over to Charlotte's horse with two soldiers at his side. The soldiers grabbed her from the horse and dragged her in front of the wizard. He reached into his robes while giving her a thin-lipped smile. "It's time to take you back to your old home. The king will want to give you a trial, just as the law demands."

Her eyes were wide, frightened.

Nepharo kept smiling. He enjoyed this, the triumph of capturing her. "King Vaygran will present you to the people tomorrow and ask them what should be done with the intruder who broke into his room and stole his sword. That's something an assassin would do, and you know what the punishment for that is." Cold laughter trickled from the wizard's mouth. "It can't be counted against the king or me if they demand your death."

Counted against them?

With a gnawing feeling of defeat, Hudson realized why the wizard cared who ordered her death. In this land, if you broke the law, that sort of deed could be exposed, written on your forehead if someone put revealing powder on you. So instead of killing Charlotte himself, the king would put her in a situation where the crowd called for her death.

Nepharo took hold of Charlotte's hair with a yank and flicked his wand at her. She immediately shrank, growing dark and furry, smaller and smaller until she turned into a gray mouse. The wizard held her by the scruff of the neck. Her tail twitched wildly, and she twisted this way and that, trying to escape.

Hudson watched, horrified. Charlotte was so small and helpless—so breakable. She was going to die, and it was his fault. She came back to Logos to help him get rid of the troll mirror. Why had he thought they could fight wizards?

Nepharo handed Charlotte to a nearby soldier and tapped his wand to his own shoulder. His black cloak wavered like a convulsing shadow, and his arms shrank and sharpened into wings. His body folded in on itself, transforming from a man into a brown striped owl with piercing yellow eyes. He flapped his wings, hovering in the air, then grasped the mouse from the soldier's hand in his talons. With a harsh screech, he flew upward into the sky.

"No!" Hudson shouted. "Don't hurt her!"

Within moments, the owl had disappeared over the treetops.

The soldier with the long mustache pulled Hudson from the horse. A couple of other soldiers stood nearby with Hudson's and Charlotte's bags, rifling through them.

The mustached soldier took hold of the end of the rope that tied Hudson's hands. "You must not be nearly as important as the girl. No fancy travel for you. And I see no point in tiring out my horse by making him carry you. You can walk for a while."

Hudson didn't respond. He felt numb.

The man tethered the rope that bound Hudson's wrists to the side of his horse, tugging the rope to secure the knot. "Keep up or you'll be trampled." With that parting message, the man ambled over to the soldiers who were searching through the bags. "Anything good?"

"Aye," one said, holding up Charlotte's compass, "but Nepharo will want it."

A soldier with a curly red beard led his horse past them on his way to the front of the group. He blew on a horn that looked like a twisted trumpet and sounded like a goat bleating in protest. "Formations!" he yelled. "We're moving out."

The soldiers shuffled off to their horses, mounted them, and moved them into a line. The mustached soldier tapped his heels into his horse's flanks to prod the animal forward, and Hudson jerked along with it. He searched the forest for a sign of the unicorns but saw no shimmer of gold or silver hidden in the foliage.

The unicorns must have seen the soldiers pursuing Charlotte and Hudson across the Land of Desolation. Had Nigel and Cecil assumed they would be killed? Was that why they hadn't stayed around? Hudson felt abandoned and then was struck by a worse thought. King Vaygran had outlawed unicorns. The soldiers might have already found Nigel and Cecil and slain them.

Not that, he thought. Hopefully, the unicorns had heard the soldiers coming and fled far away.

Whatever the case, Hudson needed to find a way to free himself. He had to help Charlotte. Had to. As he trudged through the forest alongside the horse, he desperately sifted through the possibilities. Was there some way he could knock the soldier off the horse and steal it? Probably not. Even if he managed it, he wouldn't be able to get past all the other soldiers. Could he trick one of the soldiers into giving him the disguise paste in his bag? If he had it, he could change himself into a soldier. But that wouldn't fool anyone. He would still have a rope tying him to the horse.

The horse trotted a few steps, catching up to the one in front of it. The motion yanked Hudson into a run and made the rope cut into his wrists. He would have some nasty welts there soon. Welts that . . .

And then the perfect idea occurred to him. He nearly laughed at the irony of it. The thing he wanted to get rid of so badly was about to help him. As loudly and firmly as he could, he shouted, "Listen to me, soldiers of Vaygran! I'm a wizard, and unless you let me go, I will poison all of you with a magic spell!"

Some of the soldiers snickered at this. The curly-bearded man in the front turned and sent him a hard stare. "Quiet, or I'll give you five lashes."

"You'll suffer hideously before you die," Hudson went on even louder. "It will start with boils covering your skin. Then your stomach will slowly dissolve with the rest of your insides."

He put in the part about the stomach because once everyone saw the boils on their skin, their stomachs were bound to clench. He might as well use that to his advantage.

"If you're a wizard," the mustached man said in a mocking tone, "how come you didn't change into a bird to get away from us?"

Good question.

The soldier behind Hudson let out a scoff. "You're too young to be a wizard."

"I'm not done with my magical studies," Hudson conceded, "but I still know the spell to poison you." He needed some words that sounded like a magic incantation, words the Logosians wouldn't recognize. "Frodo Baggins Aragorn Darth Vader," he intoned. "Hogwarts to you all!"

None of the soldiers snickered. Some checked their hands for boils.

They wouldn't have long to wait. It had to be close to a half hour since the soldiers had taken him.

The man with the curly beard yelled, "Halt!"

The soldiers immediately stopped their horses and peered at their commander, waiting. The curly-bearded soldier rode his horse back down the line until he reached Hudson. "I warned you," the man snarled. "Five lashes. Ten if you put up a fight."

The man dismounted and strode over to Hudson, clenching his horsewhip. "Kneel on the ground."

Hudson didn't. The boils would appear anytime now.

The bearded man grabbed Hudson's arm and yanked him as far away from the horse as his rope would allow. "Nepharo doesn't care what happens to you now that he has the girl." The man leaned in so close Hudson could see that his lips were cracked and that smudges of dirt lined his beard. "If you want to reach Grammaria alive, you'll do exactly what I say. Otherwise, I'll kill you now and be done with your nonsense."

He lifted his whip.

The mustached soldier let out a gasp of shock. He held his hands up, staring at the red marks that covered them. "Sir, look!"

As everyone watched, boils the size of quarters appeared on the man's face.

The bearded man dropped Hudson's arm and stepped away from him. "What sort of trickery is this?"

"If you want to live," Hudson said calmly, "you'll untie me, give me my things, and let me take a horse. Once I'm a good ways away, I'll counteract the spell."

The bearded man unsheathed his sword. With one quick movement, he held the tip to Hudson's throat. "You will undo whatever you've done right now, or I'll run you through."

As he spoke, boils bloomed on his hand. He let out a cry and dropped his sword, clutching at his hand as though he could scrape off the spots. All down the line, the men were groaning, calling out, cursing. They stared at their hands or felt the oozing boils on their faces. One called out, "My stomach, Captain. I think it's dissolving."

Another yelled, "Let the boy go!"

The bearded man pulled at a leather strap that hung around his neck, revealing a four-leaf clover dipped in silver. Hudson hadn't expected anybody to have one of those.

The man checked to see that the clover was still there, intact, then glared disbelieving at Hudson. "You shouldn't be able to cast a spell on me."

Apparently, the clovers only protected against wizard spells, not troll curses. Hudson couldn't let anyone figure this out. He shrugged. "Your clover must not be real. Who did you get it from? Nepharo?"

The man didn't answer. His eyes bulged in anger, and he gripped the leather string harder.

"Nepharo must not have wanted you to have anything that could protect you from his spells. You didn't really think you could trust him, did you?"

The man still didn't answer. He dropped the clover, letting it dangle back around his neck.

Hudson pointed to the horse he was tethered to. "I'll take this horse . . . unless you've decided you'd rather die instead?"

The bearded man narrowed his eyes, and his breathing came out in angry pants. "How do we know you won't leave us to die after you ride away?"

"I'll give you my word as a wizard," Hudson said.

The bearded man broke the leather strap at his neck and tossed his clover onto the ground. "I don't trust wizards. Swear by your life instead. Swear by the magic in you—that it will destroy you if you go back on your word."

"Okay. I swear by all the magic in me." Hudson lifted his hands, emphasizing that they were still bound. "Don't attempt to recapture me, though. Next time, I won't be as generous with you." He gave them a smile to show he was sincere. It probably just came out looking smug.

Minutes later, he was on the horse with both his bag and Charlotte's strapped on the saddle. He galloped through the forest, holding the compass. "Which way to Grammaria?"

The compass needle swung slightly to his right, and he headed that way.

15

WHILE HUDSON RODE, he pulled the falcon and eagle from Charlotte's bag and changed them to their normal state. "Fly to Grammaria," he told them. "Nepharo turned himself into a brown striped owl and Charlotte into a mouse. See if you can rescue her before they reach the castle."

The birds streaked into the sky, leaving only a flutter of leaves in their wake. Hudson hoped they would succeed but knew it wasn't likely. Charlotte had said shabtis had only weak magic. He was sending them up against a wizard with powerful magic.

Hudson galloped on through the forest, his mind churning. How could he rescue Charlotte? He couldn't ride as quickly as an owl could fly, and besides, what could he do once he reached Grammaria? He couldn't fight soldiers to free her. He didn't have a chance against Nepharo. But Mr. Fantasmo did.

Hudson checked the compass face. "Where is the closest exit to my world?"

The arrow shifted sharply left. The words MERMAID LAKE emerged under the glass. He had no idea how far it was. He turned his horse in that direction, jumping over a succession of bushes that looked like large, sunburned hedgehogs.

The horse wound around trees and some mushrooms big enough to actually be rooms, then trampled through a patch of catflower that meowed indignantly at the treatment. A field of tiny toadstools hopped out of his way, ribbiting in protest. After a half hour, he came upon a trail. The horse could move faster there, and Hudson pushed it to a jarring gallop. Unicorns were a much smoother ride.

An hour and a half later, he reached a large lake with a small island not far from shore. The water was so blue, from the distance it looked like turquoise paint. The pink, lilac, and pastel-yellow trees surrounding the area made Hudson feel like he'd stumbled into his sister's bedroom mural. He wouldn't have been surprised to see a few pastel teddy bears lumbering by.

While the horse drank from the water's edge, Hudson scanned the treetops, searching for something that resembled the box he'd used in the thorn tree. He didn't see anything except for some fluffy white birds that looked like snowballs with eyes. The sun had already begun to set, and before long it would be too dark to find anything. Where was the exit? After a couple of minutes, he turned his attention to the island. And there, nestled against an outcropping of blue rocks, was a wooden box. It had to be the exit.

No boats sat on the lake's shore, but a small rowboat lay pushed up on the island's shore. It did him no good over there.

He would have to swim across the lake to get to the exit box. Could he do that while carrying both his and Charlotte's bags? Probably not. When he'd fallen off the *valor* boat in the Sea of Life, his bag had been so heavy he'd needed Pokey's help to get it to shore. Well, it was about time for the bird to help again. Hudson took the magical items from Charlotte's pack and put them into his. Even in their smaller sizes, her sleeping bag and pillow wouldn't fit into his bag. He would have to leave them here.

While the horse was still drinking, Hudson dismounted and took Pokey out of his bag. With one zap from the compactulator, the bird grew, stretched, and gave a lazy yawn.

Hudson tucked the compactulator back into his pack. "I've got to get to the portal on that island. I want you to swim my bag across."

"Swim?" Pokey said, brightening. He swiveled his head, noticed the lake for the first time, and gave a happy squeak. "Fish! Beware little minnows, a mighty . . ." He didn't finish his sentence.

Something on the lake had caught his eye—a dark shadow below the surface moving toward them. Whatever it was, it was big. It skimmed along, swirling bits of leaves that floated on the lake. Hudson took a few steps away from the water.

Pokey waved his wings in alarm, scampered backward, and hid behind Hudson's legs. "Never mind. I don't want to swim anymore!"

Another dark shadow joined the first, coming toward the shoreline.

"Sharks!" Pokey squawked. "Why aren't you picking me up and running?"

"Sharks don't live in lakes," Hudson said. "And even if they did, they couldn't get to us onshore."

Pokey tugged at Hudson's leg, trying to get him to move. "Maybe it's alligators, then. Or sea lions."

The dark shapes kept coming toward them, ripples of water fleeing in their wake. When they were a few feet away from the bank, double splashes erupted in the water, and two teenage girls lifted their heads out of the lake. Mermaids. One had long dark green hair. The other's hair was purplish brown. It swayed in the current, curling around her arms. Both wore tops made of strips of clinging seaweed.

"Look," the green-haired mermaid cooed to the other. "It's a boy."

The purple-haired mermaid tilted her head and gazed at him like he was a lost puppy. "Ahh, isn't he cute?"

They both giggled.

"Um, hi," Hudson said. Charlotte had never said mermaids were dangerous, just that they were incurable flirts. Still, after his run-in with the trolls, he was nervous about meeting anyone not of his own species.

The green-haired mermaid looked Hudson up and down. "You're from the Land of Banishment, aren't you?" She swam a bit closer. "I can tell by your clothes."

"Yeah."

"That's so cool." The purple-haired mermaid came closer, as well. Their voices had a quality to them that reminded him of wind chimes, light and tinkling.

Hudson gestured to the box on the island. "I need to get to a magical exit. That's one over there, right?"

"Mm-hmm," the green mermaid purred. "What's your name?"

"Hudson. Listen, could you do me a favor and bring that boat over here so I can use it?"

The purple-haired mermaid blinked her eyes, fanning purple lashes at him. "I didn't ask whose son you were. I asked your name."

The green-haired mermaid flipped her tail fin out of the water playfully. It gleamed in the sunlight with turquoise highlights. "Maybe he wants us to guess it." She giggled another wind-chime laugh. "I'm Micaiah, and this is my sister Marissa."

Hudson shifted his legs impatiently. "Great. Nice to meet you. Can you bring me that boat?"

"Lance?" Marissa asked. "Arthur? Or maybe Orlando?"

"Alexander? Mark Antony?" Micaiah put in.

Pokey peeked around Hudson's legs. "My name is Pokey."

"Ahh," Marissa drifted closer to the water's edge. "It's so cute! It's some sort of fat, little bird with tiny wings."

"I'm a penguin," Pokey said, feathers ruffling a bit. "We live in the Antarctic, and in Chile, and on Hudson's dresser."

"I don't mean to be rude," Hudson said, forcing a smile, "but I really need that boat. A friend of mine is in serious trouble, and I have to go back home and get her father." Somehow, he couldn't bring himself to wade into the water and swim to the island with the mermaids right there. He had the uneasy feeling that if he entered their world, he would be in their power. It would be better, safer, to go by boat.

Marissa pouted, puckering her purple lips. "You don't have to go right away, do you? We just met you." She put her elbows on the bank and rested her chin in her hand. "Wouldn't you like to stay and talk? People from the Land of Banishment are *so* interesting."

"We could talk with you for hours." Micaiah pushed her long green hair off her shoulder and wound a strand around her finger. "Or days."

Any other time, Hudson would have liked sitting at the water's edge and talking with two beautiful mermaids. Now all he could think about was Charlotte, clutched helplessly in an owl's talons. "I need the boat," he snapped.

Both mermaids straightened their shoulders, offended.

Hudson cleared his throat and spoke again, this time in a calm, friendly voice. "I'd love to talk to you while I row the boat across the lake."

Micaiah and Marissa leaned together, conferring, then disappeared back into the water. They'd barely left a splash to show where they'd been.

Hudson waited and watched the water, searching for them. Were they getting the boat, or had they gotten mad and stomped off? Well, stomped off as much as a creature with fins could.

Pokey watched, too. "They liked me," he said. "I have a way with women. You, on the other hand, sucked mackerels."

Hudson clenched his hands and paced restlessly back and forth by the water's edge. Bits of pebbles crunched beneath his feet. Should he give up on the boat and start swimming across?

Although Hudson never saw the mermaids surface near the

island, the boat slipped away from the shore and made its way across the lake. The oars dangled from the boat's side, bumping against the water's surface.

When the boat was a couple of feet away, Hudson picked up Pokey and his bag and then waded the rest of the way to the boat. He was in too much of a hurry to even care that he was soaking his shoes. "Thanks," he said, climbing in. "You all are the best."

"Hey," Pokey said, flapping his wings and straining to reach the lake. "I want to swim."

"Nope." Hudson put the penguin on the bench beside him, then grabbed the oars. "I might need you later."

Pokey sat on the bench sullenly, his two webbed feet poking out beneath his white belly. He sent a dissatisfied glare in Hudson's direction.

Hudson pulled on the oars, pushing through the water as quickly as he could. Marissa glided alongside the boat, her purple hair floating around her shoulders. "We've got lots of ways to entertain boys."

Micaiah joined her at the side of the boat, swishing her tail fin back and forth lazily. "You can pretend to do all sorts of things here without ever even leaving the lake. Do you want to be an adventurer or a warrior? You could join a mermen's guild."

"I don't have time." Hudson missed the *gratitude* boat and the way it made rowing easier. His hands ached with each stroke. "I have something important to do."

Marissa giggled, then dove underneath the water. Hudson was half afraid she would think it was funny to tip the boat over, and he yanked the oars extra hard. She popped up at the back of the boat, draped her arms across the stern, then lay her chin on her arms. "Important things are always waiting to be done. I'll bet you never bothered doing them before."

Hudson hadn't seen Micaiah disappear from the side of the boat, but now she appeared next to her sister, flicking water onto him with her tail. "Boys from the Land of Banishment spend lots of time playing games. They never worry about doing anything important."

"That's not true," he said, then thought about the money sitting in his sock drawer. He was saving up for a gaming system. "I mean, we do important stuff, too. Sometimes."

The island wasn't far away now. The water beneath the boat grew light blue, getting shallower. Just a couple more minutes and he would be to the shore. He could see the trail leading to the exit box.

A jolt at the end of the boat snapped his attention back there. Marissa and Micaiah had moved to one side of the boat and pulled it in that direction, turning the boat around. "If you won't play with us," Marissa said mischievously, "we'll play with you."

"Hey, stop it!" He put his oar into the water to turn the right way.

Micaiah dove for the oar, grinning. Hudson quickly pulled both oars inside the boat so the mermaids couldn't take them.

Marissa laughed, then gave the boat a push to spin it. The boat twirled in the water, rocking back and forth.

Hudson was stuck. If he tried to use the oars again, the mermaids would take them. But if he just sat there, the mermaids would drag him wherever they wanted. He couldn't jump in and outswim them, even the short distance to the island.

"Just one game," Micaiah said, appearing at the side of the boat. "It will only take a day or two."

A day or two? He didn't want to wait even two more minutes. The daylight was already almost gone.

Pokey snorted. "It looks like they've already won the game. You might as well admit to them that you're a loser." The penguin put a wing to his chest. "I can vouch for you."

Hudson might not be able to outswim the mermaids, but a penguin could.

Hudson let out a sigh, as though conceding to the mermaids' demands. "All right. I guess I could play penguin ball for a while."

"Penguin ball?" Marissa bobbed up and down in the water. "What's that?"

Hudson feigned surprise. "You've never played?"

Pokey folded his wings in front of his stomach and shook his head. "It isn't nice to throw your shabtis."

Hudson ignored him. "It's a simple game, really. See my penguin here?"

The mermaids nodded and drew closer to the side of the boat.

"I'm going to throw him into the water, and you'll try to catch him. If you can catch him before a minute is up, you win. If you can't, I win."

Marissa tilted her head so her green hair spilled across her shoulders. "Why would it take us a minute to catch him? How far do you throw?"

"Really far."

He picked up Pokey, who squawked and pedaled his feet as though running through the air. "Don't throw me! It will hurt!"

"No, it won't," Hudson said. "Besides, you're a bird. Haven't you always wanted to fly?"

Micaiah lazily swam back away from the boat, positioning herself to catch the penguin. "Does your bird even know *how* to swim?"

"Sure," Hudson said. "Sort of."

Pokey humphed indignantly at this.

Hudson lowered his head toward Pokey and whispered, "I know how well you swim. Now show these fish-cheerleader hybrids who's boss. We're doing this for Charlotte."

Before Pokey could make further comments, Hudson hurled him into the air. The penguin soared across the lake, letting out a screech that indicated that no, he'd never actually wanted to fly. The mermaids dove into the water, zipping in the direction Pokey would land.

Hudson grabbed the oars and dug them into the water. "One," he called out. "Two." He pulled with all his might, heading toward the shore. "Remember, if it takes you longer than a minute, I win."

The penguin landed in the water with an impressive splash. He didn't surface. Penguins were slow and awkward on land, but in water they were as fast and nimble as the fish they caught.

Hudson rowed to the island, reaching it in only a few more strokes. The mermaids didn't appear again. Apparently, Pokey was giving them a good chase. That made Hudson the undisputed champion of penguin ball.

He felt a twinge of guilt for leaving Pokey behind, but the bird would probably prefer to swim around in a lake than be shoved into a bag anyway.

Hudson sprang from the boat and ran up the trail toward the exit box. He had to find Mr. Fantasmo and bring him back to help Charlotte.

FOR ALL THEIR ODDITIES, THE FANTASMOS HAD AS MANY POTS and pans in their cupboards as the Browns had in theirs. Hudson banged through several frying pans, ignoring their clangs of complaint, until he spilled out onto Charlotte's kitchen floor. Before he even pulled himself upright, he called out, "Mr. Fantasmo! Are you here?"

No one answered.

Hudson got up and went into the living room. His shoes were damp and cold, and they squeaked with every step he took.

The living room was empty. The tree's blue leaves were wilting from the branches like falling tears. Limp yellow blossoms lay scattered on the floor. Tiny red flowers had taken their place on the branches. He wondered what the red flowers meant, but he didn't have time to think about it.

"Mr. Fantasmo?" Hudson yelled, then headed down the hallway. He pulled the compass from his pocket. "I need to take you back to Logos. Charlotte is in trouble."

The only sound that answered Hudson was his own hurried footsteps. He flipped on lights and peered into each room he passed. The first was Charlotte's. A lacy green blanket lay on her bed. A mural of flowered fields covered the walls—Logos flowers in their odd varieties. Two falcons flew near the bed's headboard, suspended in the wall's sky.

The bedroom door had been closed when he and Charlotte left the house. That meant Mr. Fantasmo had been here since then.

Hudson moved down the hallway to the next room. A bathroom. He tried the door at the end of the hall and found the master bedroom. "Mr. Fantasmo!" Hudson called again, even though he knew no one was in the house. Charlotte was right about hope. It's sturdy even against obvious bleakness.

He went back down the hallway to the room with the magical supplies. Things had been pushed aside on some of the shelves. A few boxes and bottles lay on the floor as though hurriedly knocked to the ground. Someone had searched for something. Probably Mr. Fantasmo. And Hudson knew what he'd been looking for. The compass.

What had Charlotte's father done when he found her letter? Where had he gone?

Hudson looked at the shelves, wishing he knew what all these things were. Could any of them help him rescue Charlotte? A couple of silver-coated four-leaf clovers would come in handy. He picked up the jewelry box that had held them. He'd been sure there were three left, but he found only one. He took it and hung it around his neck. The box with candy hearts was empty, too, along with several other containers. What had Mr. Fantasmo done with the things?

Hudson saw an iron bar lying on the floor halfway under the shelves and grabbed it. He was going to need all the strength he could get.

He went outside, holding his jar of hope up for light. He checked first the backyard and then the front for any sign of the wizard. While Hudson called Mr. Fantasmo's name, he looked down the street toward his house. He wanted so badly to go see his mom and Bonnie, to ask for his mom's help. He couldn't. If he went home, his mom wouldn't believe him about Logos, let alone allow him to go back.

He could prove to his mom that Logos was real by having her touch the compass and taking her there.

He immediately dismissed the idea. Bonnie was too young to be left alone for hours or days. And besides, if his mom was hurt—changed into a mouse or something—he would never forgive himself.

Hudson strode back into Charlotte's house and looked around again, hoping to find a note, a phone number, some way to reach Mr. Fantasmo. A lead feeling pressed against Hudson's chest, and every passing moment made it heavier. He had been depending on Mr. Fantasmo's help. Now what would he do?

When he didn't find any way to contact Charlotte's father, he wrote a short note and left it on the tree. That way, if Mr. Fantasmo came back, at least he would know the situation.

Hudson went to the kitchen. It was after seven, long past din-nertime, but he was too worried to be hungry. He took a block of cheese from the fridge and some rolls from the counter to eat later. Then he pulled the knob on the compass. Before he could even let out a sigh of defeat, he stood on a dirt path in the Forest of Possibilities.

The night had dimmed the trees' colors into dark silhouettes, and the birds had quieted, replaced by a chorus of crickets. Hudson checked the compass. The face showed directions instead of warnings, which meant nothing dangerous was around. Good. He hoped the unicorns would show up, but he needed more than speed. He needed magical help—so much help that by the time he paid the fairies, he might not remember his name anymore. He pulled the silver bell from his bag and rang it. "I need a fairy!"

A few dragonflies darted by, chasing one another with plumes of fire, but no fairies.

Where was magic when you needed it?

Hudson held up the compass. "Which way to Grammaria?"

The needle pointed to the direction behind him, and he headed that way, still ringing the bell. He had no idea where in the Forest of Possibilities he was. He might be closer to Grammaria than he had been, or farther away. He held up his hope jar and made his way around trees and bushes the best he could.

No fairies zipped out of the foliage. Maybe they could tell he didn't have any muselings on him. Or maybe they didn't live in this part of the forest. He gave up ringing the bell and called for Nigel and Cecil instead. They could take him to Grammaria, and he could pay the river fairy to help him.

He walked for a long time, occasionally bumping into branches and frequently tripping over tree roots, before he gave up calling for the unicorns. They must be too far away to hear him. He wouldn't let himself think of the other possibility—that King Vaygran's soldiers had killed them.

For a few more hours, Hudson fought through the forest, wondering if there was any possible way he could make it to Grammaria tonight.

Finally, exhausted, he admitted that no, he probably couldn't. It would be better to sleep the rest of the night and start again at first light. In the morning, the unicorns might find him. Or at the very least, he would be able to see where he was going.

Nepharo had said King Vaygran would bring Charlotte in front of the people tomorrow, Hudson had until then to reach Grammaria and find a way rescue her.

HUDSON WOKE WHEN THE BIRDS BEGAN TO SING. THE GRAY light of dawn was returning the color to the trees and warming the cold ground. He packed his things quickly, calling for Nigel and Cecil every few minutes.

No response.

What time did King Vaygran address his people? Hudson hoped it wasn't until late in the day.

He headed off in the direction of Grammaria, still calling Nigel's and Cecil's names.

Before long, a glistening white unicorn trotted out of the trees and onto the path. He could tell right away that this was a lady unicorn. She was smaller and sleeker than Nigel and Cecil. Her dark eyes had thick lashes, and she tossed her mane in a feminine way.

"You have come here on a quest, jes?" She spoke with an exotic-sounding accent.

"Yes," Hudson said. "I need to get to Grammaria to save my friend."

"Ah," she said, taking a step closer. "An act of zee pure in heart."

"Is it far from here?"

She bent on one knee to let him mount. "Only a couple of hours if I hurry."

Relieved, he climbed onto her back. Even though he hadn't found Mr. Fantasmo, his trip to Charlotte's house had been a good thing. The compass had put him back in Logos closer to the capital than he'd originally been. The unicorn set off at a gallop. "My name is Genevieve," she said with a flourish, as though her name were an expensive dessert. "And jou are?"

"Hudson." Not wanting to be called Son of Hud, he added, "Although my father's name is actually Jermaine. My mother just liked the name Hudson."

Genevieve made tsking noises. "That was not nice of jour mother—telling everyone jou were another man's son." Then the unicorn said something in a different language that sounded disapproving.

Hudson didn't ask for a translation. "In my land, names don't mean anything. They're just names."

She gave a toss of her head so her mane swished around her neck. "Names have power. Jour people are foolish not to realize that."

Genevieve ran as fast and as seamlessly as the other unicorns had. The trees rushed by in a jumble of rainbow colors. Black-and-white birds darted overhead, chiming their melodies.

"Jou asked for Nigel and Cecil," Genevieve called back. "Jou know them?"

"Yes," Hudson said, and wondered if he should explain the whole long saga.

"They're not in this part of the forest right now. They took a girl and her companion to the Land of Desolation. Poor children. From what I understand, it was a hopeless quest. But Nigel and Cecil, they cannot say no to children with brave hearts. There are so few of those around today, jes?"

"Yes," Hudson said, hoping that number wouldn't grow any smaller. He had to find the river fairy and persuade her to help him rescue Charlotte.

AFTER GENEVIEVE DROPPED HUDSON OFF AT THE EDGE OF THE forest, he used some of the iron bar for strength and ran all the way through the farmland that led to Grammaria. When he neared the river, he saw a bird flying toward him from the city wall. A few moments later, Charlotte's falcon swooped down and landed on his shoulder.

Hudson slowed to a walk. Panting, he asked, "Did you free Charlotte?" He hoped but didn't think it was possible.

The falcon shook its head. "The owl used his magic to reach Grammaria ahead of us." He ruffled his wings in agitation. "A gallows is set up in the courtyard, and a crowd is assembling there, waiting for King Vaygran to address them. They talk of a captured assassin who broke into the king's chambers."

Hudson's stomach twisted. Plans for Charlotte's execution were already under way. He ran down the path again, pushing himself to go faster. "Do you know where they're keeping her?"

"The dungeon, probably. Bolt and I can't get close to the castle. King Vaygran has set harpy eagles in the courtyard to chase off any birds that come near."

At least the king hadn't put Charlotte to death yet. "Are there any bloodhounds around?"

"Not ones in the city that we could see. The king must have sent them all to track you and Charlotte."

That, at least, was good news. It meant Hudson could sneak into Grammaria without worrying about the dogs picking up his scent.

The falcon fluttered from one of Hudson's shoulders to the other. "People from all over the kingdom have come to see Princess Nomira's tree. In the past few days it grew taller, blossomed yellow, and then last night it blossomed red—although no one knows if the color means love, determination, or anger. Now the red blossoms are falling, too.

That struck Hudson as odd. What was happening to the princess that her tree kept changing so quickly and dramatically? Could she know that he and Charlotte had tried to rescue her? Could she know that they'd failed and Charlotte was about to be executed?

The falcon bobbed his head. "Some say it means the princess is ready to come home and rule."

Well, if she was, she couldn't pick a better time to do it. The people needed her. Charlotte needed her.

Hudson reached the riverbank. "Fly back to the city and stay as close to the castle as you can. Watch for any way you can help Charlotte."

Without another word, the bird took to the air and shot off toward the city walls. Hudson pulled the tube of disguise paste out of his bag. He needed to look like a person who fit in here. Someone with the right clothes. This was a problem, because in order for the disguise paste to work, he had to have a clear image in his mind. He considered stealing the mustached soldier's appearance, then decided against it. A lone soldier would undoubtedly be questioned about why he had returned home without his horse or regiment.

It would be better to look like an average boy. Hudson hadn't seen many of those here. He could only remember one in enough detail to be sure he got the appearance right.

He put a dab of disguise cream on the back of his hand, and the next moment he wore the clothes he first saw Proval wearing. Hudson got out the mirror and checked his face. That looked like Proval, too.

While Hudson put the mirror back, he noticed the squirrel stuffed animal wedged inside his bag. He took it out and used the compactulator to turn it full size, which wasn't much bigger than its stuffed-animal size.

Meko blinked at him, ears alert. "Where's Charlotte?"

"I'm going into the city to rescue her. You can help me by . . ." Hudson looked at the animal, unsure what to tell it. Squirrels, when you came down to it, were just rodents with fancy tails. Still, the squirrel was waiting for instructions with such devout intensity, Hudson had to include him in the rescue plan. "I'm not sure yet. Ride quietly in my bag. I might need you to bite someone later on."

"Yes, sir." The squirrel scampered inside, then poked out his head, watching for danger.

Hudson set out toward the city drawbridge. He hoped no one inside the city knew Proval, or knew he was a troll.

16

HUDSON HAD ONLY seen Grammaria during the night. The area outside the city was a much busier place by daylight. People were coming and going on the road that led to the city, most riding animals but some on foot. A large drawbridge stretched over the river, and a line of people stood on it, waiting to enter. Two armed soldiers stood guard at the city entrance, checking people's wares.

Hudson didn't go directly to the drawbridge. He walked to the riverbank and sat down as though resting. He pulled the fairy bell from his pack and rang it, making sure to keep it hidden from anyone who might be watching. "I need a fairy," he whispered.

Nothing happened. No fairy zipped out of the tall grass growing at the water's edge.

He rang the bell several more times, each time calling a little louder. Where was the fairy now, when he desperately needed her?

Hudson rang again and again, waving his hand so quickly he probably looked like he'd burned it on something. Finally, the river fairy emerged, yawning, from a clump of grass on the bank. Her hair was disheveled, and instead of a dress, she wore foamy pajamas and a pair of fluffy slippers. She slowly flitted over to Hudson, landing on a wildflower near his knee. Her wings had been as pale and shiny as moonlight before, but now they looked like yellow butterfly wings. To anyone who wasn't close by, that's all she would seem to be.

She pushed her tangled hair out of her face and glared at him. "Stop ringing that infernal bell while I'm sleeping. Hasn't anyone ever told you it isn't wise to tick off a fairy?"

"Sorry," he said. "I really need your help."

She fluttered her wings angrily at him. "Then it's especially unwise to tick me off, isn't it?" She motioned to the drawbridge. "You don't need help crossing the river. Just walk over the bridge."

Hudson lowered his voice and bent down closer to her. "Charlotte was captured by King Vaygran's wizard. She's being held captive—probably in the castle somewhere."

The fairy wiped her eyes tiredly. "That's lovely. I'm going back to bed. Don't ring that bell again unless you want it lodged someplace unpleasant." She lifted off the flower.

"Don't you care?" he asked. "They're going to execute her."

Hudson hadn't realized the squirrel had climbed out of his leather bag until it scampered onto his shoulder and perched there, baring its teeth. "Do you want me to bite her, sir?"

"No," Hudson said, and shooed the squirrel off his shoulder. "We need her help."

The fairy flew higher, unconcerned. "You know, mortals commit injustices every hour of every day. If fairies tried to right them all, our magic would be spent before breakfast."

"You don't have to right them *all*, just this one."

Meko climbed onto Hudson's other shoulder. "If I jumped really high, I could bite her."

"No," Hudson said, and shooed the squirrel again.

The fairy fluttered in front of Hudson in the scrambled pattern butterflies use. "Righting, like writing, is best done by people." She let out a tinkling laugh. "That should be Grammaria's motto. The one about peace, prosperity, and unity never really worked."

"I'll pay you a remembrance," Hudson said before she flew away. "When King Vaygran brings Charlotte before the people, turn her into a bird. Then she'll be able to fly to freedom."

The fairy paused, hovering at Hudson's eye level. "You say Nepharo captured her?"

Hudson nodded.

"Did he tie her arms with silver rope?"

Hudson nodded again, surprised that the fairy had guessed this detail.

She shook her head sadly. "He used enchanted ropes that will bind her no matter what species she changes into."

"But . . ." Hudson stared at the fairy bleakly. He had depended on having magic to help him free Charlotte. Now he felt like someone had pushed him to the ground.

The fairy must have thought he didn't understand. "Even if I changed your friend into a bird, she would still be a bird with her wings bound. She wouldn't be able to fly."

He held his hands out, pleading. "There must be something you can do."

"Yes," the fairy said, yawning. "I can put in earplugs. Executions are such noisy affairs." And with that, she flew off and disappeared into the plants that grew along the riverbank.

The squirrel scampered back onto Hudson's shoulder. His nose twitched in dissatisfaction. "You should have let me bite her."

Hudson let out a sigh and set off toward the bridge. "Stay hidden. We don't want to draw attention to ourselves."

He was going to have to do this himself. He would carry out Charlotte's original plan, which he hadn't been thrilled about even before a rescue attempt was part of it. Now it would be even more dangerous.

He would join the crowd in the courtyard waiting for King Vaygran's speech. When the king came out on his balcony to address the people, Hudson would throw the bag of revealing powder on him. That part he felt confident about accomplishing. If he could get close enough to the balcony, his baseball training would do the rest.

He hoped Charlotte was right about the way the Grammarians would react when they saw their king clearly. If the crowd realized their king was a tyrant, at the very least they would demand Charlotte's release. Hopefully, the crowd would also grab some pitchforks, or whatever Grammarians used when they rioted; and the king would be so busy dealing with them Hudson could free Charlotte, and they would be able to get away.

If the crowd did nothing, though—if they didn't care that their king was a tyrant, or if they were too afraid to stand up to him—both Charlotte and Hudson would be killed. Everyone would know who had thrown the bag of revealing powder at the king. He wouldn't be able to get away.

Hudson took his place in the drawbridge line behind a portly merchant, his wife, and two daughters. With luck, the guards standing at the entrance would think he was part of their group and not question him.

Hudson had put the compass and disguise paste in his pockets in case the guards searched his bag. Now he worried that the guards might search his pockets. Maybe those magical items would be better off buried underneath the other things in his bag. After all, when the guards found a live squirrel sitting inside, they probably wouldn't dig too deeply in the rest of it.

I went out to the forest to catch something for my dinner, he would explain if questioned. *Sadly, I could only find this squirrel.* It sounded plausible—pathetic, but plausible.

The line moved forward. The guards didn't seem to be checking people's things too thoroughly. Good.

Finally, it was the merchant's turn. One of the guards motioned him to come to the entrance. "What's your business here today?"

The merchant pulled back a covering on the cart, revealing word-shaped cinnamon rolls. The mouthwatering smell drifted back to Hudson, reminding him that he hadn't eaten much today.

"I'm selling in the marketplace." The merchant smiled and gestured to the sign on his cart. It read DON'T EAT YOUR WORDS, EAT OURS. "I've the best cinnamon synonyms in the kingdom." The merchant picked up an iced *delight* and an equally delicious *pleasure* and handed them to the guards. "Sample them if you like—a pair costs a copper. You won't find a better deal anywhere."

The guards eagerly took the cinnamon rolls and bit into them. The guard closest to the cart called to someone over his shoulder. "Is he hiding anything, boy?"

A voice behind the guard said, "Only that he eats more of his profits than he lets his wife know."

This response brought an indignant humph from the merchant and a glare from his wife. Although whether she was glaring at her husband or the boy who'd spoken was unclear.

Who had spoken? Hudson took a step to his right and craned his neck, trying to see around the guards. He caught sight of a stool and the pair of legs sitting on it but couldn't see more than that.

The guard sent the merchant an apologetic look, then called over his shoulder. "The king pays you to uncover conspiracies, not harass his good people."

The words sent a ripple of fear down Hudson's spine. Glamora said trolls could tell what a person was hiding just by looking at him. Was there a troll sitting behind the guards, helping them search people? Hudson wished he could check his compass, but he didn't dare take it from his pocket while the guards were watching.

The second guard took another bite of his synonym and waved for the merchant to pass by. "Have a good day in Grammaria. There's a fine crowd today."

Hudson knew he should go forward with the merchant's

family, but for a moment he stood fixed to the spot. The boy behind the guard—had Hudson heard his voice before? He wasn't sure.

He wanted to turn around and run back across the drawbridge and find some other way to get across the walls. No, that would be worse. It would call attention to him. The guards might chase him if he fled.

With his head down, Hudson followed after the merchant's family. He kept his walk casual, a saunter that said he belonged with the others. His heart banged against his ribs with fear. *Don't notice me*, he thought.

He kept his gaze on the guards' boots, unable to bring himself to look over at the boy. With each step Hudson took, Glamora's words grew louder in his mind. *Trolls can tell. . . . Trolls can tell.*

No, King Vaygran wouldn't employ trolls. Not when he had so much to hide. And yet what else could the guard's question and the boy's answer mean?

Hudson passed the first guard. In another moment he would be past the second, too. This was almost over.

"Stop!" The boy's voice was loud and sharp.

The merchant's family immediately halted. Hudson looked over and found himself staring into Proval's face. *He* was the one helping the guards.

Proval stood and pointed a finger in Hudson's direction. "That boy looks exactly like me. Could you honestly not tell on your own that he's an impostor who's up to something?"

Hudson didn't wait for the guards' response. He sprinted

forward, knocking into the merchant's wife and then pushing around her. Proval leaped at Hudson, arms outstretched to seize him.

Hudson jerked to the right, avoiding capture. Proval's momentum carried him forward, and he fell to the ground, blocking the way of the guards who came after Hudson.

As Hudson sprinted into the city, he heard Proval let out an "Oww!" and then yell, "You stupid oaf!" One of the guards must have trampled him.

Crowds of people milled around the streets, dressed in the tunics and dresses that Hudson had grown used to. Some pushed carts full of wares. Hudson ran on, heading toward a side street in an attempt to lose the guards. The road was narrow and lined with stalls on both sides. Shoppers carrying baskets and bags gathered in clumps or wandered between stalls. Hudson darted around a booth selling homonyms. "Two for the price of one!" a man barked out. "Get your alouds allowed! Buy your byes! Too for the price of won!"

Hudson slowed his pace in the hope that if he walked, he would blend in with the other villagers strolling around. A guard behind him yelled, "There he is! The brunet boy in the green tunic!"

So much for blending in. Hudson ran down the street again, weaving around shoppers the best he could. After a couple of minutes, he got caught in a crowd of people gathered to see a demonstration. He slowed to a near standstill as he wedged his way through them.

"Need a bargain?" the salesman called, holding up a shiny

brass *fit*. "Look no farther than this all-purpose word. It's a noun, it's a verb, it's even an adjective." The man held the word above his head, showing it off. "Impossible, you say? Not for this three-letter wonder."

Hudson glanced over his shoulder. Three more soldiers had joined the chase. All five headed down the street, pushing through the throng of shoppers.

"Don't have a fit. It will always fit. And with it, you'll always look fit."

The villagers clapped in appreciation. Hudson jostled through people trying to go one way, then another. He barely made any forward progress. The soldiers had almost reached the crowd, and it wouldn't take them long to clear people away.

He couldn't hide—but then again, maybe he could. The soldiers were looking for the brunet boy in the green tunic. Hudson took the disguise paste from his pocket and squeezed dabs on each of his fingers. He managed to drop the lid in the process. There wasn't time to look for it.

He touched a dab of paste on the man in front of him and pictured Proval wearing the same green clothes that Hudson now wore. He did the same to the woman beside him and the two teenage boys to his left. Now instead of one imitation Proval, there were five. As he touched more people in the crowd, the duplicates grew until ten exact images of Proval clustered around him.

Hudson used the residual paste on his fingers to change his appearance. He didn't want to risk getting any of his features wrong, so he imagined that he looked like himself—himself wearing the rough brown clothes and a straw hat he saw on another boy in the crowd.

The villagers who'd been turned into Provals began to notice the change. They gaped at the identical people around them and then saw their own clothes, arms, and hands. Several of them cried out in confusion.

"What sort of devilry is this?" a Proval with a deep voice asked.

"Who are you?" a Proval with a woman's voice demanded.

"What's happening?"

"Do I look like that, too?"

The soldiers' gazes ricocheted among the different Provals in confusion. "Which one is he?" one of them called. "I lost track."

"Round them all up!" another soldier said.

If the ten villagers were distressed to find themselves looking like the same teenage boy, they were downright panicked to see soldiers coming at them with swords drawn. Several dropped their parcels, two screamed, and each of them pushed and shoved past the people around them.

It didn't take long for the crowd to disperse. Men with swords tended to do that to a crowd.

Hudson shouldered his way past a few people and ran down the street. Everyone was hurrying away from the soldiers, so he didn't even seem out of place. He made his way back to the main street and then headed to the castle courtyard.

The castle seemed much farther away, now that he wasn't flying the distance. When a wagon filled with orange hay slowed at an intersection, Hudson jumped onto the back and caught a ride down the street.

He worried about wearing his normal face. He had used it because, at the moment, it was the only face he could think of clearly. He reached into his pocket for the tube so he could change himself into somebody else. And then he reached into his other pocket. Even though he went through this process several more times, the results didn't change. The tube of disguise paste wasn't there. He'd lost it. Hudson searched the hay beside him. He looked down the street, hoping it had fallen out recently. It was nowhere.

He gritted his teeth and cursed his luck. The guard at the castle garden had seen his real face. The soldiers here were probably looking for someone who fit his description.

As the wagon neared the castle, Hudson slid off the back and walked the rest of the way to the courtyard. He knew he couldn't stay there long. In about a half an hour, anyone around him would break out in boils.

At the back of the courtyard, a crowd of people surrounded Princess Nomira's tree, surveying it with shaking heads. Hudson nearly gasped at the change in it. It had grown bigger, with thin new branches everywhere, but it looked as though someone had thrown poison on it. The branches were not only wilted, but they had also dropped leaves everywhere. The ground was covered in a limp blue carpet. What had happened to the princess to make her tree change like that?

King Vaygran's tree was a massive thing, with thick steel-colored branches that twisted upward. Its blue leaves were so dark they looked black in places. Several of the branches were bare, and thorns ran along the trunk.

Hudson pulled his hat down, hiding as much of his face as he could. He walked across the courtyard, where hundreds of people had congregated in front of the balcony, waiting for the king's speech. Women and men stood pressed close together, talking in so many conversations the noise sounded like waves crashing into a shore. Some younger children played along the edge of the courtyard, laughing as they tossed a hat back and forth between them. Merchants walked around the courtyard, selling *wares* and *where's*.

The people's happy chatter seemed a stark contrast to the gallows that waited to the left side of the balcony. A noose hung from the center, unmoving, even though a breeze swept across the courtyard. Two soldiers stood at attention on each side of the castle doors, swords hanging at their sides. They didn't seem to be looking for anyone in the crowd, just guarding the castle's front doors. Hudson pulled his hat down a little more anyway.

A pair of large birds—harpy eagles, the falcon had called them—sat on the turrets above the balcony. They had gray checked wings and large feathers circling their heads like lion manes. Three more harpy eagles perched around the castle, watching the crowd with darting black eyes. Charlotte's birds wouldn't be able to come close to this place.

Hudson hated seeing the gallows, hated the thought that King Vaygran might send Charlotte there before Hudson could stop him. He wished he had some magical item that would sabotage the contraption, then realized he did. Sometimes magic came in small packages—in this case, a small, furry rodent package.

Hudson slipped his pack from his shoulder and opened the flap. Immediately, the squirrel poked a twitching nose out. "Are we there? Where's Charlotte?"

"Shhh," Hudson whispered. "I need you to do two things. Go to the gallows, climb up the side, and gnaw the rope. Cut through enough of it so it will break if they hang Charlotte. But don't cut enough that the soldiers notice the noose is hanging by a thread. Can you do that?"

Meko nodded and lifted his paws, eager for the next instruction. Which was good, because there were more ropes that needed gnawing.

"When they bring Charlotte out, sneak over to her and chew through the ropes tying her up. If she's bound with chains, see if one of the people near her has the key to the lock. Steal it if you can, and unlock her chains. Oh, and watch out for harpy eagles." He opened the bag wider. "Go."

The squirrel shot out of the pack, zipped across the ground, and disappeared among the feet of the crowd.

Hudson wished he could move through the crowd so easily. More people were coming into the courtyard with every passing minute. He needed to be close enough to the balcony that he could be sure to hit King Vaygran with the pouch of revealing powder. Hudson also wanted to be close enough that Charlotte would see him and know he'd come to help.

He strained his head, peering around the people who stood in front of him. How could he get closer? It was then that he saw more soldiers striding into the courtyard from the street. About ten of them, and they weren't alone. Four villagers stood beside them. Hudson recognized three: Glamora, Proval, and Rex. The other woman with them was undoubtedly also a troll.

Hudson let out a groan. Even if his hat completely concealed his face, it wouldn't keep him from the trolls' detection. Trolls could tell what a person was hiding. As soon as they saw him, they would know he hadn't come here to listen to the king; he'd come here to stop him.

Hudson turned so his back faced the trolls. *I'm not hiding anything*, he told himself. *I'm proud of what I'm doing.* He hoped thinking these thoughts would shield him from the trolls' powers. As he pressed into the crowd, he tapped a woman on the shoulder. "I'm Hudson Brown."

She cast him a questioning look, as though wondering if she should know him.

"I'm here to rescue Charlotte," he said in an offhand manner. "I'm from Texas, and I was a jerk at school for not sticking up for her."

The woman's eyebrows drew together in confusion. "What?"

He didn't explain, just went on spouting off things he wanted to hide. "I have a troll mirror, I escaped from soldiers, and I changed a bunch of people in the marketplace into Provals."

The woman cocked her head. "Do you feel faint, young man?"

"I'm not hiding anything," he told her. "It's out in the open now. Could you let me through? I've got a bag of revealing powder to throw at the king."

Rude behavior may get you nowhere in life, but crazy

behavior will take you all sorts of places. Most people prefer you go there alone.

With her eyebrows still drawn together in question, the woman stepped aside and let Hudson pass. He squeezed by six more people and then got stuck in the crowd again.

A glance over his shoulder showed him that the soldiers were pairing off with the trolls and positioning themselves on all sides of the courtyard. They would methodically scan the crowd, searching for someone who was hiding who he was. Hudson didn't know if his confession had shielded him from troll scrutiny. Even if it had, he didn't have long. Soon everyone in the crowd except him would break out into boils. If the trolls hadn't found him before then, they would know who he was after that.

What if the king didn't come out for hours? Could Hudson leave every twenty minutes and come back? He didn't let himself think about that, or about the other ways this plan could go wrong. In order to have a sure shot, he needed to get closer to the balcony. As he jostled around people, he listened to their conversations. Everyone spoke about either the tree or the assassin. They seemed to think King Vaygran had caught the assailant in the very act of wielding the king's sword against him.

Hudson was nearing the front of the crowd when the trumpets sounded, announcing the king's arrival. Two men in red tunics and leggings marched onto the balcony, each with a loopy trumpet pressed to his lips. A third red-tunicked man strode out and draped a flag across the balcony railing that depicted the king's tree underneath the phrase PEACE, PROSPERITY, UNITY. IT'S THE LAW.

While the red-tunicked men retreated back inside the castle, King Vaygran strolled out, arms raised as though he wanted to embrace the crowd. He wore a gold crown perched high on his thick black hair, and his long blue robe dragged across the balcony like a trailing storm cloud. He looked tall, noble, and utterly powerful.

He stepped over to the railing, and the crowd cheered so loud the noise rang out through the courtyard. Behind him, Nepharo and a soldier half dragged, half carried Charlotte onto the balcony. Her hair had been blown into wild disarray, and her eyes were wide with worry. She was still gagged and bound by the silver rope, and more surprising, she still wore Macy's face. Hudson had expected Nepharo to use revealing powder on her. Maybe he didn't want people to know she was Fantasmo's daughter. No point in alerting any friends who might help her.

While the people around Hudson continued clapping, he slipped his bag off his shoulder. Time to get out the revealing powder.

Nepharo gazed at the gallows with smug satisfaction and dragged Charlotte closer to the balcony railing. King Vaygran held up his hand to silence the crowd. Rings glittered on his fingers, tossing the light away from him like a sunburst. "People of Logos, I bring before you one of the assailants who broke into my chamber and seized my sword."

Hudson found the bag of revealing powder and took it out.

"My soldiers apprehended her," King Vaygran continued, "and now I bring her before you so you can decide her fate."

The fate King Vaygran wanted for her was pretty clear, since he'd already set up the gallows.

"Hang her!" a man in the crowd shouted.

"Death to traitors!" Someone else shouted. Several people joined in agreement. One finished with, "And let that be a warning to all would-be assassins!"

Hudson shifted a step to his left, away from a tall man who stood in front of him. As he did, Charlotte's gaze found him. He couldn't see her smile through the gag but was sure she had. The corner of her eyes crinkled in relief. She knew he was here to carry out her plan and thought it would work.

Hudson was considerably less sure. When you came down to it, nothing had worked the way they thought it would. The bee had told him rescuing the princess was a process. If that was true, then the Cliff of Faces sure hadn't known the process. They'd sent them to an empty tower in the Land of Backwords.

King Vaygran held up his jeweled hand to silence the crowd again. "I would not issue such a serious verdict on one so young. If the girl is to die, it must be because the people insist upon it. It must be your devotion to me and abhorrence of her crime that lead to her punishment."

Voices all over the crowd erupted in agreement, insisting that assassins be punished. Hudson fingered the bag of revealing powder, getting a feel for its weight. He loosened the tie a bit and made a quick check of the soldiers' positions. The ones to his left still stood, hands on their swords, peering into the crowd. The ones on his right—oh no, Proval was staring right at him.

The troll boy grinned in gloating triumph and pointed out Hudson to the soldier next to him.

Hudson didn't have any more time to spare. He turned back to the balcony. Charlotte was waiting with tense anticipation. *Throw!* Her eyes told him. *Throw now!*

It was during the moment when he wound his arm back that he figured out the riddle in the Cliff of Faces' answer. The face on the cliff had said that if Charlotte and Hudson walked into the tower, the princess could walk out. There was only one way that answer was the truth, and the possibility made Hudson inwardly gasp.

The facts, he suddenly realized, had been there all along, scattered puzzle pieces waiting to be snapped together. In a whir of understanding, the pieces came together now.

Disguise paste changed the way a person looked—permanently, unless revealing powder changed them back to their original form. Which meant Charlotte could have looked completely different in Logos than she had when she came to Texas. Aziz Fantasmo was hiding her, so he would have changed her looks along with her name.

Hudson didn't know what Charlotte actually looked like.

Charlotte's memories were cut into ribbons. She hadn't done that—she wouldn't have, at least not without writing down what memories she was losing. A wizard had done it. One who'd made a calculator.

And a wizard had taken Princess Nomira from the tower at Backwords to someplace where she could live a safe, normal life.

What better place than the Land of Banishment?

The Cliff of Faces hadn't given the wrong answer, after all. The princess *had* walked out of the tower. He and Charlotte just hadn't realized it.

Hudson could hear the soldiers coming toward him, pushing their way through the crowd. "Out of the way!" they barked.

He threw the bag of revealing powder. It arced up toward the balcony high and fast, then struck dead center into Charlotte's chest. A small cloud of powder shot into the air, covering her, glistening like glitter as it fluttered to the ground. Her eyes blinked in anguished disbelief. She thought he'd missed. But he hadn't. He'd been aiming for Charlotte.

17

THE COLORS AND shape of Charlotte's clothes ran together and drained away. Her hair darkened and grew longer, and her features changed. She wasn't Charlotte—not the redheaded girl he'd gone to school with in Houston. The girl on the balcony looked a bit older than the picture Hudson had seen of her in Scriptoria, but it was definitely Princess Nomira. Charlotte had been the princess all along. She just hadn't been able to remember this fact.

A series of gasps went up from the crowd. "It's the princess!" several people yelled. Followed by "Why is she bound?" and "Release her!"

Someone yelled, "King Vaygran wanted to trick us into executing the princess!"

Even the soldiers halted where they stood, gaping open-mouthed at Charlotte instead of coming after Hudson.

She stared at Hudson, her eyes circles of surprise. She was putting the pieces together, understanding what the gaps in her memory actually meant. Aziz Fantasmo wasn't her father. He'd been King Vaygran's wizard, the man assigned to guard her at the tower in the Land of Backwords. After he'd changed loyalties, he'd done something to her memories and taken her to Texas to hide.

Nepharo glared at the crowd and fingered his wand. King Vaygran strode over to her, the anger flowing off him like heat waves. "She isn't the real princess!" he yelled. "It's trickery. That boy hit her with magic powder to change her appearance." He pointed at Hudson. "Guards, grab the boy and bring him to me."

The soldiers tried to push through the crowd again, although fewer people moved out of their way now. Still, Hudson couldn't escape from the courtyard, not when so many people surrounded him, pinning him in place.

"She *is* the princess," Hudson shouted. "I threw revealing powder on her! King Vaygran knows she's the princess, and that's why he's trying to kill her!"

This caused another murmur to go through the crowd. "Let the girl speak!" several people yelled.

Someone called, "Those of us who knew her will recognize her voice. Ungag her."

"No!" the king snapped. "If she speaks, she might cast a spell upon you." He glared at Charlotte, enraged. "She might be a wizard. I'll have Nepharo question her in private, where he can protect himself from her magical treachery."

The crowd seemed torn by this statement. Some nodded, while others protested. "How will we ever know the truth?" a woman called out.

"If it's the princess," a man yelled, "she'll know where the scepter is. Ask her. Have her write the answer."

King Vaygran put his hand to his chest and forced a benevolent smile in the crowd's direction. "You need to trust my judgment on the matter. Haven't I served you well this past year? Haven't I brought you what none of my predecessors could? I've given Logos peace, prosperity, and unity."

This statement didn't rouse the support King Vaygran had hoped for. Murmurs turned into mutters of complaint.

The king pointed at Hudson. "It's that boy who's sowing disunity, and he'll be punished for it."

The soldiers pressed closer to Hudson. Nepharo stepped to the edge of the balcony and held his wand outstretched, perhaps shooting a spell in Hudson's direction. Nothing happened. Hudson's clover was protecting him.

The wizard was so busy with his wand-waving he didn't notice that the squirrel had shimmied up the castle wall and run across the balcony, but Hudson saw it.

"It isn't your kingdom," he yelled. "Princess Nomira is the rightful ruler. Cut through her ropes right now!"

He didn't expect Vaygran to do it. The instruction was for the squirrel. Meko darted behind Charlotte and disappeared from Hudson's view. If she felt the squirrel biting at the rope, she gave no indication of it. She gazed stoically out at the people.

The soldiers who had pushed their way through the crowd finally reached Hudson. One grabbed his arm roughly and yanked him sideways. The second grabbed hold of his other arm. "She is the princess," Hudson yelled again. "Rescue her before King Vaygran kills her!"

People in the crowd began talking in so many heated conversations no one heard the next few words the king said. At least a dozen men pushed toward the castle doors, demanding to be let inside so they could see the princess themselves. Other people cried out, "Let us examine the girl! We insist on it!"

One of the guards stationed at the doors pulled out his sword, but he tried only halfheartedly to keep the men outside. The other soldier had left his post and gone into the courtyard to see Charlotte himself. "It looks like her," he called back to the other. "It might be the princess."

King Vaygran's eyes darted over the crowd, worried. He grabbed hold of Charlotte's arm to keep anyone from spiriting her off.

It was a mistake. The revealing powder glistening on her skin affected him, too. He'd apparently used some sort of magic to enhance his royal appearance, and once he touched the revealing powder, he shrank several inches. His features grew sharper, less handsome. Instead of glowing with warmth, his eyes looked as cold and dark as stones. Charlotte had said revealing powder also revealed crimes. Two words took shape across his forehead, glowing red like brands: IMPRISONED NIECE. Other sentences were written below these words, but they were too small to see from far away.

The crowd stared at him in wonder, their conversations now spinning around the revelation. "The girl must be the princess!" a man yelled. "He imprisoned her last night."

"No," someone else answered. "Those words mean that he unlawfully imprisoned her a year ago. He didn't send her away to protect her. We have proof of that now."

King Vaygran realized what had happened and jerked his hand away from Charlotte. It was too late, though. The words stuck.

"If that's not the real princess," a woman shouted, "then where is she? Bring her forth!"

"Let us ask the girl questions!" someone else demanded.

"That's why the princess's tree is dying!" a woman yelled, pointing at the king. "You're trying to kill her!"

The crowd rumbled with agreement, and several people shouted, "Release her!"

The soldiers pulling Hudson slowed down. No one moved out of their way now, despite the soldiers' commands.

King Vaygran stepped forward and planted his hands firmly on the railing. "I am the king! I decide what happens to impostors. Anyone who thinks differently will answer to Nepharo."

At the sound of his name, Nepharo gave the crowd a thin-lipped smile, as though the masses below him were unruly children who needed discipline. He held up both hands and grew larger and taller, each moment adding height. His fingers stretched into sharp gray claws, and his skin turned dark red and scaly. A tearing sound came from his back as wings sprouted, unfurled, and flapped angrily. His neck jutted out unnaturally, and for a moment he looked like some horrible genetic accident—a dragon with a man's face—then his beard disappeared and was replaced by snapping jaws and a reptilian snout.

He leaped onto the balcony railing, making it creak beneath his weight, and lifted his head in a roar.

Gasps and shrieks went up from the crowd. The people

nearest the balcony backed up, knocking into those behind them. Several people cowered, covering their heads with their hands. Some near the street fled out of the courtyard.

Others stood firm, glowering at the king. "It's definitely the princess," a man behind Hudson called out. "Or King Vaygran wouldn't be threatening us."

People around him shouted their agreement.

Charlotte still stood silently, her dark eyes watching the crowd. Only Hudson noticed that the ropes around her ankles were slack. The squirrel had managed to bite through them.

King Vaygran scowled down at the crowd. "All of you, go back to your homes. This is over."

The instruction didn't apply to Hudson. The soldiers tightened their grip on him. One gave Hudson a vicious pull forward.

A voice in the back of the courtyard yelled, "This is *not* over!"

Despite the soldiers tugging him, Hudson turned hopefully to the voice. He recognized it. Mr. Fantasmo had come.

The wizard rode on a silver unicorn—Cecil. Instead of the corduroy pants and Hawaiian shirts Hudson was used to seeing him wear, Mr. Fantasmo had on a shimmering blue robe. He held his wand outstretched and pointed at the balcony. "Release the princess now!"

King Vaygran's eyes narrowed. "Traitor," he growled, then motioned to Nepharo. "Kill him."

The dragon leaped into the sky, wings flapping in great, angry beats. A screech blasted from his mouth, so loud and shrill the air shuddered with the sound of it. He soared toward Mr. Fantasmo, claws outstretched.

Mr. Fantasmo pointed his wand at the dragon and yelled, "Downdraft!"

Hudson realized why Mr. Fantasmo had said these words. A four-leaf clover protected Nepharo from other wizards' spells, but Mr. Fantasmo could still cast a spell on the air around the dragon.

Sparks shot from the end of Fantasmo's wand, swirling around the dragon like a fireworks explosion. Nepharo tumbled, careening downward, wings flailing.

The people beneath the dragon screamed and pushed at one another to get away. Right before crashing, Nepharo righted himself, let out an enraged shriek, and rushed upward into the sky. With a beat of his wings, he shot toward Mr. Fantasmo again. Flames flickered in his widening mouth.

Cecil reared, his horn raised and glistening, sharp as a knife. The dragon pulled away to keep his distance from the unicorn, then breathed a stream of fire at them.

Mr. Fantasmo aimed his wand and shouted, "Extinguish!"

The fire dissolved into a cloud of smoke, covering the area so completely Hudson couldn't see the unicorn or rider.

The soldiers tightened their grip on Hudson. All around them, people jostled and shoved through the crowd. Some were getting away from the fighting. Others made their way to the castle doors. Hopefully to help Charlotte.

One of the soldiers holding on to Hudson pushed a couple of people standing in the way. "Let us through!"

No one paid attention to them.

Hudson planted his feet and twisted his arms, trying to break free from the soldiers' grip. He needed to get away. He needed to get to the balcony to help Charlotte.

Three dark shapes streaked by overhead. It took Hudson a second to realize what they were. Charlotte's eagle and falcon had joined the fray, and another bird was with them. A pale brown falcon. Somehow Hudson knew it was the princess's pet falcon. Wherever it had been, it had recognized its owner and had come to help her. They zoomed toward the castle, trying to get to her.

Harpy eagles chased after them, tailing so closely the birds didn't dare land. Instead, they swooped back and forth around the balcony, nearly knocking into King Vaygran. He covered his head with one hand and waved the other madly at them.

Charlotte still stood exactly where she had been. Why hadn't she run away, now that her feet were unbound? She was moving her shoulders, probably working to free the ropes around her wrists. He couldn't tell if the squirrel was still there, gnawing away at them.

The soldiers yanked Hudson a few more feet toward the castle. He dug his feet in, checking over his shoulder on Mr. Fantasmo. As the smoke cleared in the back of the courtyard, not one but two unicorns took shape in front of the royalty trees. Nigel stood at the back of the courtyard now, too, and another person rode on his back.

Hudson stared at the sight. It couldn't be. And yet the image remained the same. The man had short-cropped brown hair, a wide nose like Hudson's, and a muscled build. A Marine build. His dad was sitting on Nigel's back. His dad. How had he gotten here?

Mr. Brown had never used the sword from his Marines dress uniform, but he held it now, pointing it at the dragon.

"You come any closer," he called in his soft Texas drawl, "and we'll be having some dragon shish kebab."

Hudson gaped at his father, stunned. Amazed. Afraid. Could his dad fend off a dragon, even with Mr. Fantasmo's help? Hudson wanted to call out to him but didn't dare. It would be dangerous to distract his father while he was fighting Nepharo.

Hudson yanked at the soldiers' grip again, this time finding added strength. His father was here. He and Mr. Fantasmo had come to help, and Hudson wasn't about to let a pair of soldiers drag him away to a dungeon somewhere.

He wrenched one arm free, then tugged the other free, too. Before either of the soldiers could grab him, he darted away into the crowd and the smoke.

He had one moment of indecision. Did he go to help his father or Charlotte?

Charlotte.

His father would want him to help her first.

Hudson headed in that direction, not sure how best to get to the balcony. There were some men gathered around the castle doors, and by the looks of it, they were having a yelling match with one of the guards stationed there. Was there another way he could make it to her? Could he scale the castle wall? Maybe it would be easier to climb the gallows and use the rope to swing himself over.

He noticed, vaguely, that people were developing faint red spots, the telltale sign of boils. With everything else going on, no one seemed to notice or care—yet.

Charlotte stood in the same place on the balcony, arms tugging at her ropes. King Vaygran crouched nearby, batting at a falcon that zoomed around him. It was quickly followed by the larger harpy eagle. "Where are the rest of my wizards?" he screamed.

An especially loud dragon roar drew Hudson's attention back to the fight behind him. The dragon lunged downward, his red coloring making him look like a smudge of blood against the sky. With outstretched claws, he streaked toward Hudson's dad.

Hudson watched, frozen, a silent *No!* on his lips.

Nigel reared, kicking his front hooves upward and swinging his horn threateningly. His gold mane glowed bright and hot, burning like fire.

Again, the dragon pulled away, but not fast enough. Mr. Brown arced his sword, and with a flash of silver and a loud crack, it slashed through a claw, severing it. The dragon screeched in pain and whipped his scaly tail into Mr. Brown. The blow knocked him off the unicorn and toppled the sword from his hand.

The dragon turned, ready to dive down and strike. Mr. Fantasmo held both arms aloft and shouted, "Whirlwind!"

Dirt, leaves, and bits of grass twirled upward, spinning faster and faster. The dragon growled and snapped his jaws, flying higher to avoid the whirlwind's reach.

Mr. Brown grabbed his sword again, took hold of Nigel's mane, and pulled himself onto the unicorn.

Hudson turned back to the castle and pushed that way again. He needed to help Charlotte.

Her hands were free now, and the squirrel climbed to her

shoulder, chittering proudly. Charlotte tugged the gag off her mouth and took a step toward the crowd. "People of Logos!" she called. "I *am* the princess!"

King Vaygran straightened, ignoring the swooping birds for the first time. "Silence!"

His face twisted with such rage, Hudson knew he would do something horrible to Charlotte—stab her or throw her off the balcony. Hudson reached into his leather bag, looking for something to throw. His fingers curled around the jar of hope.

He wound his arm back and hurled the bottle at the king. It flew through the air, spinning, until it smashed into King Vaygran's shoulder.

The king gripped his shoulder and swung around to see what had hit him. Charlotte moved away from him but didn't run inside the castle as Hudson had expected. She might be able to get away if she went inside. She knew her way around, knew secret passages.

He searched his bag for something else to throw and found the metal box of Valentine's candy.

Charlotte went to the railing, her hand held out toward the back of the courtyard. "I need my scepter! I'm ready for it now!"

At first, Hudson thought she was talking to Mr. Fantasmo. Did he have her scepter? With the whirlwind swirling near him, he probably couldn't hear Charlotte.

But her eyes were fixed on her tree. It was no longer shedding leaves or wilting. The branches stood tall and straight, new leaves already budding and stretching. A large white blossom grew in the middle of the tree. No, not white—crystal—a diamond as big as a doorknob. Sunlight hit its sides and sent flickers of colors shimmering outward.

The leaves at the base of the crystal peeled away, and Hudson realized it wasn't a flower at all. It was the top of a scepter. It had been inside Charlotte's tree all along.

She reached out, beckoning the scepter to come to her.

King Vaygran strode toward her again. Hudson wound his arm back and threw the metal box of Valentine's candy as hard as he could. It whirred toward the balcony, hitting King Vaygran smack in the middle of his forehead. His head snapped back, and he stumbled and fell backward.

Ah, love was good.

Charlotte's scepter arced through the air, flying across the courtyard until it landed in her hand. Immediately, the crystal glowed blue and bright like the tip of a flame.

She pointed the scepter at the dragon, who was flapping his wings and snapping at the whirlwind. "Return to your true form!"

A blaze of light hit the dragon and wrapped around him. He shrank, his colors fading, and then his scales fell away like dry leaves in a storm. He flailed in the air on ever-dwindling wings and then sank to the ground, a man again.

Charlotte turned back to King Vaygran. He trembled at the sight of the scepter in her hand and scooted away from her.

She pointed the scepter at the discarded rope lying on the floor. "Tie him."

The silver ropes quivered to life and slithered over to the king, no longer ropes but silver snakes that hissed angrily.

"Stop!" he yelled, and tried to knock them away. Some of

the pieces wound around his ankles, biting their tails to bind him. Others wriggled up his legs, slid across his torso, and made their way to his wrists. He slapped at them uselessly.

"I never hurt you," he cried. "I sent you away for your own good! You couldn't rule. You were just a child."

She didn't lower her scepter. "I'm not just a child anymore."

King Vaygran struck a snake that was twining around his arm. "I did it to protect you!" Instead of falling off, the snake bit the king's finger, then wound around his hand. Other snakes made their way—clinging, squeezing—until they bound the king's arms, too.

"I'll protect you the same way you protected me," Charlotte told him. "With banishment."

A crowd had gathered underneath the balcony again, and they let out a cheer.

Charlotte, it was clear, was back in power.

She pointed her scepter upward, using it to turn the harpy eagles into bursts of confetti. Hudson turned away from the castle and made his way across the courtyard toward his father.

While Mr. Fantasmo tied Nepharo with silver cords, Hudson's father looked out over the crowd, searching. His eyes connected with Hudson's, and relief washed over his face. He grinned broadly and held his arms open.

Hudson weaved around people who were heading to the balcony. More and more had joined the throng, pouring in from the streets of Grammaria. Everyone, it seemed, wanted to see what was happening at the castle.

At last, Hudson broke free from the crowd and ran the last

few steps. He wrapped his arms around his dad, holding him tightly. The hug felt warm and reassuring. It felt like home. Neither let go for a long time.

Finally, Hudson asked, "How did you get here?"

"That's quite a story." Mr. Brown stepped away from Hudson, checking him over for injuries. "I flew home to Houston early to surprise everyone. Bonnie said you'd gone off to some enchanted land with Charlotte, but I figured you were just teasing her. I went over to Charlotte's house to haul you home and unenchant you. When I got there, Mr. Fantasmo was packing a bag, ready to go after the two of you. It took me about ten seconds to realize you were in real danger."

"Oh," Hudson said. "Sorry about that."

"I insisted on coming with Fantasmo, and ever since, we've been running all over Logos searching for you." Mr. Brown patted Hudson on the shoulder. "I'm proud of what you did today, of the way you helped Charlotte." The smile stayed fixed on his face. "That doesn't mean you're not grounded for the next month, because you are." He kept patting Hudson's shoulder. "Really, really grounded."

18

MR. FANTASMO AND Mr. Brown thanked the unicorns profusely for their help. Profusely in this case meaning that Mr. Brown made them honorary Marines, and Mr. Fantasmo waved his wand and gave them wings.

"As I promised," Mr. Fantasmo told them, "I won't zap you around Logos again. You can fly out of Grammaria and avoid the crowds that way. The wings will disappear when you land in the Forest of Possibilities."

Cecil opened his wings to examine his silver feathers. "I don't think I'll land for a bit. I'll try my hand at being a Pegasus."

Nigel spanned his own wings, sweeping them up and down. "Tell the princess we're glad she's returned. She'll be a much better ruler than that sour fellow."

Cecil swished his tail in agreement. "I suppose this means we'll be legal again." Under his breath, he added, "Pity. I made a rather good bandit."

The unicorns turned to go, and their hooves clacked against the courtyard stones.

"Thank you!" Hudson called after them. "We couldn't have done it without you!"

Nigel looked over his shoulder and nickered approvingly. "Farewell Fantasmo, Hudson, and Hud."

He turned back to Cecil, and the two unicorns trotted a few steps before leaping upward. Their silver and gold wings sliced through the air, lifting them into the sky.

Mr. Brown shook his head as he watched them go. "The unicorns called me Hud the entire day. They said it would be insulting to call me anything else."

Hudson smiled and tried to explain. "Names are important here. And changeable."

While Mr. Fantasmo directed the soldiers to take Nepharo to the dungeons, Hudson and Mr. Brown made their way toward the balcony. Charlotte was addressing the people, answering their questions. While they walked, Hudson related how he and Charlotte had looked for the princess in the Tower of Backwords and afterward been caught by Nepharo's men.

Hudson's father made unhappy grumbling noises during the story, as though he wanted to knock some soldiers' heads together—or maybe just knock Hudson's and Charlotte's heads together for tromping off into danger.

Hudson had just gotten to the part where he'd tricked the soldiers with the troll curse when a woman in the crowd called out to Charlotte, "Your Highness, when we demanded your release, King Vaygran's wizard must have cursed us with boils."

She held up her arms to show her spots. "Please, Your Majesty, make the wizard reverse the spell!"

Charlotte nodded at the woman. "Don't worry. I know how to cure you all." Her gaze swept over the crowd until she found Hudson. She motioned to him. "Come here and throw me the mirror."

The crowd around Hudson parted, making room for his father and him to reach the balcony. As Hudson walked, he remembered various PE softball games where Charlotte had loitered in the outfield, paying more attention to the grass at her feet than the ball whizzing toward her. "Are you sure you want me to throw this? No offense, Charlotte, but I've seen you catch."

She arched an eyebrow at him, looking imperial. "Trust me. Throw it."

Hudson sighed, hoping troll mirrors didn't break easily, and lobbed it to her as gently as he could.

Charlotte pointed her scepter at the flying mirror, and instead of continuing to soar, it slowed and floated gently into her outstretched hand. "I accept this mirror from you, knowing its magical properties."

She tapped the mirror with her scepter, and it vanished from her hand. Immediately, the boils that covered everyone's skin vanished, too.

The crowd gave Charlotte another round of applause. One of the soldiers, perhaps because he was worried about retribution, shouted, "Long live the princess!"

The other soldiers joined in the cheer, and the rest of the crowd followed until Hudson was sure the whole city could hear the chant. Charlotte smiled at them, a happy, reassuring smile.

As though the crowd had agreed upon it beforehand, everyone began singing the Logosian national anthem.

The anthem turned out to be nine verses long. Hudson supposed that was inevitable in a country where people loved words. While the people sang, Charlotte ordered some of the soldiers to take King Vaygran to the dungeon until she arranged for his banishment. They carried him off during the fourth chorus.

After the song ended, Charlotte looked out across the crowd. "I need to talk with my fa—um—wizard." She motioned to Mr. Fantasmo, who had joined Hudson and Mr. Brown in the crowd.

Charlotte wasn't any taller than she had been when Hudson went to school with her in Texas, but she seemed more regal now. She stood straight, chin lifted. Her long black hair looked nothing like her old unruly red hair. Freckles no longer dotted her skin, and the upturned elflike nose was gone, too. Her eyes seemed the same, though, large and kind.

At Charlotte's words, Mr. Fantasmo grew a bit paler. His pretense of being her father was gone now. She knew the truth. He was only a wizard, and one who had helped Vaygran keep her prisoner before he switched loyalties.

Fantasmo lifted his arms so his long sleeves looked like dark wings. Then, faster than Hudson could see the change coming, the wizard turned into a speckled brown owl. He flew over the crowd with quick wingbeats and landed on the balcony railing.

The bird hung his head, then flapped off the railing and hovered before Charlotte. He transformed back into his human form, his head still bowed.

"You're not my father." Her voice sounded sad and heavy. "You changed my memories and tricked me about my identity. Why?"

He didn't meet Charlotte's gaze. "You weren't ready to fight King Vaygran or rule, and until you were, knowing that you were the princess only made you miserable. You felt the responsibility of your people's suffering, and it made you ill with worry. I was going to give you back your real memories when you were older, so you could return and challenge him, but I thought it would be years until you were ready. " His head drooped even lower. "I ask forgiveness for underestimating you."

She considered his words, then stepped toward him and touched his sleeve. "Of course I forgive you. You took care of me like a father and fought Nepharo in order to protect me. For that, I will always love and thank you."

Mr. Fantasmo looked up at her for the first time. His shoulders lifted with relief. "Thank you, Your Highness."

"Will you be my top wizard and adviser?"

He smiled, happy again. "I will."

She reached toward him with arms outstretched, and he gathered her into a hug. For a moment, they stood like that, her head resting against his chest. When he released her, the pride was evident in his eyes. "This quest has strengthened you. You are now truly a princess who sees."

Charlotte nodded. "My name will no longer be Nomira. It

won't be Erica, a ruler, or Charlotte, one who is free. Now my name is Colette—victory for the people."

The crowd clapped and cheered at this announcement, then burst into the national anthem again. They might have gone on singing it all night if Charlotte—Hudson couldn't think of her as Colette, even though the crowd had instantly incorporated her new name into the national anthem—hadn't cut the song short.

She called for Hudson and Mr. Brown to join her on the balcony. As Hudson walked to the castle, he looked around for Proval and Glamora. They were nowhere in sight. He checked the compass. No warnings appeared on its surface. He supposed the trolls had fled Grammaria as soon as they realized Vaygran would no longer rule the city.

Good riddance.

Charlotte ordered King Vaygran's wizards, advisers, and officials to come to the balcony to explain their part in King Vaygran's government and to swear an oath of loyalty to her. It was easy to see that they supported her, since they hadn't come to King Vaygran's aid while he fought her.

After she finished taking oaths of fealty from the wizards, she decided which of the castle guards to pardon. This involved a lot of kneeling, and quite a bit of pleading on the part of the guards, since some of them had dragged Charlotte, bound and tied, before King Vaygran. Others had constructed the gallows she was supposed to hang from.

In the end, she forgave most of them. The only ones she sent to stockades were the ones who had still followed King Vaygran's orders after it became clear that he was trying to kill her.

Charlotte then thanked the crowd for their support, told them she needed to meet with her advisers, and said she would address the people of Grammaria again tomorrow. As she turned and went into the castle, the people sent out a final cheer.

Hudson, Mr. Brown, and Mr. Fantasmo followed her inside. It was odd to see long black hair swishing down her back. It would take some getting used to. *She's still Charlotte*, Hudson told himself. Still the same on the inside, no matter what she looked like on the outside.

Servants lined the large hallway, all bowing to her like trees in a windstorm. "We're so glad you've returned," one man said. A woman teared up and kissed Charlotte's hand.

Charlotte murmured her thanks to them and walked to a large meeting room. She swept inside and waited for Hudson and the others to follow her.

Once inside, she shut the door and leaned on it. Her regal bearing slipped away and her brown eyes grew anxious—or maybe it was just exhaustion. "I need my old memories back. I can't run a country if I have amnesia."

Mr. Fantasmo nodded. "Where is the calculator? I saved them there."

"I have it," Hudson said, getting it from his pack. He'd had no idea how valuable the contraption was and was glad Nepharo hadn't seen it when he'd captured them. He might have guessed what it was and destroyed Charlotte's memories.

Mr. Fantasmo took the calculator from Hudson and looked at it sadly.

At first, Hudson didn't understand why anyone, especially

Mr. Fantasmo, would be sad at this moment. They had defeated King Vaygran and returned the princess—returned Charlotte—to the throne. This was the definition of happily ever after.

The very next moment, Hudson understood the sadness. When Charlotte's memories returned, she wouldn't be Mr. Fantasmo's daughter anymore. And she also wouldn't come back to Texas and go to school with him again. That thought took some of the happiness out of ever after.

Mr. Fantasmo pushed several buttons on the calculater, putting in a sequence of numbers—some sort of code. "I'll also take away the memories I added about you being my daughter. My own daughter will be happy to have them back."

"Your daughter?" Charlotte repeated. "You have a real daughter?"

He punched in a few more buttons. "She's grown up now, but you always reminded me of her." He paused, noticing Charlotte's distress. "Don't worry. She gave her memories to you willingly. We thought that if you believed you were my child, you wouldn't be so homesick for Logos."

Well, Mr. Fantasmo had either underestimated Charlotte's bravery or her foolishness. Sometimes it was hard to tell one from the other. Or perhaps, Hudson thought, looking at the determination in her expression, perhaps sometimes the knowledge of who you were ran deeper than your memories.

While Charlotte waited, she fingered the scepter, making lights flicker on its jeweled surface.

Hudson gestured to it. "If you don't remember hiding the scepter, how did you know where to find it?"

She gazed at the scepter as though still amazed she had it. "I asked myself where I would have put it if I was the princess. Inside the heart of the tree seemed like the safest place to hide something."

Fantasmo lifted the calculator, pointing it at Charlotte. "You're ready to take your memories back—the bad along with the good?"

"Do I have to take the bad memories back, too?" she asked.

"One without the other is a dangerous thing," he said. "Wisdom requires both."

She took a deep breath, bracing herself. "Then give me both."

Mr. Fantasmo pushed the last button, and a flash of light went off from the calculater. As though something physical had hit her, Charlotte stepped backward, her eyelids fluttering. When she righted herself, she glanced around the room with sudden recognition. "I remember everything," she said with happy awe. The next moment, her voice lost some of its excitement. "I remember everything."

Mr. Fantasmo put a consoling arm around her shoulder. "Wisdom requires both."

She nodded, swallowed, and leaned into him a bit. Her gaze went around the room again. "My father used to meet in here with the leaders of the different guilds. He made me stay and listen so I would know how the guilds worked, but I always thought it was boring and drew pictures instead of paying attention."

Fantasmo gave her an encouraging smile. "Perhaps you won't find it so boring anymore."

"I should have listened better," she said. "I don't know enough about running a country."

"I'll help you," Fantasmo said. "As will your other advisers. You still have time to learn everything."

"Time," she repeated, and her gaze went to Hudson. "We need to pay the Cliff of Faces our year."

"Right," Hudson said, and then scowled.

Mr. Brown tilted his head. "Come again?"

Charlotte explained how they had gone to the cliff and asked their questions. At the end of the story, Hudson let out a grunt. "Seeing as Charlotte turned out to *be* the princess, it doesn't seem worth a year of my life."

Mr. Fantasmo sighed in agreement. "Sometimes education can be costly."

Mr. Brown stepped in between Hudson and Fantasmo, his hands raised in protest. "Wait—a cliff of faces bought a year of Hudson's and Charlotte's lives? That can't be legal. What kind of contract is that?"

Mr. Fantasmo sighed again. "One that must be taken at face value, I'm afraid. Magic has its own laws, and they must be obeyed."

Mr. Brown shook his head, and his expression darkened. "No way, no how. I'm not letting anyone or anything take a year of my son's life. If the debt has to be paid, I'll let them take one of *my* years instead."

"Unfortunately," Mr. Fantasmo said, "one cannot pay the price of education for someone else." He held up his hand, warding off the objection already coming from Mr. Brown. "Some people try, but it never works. It's up to each person to decide what they'll learn and what price they'll pay for knowledge." He forced a smile. "If the children have learned well, then the education is worth it."

Mr. Brown let out a frustrated growl that indicated he didn't agree.

"We'll set off tomorrow," Mr. Fantasmo said, apparently immune to Mr. Brown's disapproval. "Now I must take the princess to see her other advisers."

Charlotte looked at Hudson wistfully, and for a moment he thought she was going to ask him to come with her, but then she glanced at Mr. Brown and seemed to change her mind. When she turned her attention back to Hudson, she said, "You should show your dad around Grammaria. The two of you are heroes now. The people will want to thank you."

"Okay," Hudson said, even though he didn't want to go talk to a lot of strangers.

"And of course, I do, too," Charlotte said.

"Do what?" Hudson asked.

"Want to thank you," she said, and added almost shyly, "and I think you're heroes."

Hudson smiled, glowing at the compliment. "Thanks."

She smiled back at him. "Thank you. For everything." Then she turned and walked away with Mr. Fantasmo.

HUDSON AND HIS FATHER DECIDED TO SKIP TOURING GRAMMARIA and went to a large game room in the castle to play the Logosian version of basketball. Instead of using a ball, you pulled a word out of a bin. Groups of letters appeared around the room on different baskets. You had to figure out which groups of letters would make a word if you threw your word into the basket.

Hudson reached into the bin and pulled out the word *cat*.

It was furry and purred. It also stretched its *t* around like a tail. "I can't dribble this," Hudson said. "I'll hurt it. Besides, if I throw it, it might scratch me. We should exchange it for another word."

Cat went all bristly, as if Hudson had offended it. The word curved itself into a ball and waited. So Hudson dribbled it. It purred again.

Really, he would never get used to Logos.

Hudson scored with *catch, scatter, catalog,* and *educate*—he couldn't forget *that* word. His dad went for the fancier shots and got *advocate, duplicate, category,* and *disqualifications.* While they threw and rebounded, they talked about the places they had been in Logos. They also talked about how much Bonnie would have loved it here, and how much Hudson's mom would have hated it—at least the dangerous parts. He wasn't sure he should tell her about breaking into King Vaygran's room and stealing his sword.

It felt good to talk to his dad like they used to. Hudson was going to write down this memory to make sure he could hold on to it forever.

HUDSON AND CHARLOTTE DIDN'T GO TO THE CLIFF OF FACES the next day. Charlotte addressed the Logosians in the morning, telling them she'd sent King Vaygran to a secure place out of the country.

She had, in fact, sent him and several guards to the gray tower in the Land of Backwords, the same tower he had imprisoned her in for eight months. She told Hudson about it at breakfast. "We'll see how he likes performing for the dust bunnies for a while."

Charlotte also outlined new policies for Logos, striking down many of King Vaygran's laws. The ten villagers who had been disguise-pasted into looking like Proval came to the courtyard and begged for her help in restoring their identities. She used some revealing powder to change them back to their normal selves. She reported that a team of wizards would study the spell Nepharo had cast on the Land of Scholars to see if they could find a way to locate and retrieve the lost people.

While the crowd was cheering at this news, the soldiers who had first captured Charlotte and Hudson returned to the castle. They were surprised to find King Vaygran deposed and Princess Colette ruling. They were even more surprised to learn that the girl they had captured was the princess and that they were almost accomplices in her death. Mr. Fantasmo brought the soldiers to the balcony, where they knelt before her, hats clenched in their hands, apologizing to the point of groveling.

Charlotte regarded them without showing emotion, either anger or pity. "You might not have known you caught the heir to the throne, but even the lowest-born citizen of Logos has rights. From the moment my uncle had discovered that Hudson and I wanted to free the princess, you hunted us like criminals."

The soldiers' leader, the man with the curly beard, put his hand to his chest. "We only followed the king's orders, Your Highness. He told us you were dangerous enemies. If we had refused him, the king would have thrown us in his dungeons."

Charlotte didn't speak for a moment. She lifted her chin, eyes firm. Several of the soldiers gulped nervously.

"On the day you chased us into the forest," she finally said, "a polar bear, a wolf, and a tiger fought your bloodhounds so I could escape. What happened to them?"

The bearded man fingered his clenched hat. "They weren't killed," he said, offering this news with emphasis. It was clearly the good news that would shortly be followed by bad news. Bad news often tags along like that. "When Nepharo realized they were magical animals, he thought he could get information about you from them." Another gulp. "After the dogs brought them down, we tied them up, and Nepharo questioned them. They weren't what you would call cooperative, so the wizard sent them to the castle so they could be questioned later."

"They're here?" Charlotte asked, brightening.

The soldier nodded. "They should be."

Charlotte turned to Mr. Fantasmo. "Can you check the dungeons for them?"

While he left to do that, she had the soldiers swear an oath of loyalty to uphold her laws. Hudson imagined she would spend a lot of time trying to straighten out the messes King Vaygran had caused. When the soldiers had finished, Charlotte sent them away and said her good-byes to the crowd, then she and Hudson made their way through the castle hallways.

"I hope my animals are all right," she said, hurrying so quickly Hudson could barely keep up with her. "Why didn't I have someone check the dungeons earlier?"

They rounded a hallway, and the dungeon doors came into sight, swinging open. Mr. Fantasmo was holding them open for the animals. The polar bear loped out first. His fur was so matted and dirty he looked more like a brown bear than a white one. He was favoring one paw, moving slowly. The tiger limped out after him. She had several gaping holes in her fur, slashes where the bloodhounds had ripped into her. Bits of stuffing poked out everywhere. One of her ears was torn loose, and a piece of her tail was missing altogether.

Charlotte ran toward them, arms outstretched. "Chancellor! Blaze! It's me!"

They recognized her voice. Their ears perked up, and both immediately hobbled toward her. The polar bear bellowed in happiness, and the tiger let out a rumbling purr.

She hugged the polar bear and petted the tiger, both of whom licked her face in appreciation.

The wolf hobbled into the hallway last. His side had been shredded and was nothing but loose stuffing. His tail was in tatters. One paw hung by a thread. He took two steps, whimpered, and fell to the ground.

Charlotte left the polar bear and tiger and knelt down beside him. She gingerly stroked his head. "It's all right," she told him. "We'll have you sewn up, and you'll be as good as new."

The wolf rested his muzzle against Charlotte's leg. His eyes were sad, and his ears drooped. "I'll never be as good as new again."

Charlotte kept petting his head. "You'll be better, because the scars you carry are proof that you love me."

THE PALACE SEAMSTRESSES SPENT THE NEXT COUPLE OF HOURS restuffing and stitching the animals. They were patched, bathed, dried, fluffed, touched up, and given seats beside Charlotte to watch a celebration in her honor.

As soon as it got dark, the wizards put on a fireworks display. Lighted words zipped through the air—*shine, dazzle, sparkle*—crackling and popping before they faded away.

The party could have easily stretched into a weeklong event, but at the homonym feast that night, Mr. Brown reminded Charlotte that he and Hudson needed to go back to Texas. "We've been gone for too long," Mr. Brown said as he scooped some green *P*'s and golden *karats* onto his plate. "My wife and daughter must be worried sick about us."

Mr. Fantasmo buttered a freshly baked *role*. "Don't trouble yourself about that. I sent a messenger to your wife last night telling her the good news."

Hudson dipped his spoon into a chocolate *moose*. "How did you do that?" Part of him dreaded going home, where things were so ordinary and dull. If he still had a way to communicate with Charlotte, it wouldn't be quite so bad.

Charlotte raised an eyebrow at Mr. Fantasmo. "I thought you said it was nearly impossible to send people to the Land of Banishment."

"People, yes." Mr. Fantasmo took a bite of a juicy red *beat*. "Bugs, however, can get through to just about anywhere. I simply wrote out a message to Mrs. Brown, enchanted a cockroach so it felt compelled to deliver any messages given to it, and then I sent the bug on his way."

"You sent an enchanted cockroach to my house?" Mr. Brown repeated.

Hudson's mother didn't like bugs. Especially cockroaches. She had probably killed the thing on first sight.

Charlotte cut into a roasted *meet*. "Cockroaches are so small. How could it have delivered a message that Mrs. Brown would even see?"

"Oh, I took care of that," Mr. Fantasmo said with a wave of his hand. "Part of the enchantment is that the bug grows two feet as soon as it enters the Browns' house."

Well, that had probably been an interesting sight. Hudson could just imagine his mother finding a two-foot cockroach wandering around the house with a letter grasped in its pincers. The next moments had no doubt been filled with a lot of shrieking and objects being hurled at the insect. Hudson probably shouldn't have laughed at the thought, but he did.

"Great," Mr. Brown said, sounding less than happy. "That is very . . ."

"Reassuring," Mr. Fantasmo supplied.

"Yeah." Mr. Brown cleared his throat and shifted in his seat. "But we should still get home as soon as possible."

THE NEXT DAY, HUDSON, MR. BROWN, CHARLOTTE, AND Mr. Fantasmo set out on horseback to go to the Cliff of Faces. As they went down the streets of Grammaria, the stone bee flew up to Charlotte. "Welcome home, Your Highness."

"Thank you," Charlotte said. "And thank you for your help earlier."

As Hudson remembered it, the bee hadn't been that helpful. The bug had said, "The princess is closer than you think, but rescuing her is a process, not an event."

Hudson narrowed his eyes at the hovering bee. "Did you know all along that Charlotte was the princess?"

"Her looks changed," the bee said, "but her voice didn't. Bees notice those sorts of details."

"I came alone to ask you the question," Hudson pointed out. "You never heard Charlotte talk."

"I didn't hear her," the bee said, flying in a lazy circle above Hudson's head. "The other bees did, though, and we're very social. It's hard to keep secrets from us."

Charlotte frowned at the bee. "If you knew I was the princess, why didn't you tell me?"

The bee bobbed up and down in the air between Charlotte's and Hudson's horses. "It wasn't enough that *I* knew it. *You* had to know, and you wouldn't have believed me even if I'd told you. Just like Hudson wouldn't believe me if I told him he would one day be the president of his land."

Hudson sat up straighter in his saddle. "What?"

The bee didn't answer, just flew higher.

"Wait," Hudson called. "Was that just an example, or am I really going to be president?"

The bee buzzed upward in a spiral. "You'll have to find out yourself." Then the bug zipped off toward the castle garden.

The squirrel ran across Charlotte's shoulder, nose twitching at the departing insect. "If you ask me," Meko said, "bees are a bunch of gossiping biddies."

No one had asked the squirrel. Still, Charlotte petted him. He arched his back in pleasure and ruffled his tail. Ever since Meko had cut through her ropes, he'd insisted on being her bodyguard. She let him ride around on her shoulder a lot. The squirrel was perpetually fluffed up with pride about this.

When Charlotte went through Scriptoria, the people lined the streets and applauded. Hudson recognized a few of the merchants. Madam Lola, who made renouned baked words, clapped the loudest.

Before long, the group reached the Sea of Life. A mild breeze blew across the water today, and the sea looked an inviting turquoise blue. Instead of smelling of salt, danger, and things lurking near the bottom, it smelled of warm summer days and friendship.

As Hudson dismounted his horse, he turned to his father. "Guess which boat will get us safely across."

Mr. Brown slid from his saddle and tied his horse to a hitching post near the docks. He squinted at the names written on the boats. "Is there one that says '*Have a platoon of Marines watching your back*'?"

"I don't think so."

The rest of the group tied their horses to the post, as well. Hudson waited for his father's guess. "*Love*," Mr. Brown said.

"That's what I thought," Hudson said as the group headed toward the docks. "It took us most of the way there and then sank."

"Love," the squirrel called over, "isn't always smooth sailing."

"But," Hudson added, "when you've got to throw something at King Vaygran, love—or at least a sturdy box of Valentine's candy—is all you need."

"*Endurance?*" Mr. Brown guessed. "Because you've got to endure to get to the end?"

Hudson shook his head.

"*Endurance* is a sturdy boat," Mr. Fantasmo said. "Most of these boats can make the trip on a good day. However, when the storms come and the waves get high, *gratitude* is your best bet."

The group reached the dock and walked down to the *gratitude* boat. Mr. Fantasmo stepped into it, pushing his robes aside so he could sit down on the bench. "The secret is attitude—it's built in."

Hudson was sure that made sense, in a Logosian sort of way.

The bench wasn't big enough for all of them, so Mr. Fantasmo and Mr. Brown worked the oars while Charlotte and Hudson sat together in the back. As the boat slid across the water, everyone took turns saying what they were grateful for. It should have been easy for Hudson. Things had turned out so well. But he couldn't stop thinking about the year of his life he was about to lose.

An entire year. You could do a lot in that time. Learn things, go places, build stuff. Spend time with friends and family. There was so much to do when you thought about it.

"I'm thankful Hudson and Charlotte are okay," Mr. Brown said. Earlier, when Hudson asked if they could keep calling her Charlotte, she said, "Of course. I know how hard it is for people from the Land of Banishment to change." Which was probably not a compliment, but Hudson decided not to take offense anyway.

Mr. Fantasmo pulled on his oar, leaning into it. "I'm thankful Colette knows who she is and has forgiven me for being part of her imprisonment." He smiled at Charlotte.

She smiled back. "I'm thankful you took me to the Land of Banishment. I was safe, and Hudson and I became friends."

She grinned at Hudson, and he wanted to agree, but it would be too embarrassing in front of their fathers. Then he followed his inner compass and said the words anyway. "I'm glad we're friends, too."

"I'm glad you're glad," she said, and neither of them mentioned he would be leaving soon.

19

WHEN THEY GOT to the island, the group trudged up the path to the Cliff of Faces. Each step Hudson took reminded him of the deal he'd made. Really, for twelve months of his life, the faces should have been a little more helpful. Would it have been so hard for the rock dude to say, "Hey, the princess is standing right next to you"?

Then again, maybe the stone bee was right. It wasn't enough for Charlotte to know who she was. While she was imprisoned at the tower, she knew who she was, and it hadn't done her any good. She needed to get to the point where she stopped hoping for someone else to depose King Vaygran and was willing to do it and rule Logos herself.

The group hiked up the dirt path, past scraggly bushes with leaves like curling shells, past seagulls whose wings and beaks were shaped like C's. At last, they stood at the tall grayish-brown cliffs. They seemed bleak and imposing.

Two spots on the cliff wall blinked. The jagged lines on the rock deepened and moved until a face took shape. A weathered old man with a mossy beard peered out at Hudson and Charlotte. "I see you found the princess," he said.

"Yes," Charlotte said, "we did."

Hudson sighed. This was it. "We've come to pay our time for the answers you gave us."

As soon as he spoke, two colored piles of coins appeared on the ground beside them. Hudson's name floated above one, and Charlotte's name—now Her Highness Colette—floated above the other.

Mr. Fantasmo nudged her forward. "The law must be satisfied, Your Majesty."

She took a deep breath and walked over to her pile. Hudson went to his, as well. He looked down at the coins—the years left of his life. Instead of pictures of presidents, each coin was stamped with a likeness of Hudson, a silhouette of him looking off into the distance. Even though it was a substantial pile, he didn't want to give any of them up. Charlotte had already picked up a coin, though, so he took a dull brown one from the top of the pile and joined her at the cliff wall. He hoped the dingy color of the coin meant it was a year Hudson wouldn't enjoy much anyway.

Two more faces appeared in the rock wall in front of them, one resembling Hudson, the other Charlotte. The rock Hudson frowned. "Well, get on with it," he said, in a voice that sounded much older than Hudson's. The face's lips thinned until they became a waiting slot.

Hudson gingerly slid his brown coin into the face's mouth. No magic happened. Nothing whooshed out of his body. He didn't feel different. He had wondered if he would age a year in an instant. That, at least, would be cool, because then he would be taller. But he didn't change. Neither did Charlotte.

He half expected the rock Hudson to lick its lips, savoring his year the way the fairies savored memories. Instead, after a moment, the face spit the coin back out, making it tumble onto the ground

Hudson picked up the coin and turned it over in his hand. It was now the color of fresh gold.

He looked over at Charlotte and saw that she held a golden coin, too.

"Why did we get a coin back?" he asked.

The stone Hudson winked, and his slot mouth lifted into a smile. "Because time well spent is never really lost."

"And," the rock Charlotte added in a voice that sounded old and stately, "a quest for knowledge generally makes you richer than when you started, at least in the ways that matter."

Both faces faded back into the cliff wall, becoming jutting patches of grayish-brown stone again.

Hudson held up the coin. "We didn't lose a year, then?"

Three rock faces formed in the wall in front of him, noses and chins suddenly protruding out.

"Yes."

"No."

"Define *lost*."

Hudson glanced at Mr. Fantasmo to see if he knew which

answer was correct. The man only shrugged. "It's not a question I would pay to have answered."

Charlotte walked to her pile of coins and dropped her gold coin on the top. "Our pile of life is richer. That's enough."

Hudson tossed his coin back onto his pile, as well. "Thanks," he told the faces.

The faces nodded and faded back into the cliff until the only thing that remained were the thin lines where their mouths had been.

Mr. Fantasmo put his hand on Charlotte's shoulder. "Sometimes magic turns out better than you expect."

Hudson's dad turned away from the cliff, his stance more relaxed now that the faces were gone. "Well, I guess it's time for us to head home."

Hudson didn't move. "Where's the nearest portal back to our world?" He had heard Mr. Fantasmo and his father talking about it in Grammaria, but Hudson purposely hadn't paid attention. He didn't want to think about it. He hated good-byes. This one would be especially hard.

"It's on the top of the bluff." Mr. Fantasmo pointed to the far end of the cliffs, where a trail curved around the side. "It will take you a few hours to get to the peak. Once you're there, you'll see it."

"Oh." Hudson felt like his stomach had folded in half. He and Charlotte stared at each other in a hesitant sort of silence.

Mr. Brown reached out and shook Mr. Fantasmo's hand. "I guess this is where we part ways. Thanks for your help."

Mr. Fantasmo gave a curt nod of his head. "And yours."

Charlotte forced a smile at Hudson. She still didn't say

anything. After a moment, she looked at her feet. It was the first time in days that she didn't seem regal and confident. She was just Charlotte again, a girl who didn't know what to say.

Hudson pulled the compass out of his pocket and held it out to her. "This is yours."

She didn't take it. "I thought you might want it." Her eyes met his, questioning. "I mean, if you ever wanted to come back for a visit." She shrugged. "I mean, since I don't need it anymore."

Hudson smiled, and his stomach seemed to unfold. "I know what you mean." He slipped the compass back into his pocket. "I'd like to come back for a visit. It would be nice to check up on the unicorns . . . and things."

She smiled back at him. "I know what you mean."

"Good."

Mr. Brown turned toward the trail. "Hudson, are you ready to go?"

He wasn't and he was. Either way, he didn't have a choice. It was time to return to Texas. Charlotte and Hudson stood looking at each other for a moment longer. He reached out and gave her a quick hug. She wrapped her arms around him and made it into a longer hug.

"Good-bye," she said. "For now."

WHEN THEY REACHED HOME—COMING OUT OF THE COAT CLOSET this time, instead of the kitchen cupboards—Hudson's mother was the first to see them. Her hair was pulled back into a ponytail, she didn't have makeup on, and she was dressed in a pair of old jeans, as though she hadn't bothered to go to work today.

She let out a happy gasp and rushed over, arms open wide. She hugged Hudson, dropped kisses on his forehead, and checked him over for injuries. She also grounded him—which was sort of unnecessary, since his father had already done that—and told him that he was never, ever, to run off to another realm without discussing it with his parents first.

You would think saving a country from a tyrant would automatically get you out of being grounded, but no.

Mrs. Brown then hugged her husband and checked him over, too. When she was assured that they were both all right, she took Mr. Brown by the arm and smiled in a gritting-her-teeth sort of way. "Although I really appreciate the message y'all sent about being safe, next time could you think of a way to send one that *doesn't* involve a two-foot-long cockroach? You could just text me, for example."

Mr. Brown pulled her into another hug. "Sorry about that, baby. Fantasmo sent the bug." Mr. Brown tilted his head to better see his wife's face. "Did you kill the messenger?" He let out a low chuckle. "How much Raid did that take?"

"Oh, I didn't kill it," Mrs. Brown said. "Bonnie wouldn't let me. She named the thing Fredericka and wants to keep it as a pet."

"Are you kidding?" Hudson looked around the living room and kitchen for his sister. "You already let her keep a kitten. She can't have a mutant pet cockroach, too."

Mrs. Brown shook her head. "I tell you what, if Bonnie doesn't keep an eye on that bug, Fredericka is going to up and eat the kitten."

"Do cockroaches eat cats?" Hudson pulled off his jacket and hung it in the coat closet. Besides the rips from the thorn tree, it was now also stained. Didn't matter. He would keep it because it reminded him of Logos and Charlotte.

"That cockroach eats everything," Mrs. Brown said. "Even things that aren't polite to mention. It's all I can do to keep it out of the garbage can. I'm constantly smacking its little antennae."

Mr. Brown pulled off his coat and hung it with Hudson's. "Why haven't you gotten rid of the bug before now?"

She raised an eyebrow at him. "And just how am I supposed to get rid of a two-foot cockroach? Give it a satchel full of garbage and send it on its way?" She put a hand on her hip. "I was waiting for you to come home so you could shrink it and dispose of it somehow. Then we could tell Bonnie it went home to live with its family."

Mr. Brown ran a hand over his short hair. They didn't have a compactulator, and Mr. Fantasmo hadn't told them how to shrink the bug. He probably hadn't taken into consideration that anyone would be bothered by a two-foot messenger cockroach.

"Where is Bonnie now?" Mr. Brown asked.

"In her room playing with Fredericka."

Mr. Brown walked toward the hallway. "Bonnie?"

From her bedroom, Bonnie let out a squeal of glee, and her footsteps pounded down the hallway. "Daddy, you're home! Did you find Hudson?" She rounded the corner, pigtails flapping, and launched herself first at their father, then at Hudson. She smelled of strawberry shampoo and peanut butter. "What took you so long?" she asked. "We were worried!"

Long? Bonnie obviously had an overly optimistic opinion of Hudson's tyrant-fighting abilities.

After finishing her hug, Bonnie let Hudson go and excitedly jumped up and down on the balls of her feet. "You gotta meet Fredericka. She's the smartest cockroach in the whole world. I want to take her to school for show-and-tell, but Mom says I can't. She says she'll scare people. But Fredericka is a nice cockroach."

Bonnie took Hudson's hand and pulled him to her room. There, sitting at Bonnie's play table, was Fredericka, the two-foot-long cockroach. Most bugs have hideous faces, and Fredericka was no exception. The huge cockroach would have looked like something out of a horror show, except she was dressed in one of Bonnie's ballerina tutus with a feather boa draped around her thick brown neck.

Bonnie had laid out peanut-butter-and-jam sandwiches, Cheetos, and some old marshmallows on her tea set. The peanut-butter jar sat open on the table, a messy knife lying across the top. The cockroach shoveled part of a sandwich and several Cheetos into her mouth using four of her legs.

Disgusting. "That is just wrong," Hudson said.

"You're telling me," Mrs. Brown said. "I didn't raise my baby girl to play with cockroaches."

"I'm not eating that peanut butter," Mr. Brown said. One of Fredericka's legs had dipped into the jar and grabbed out a glob.

Bonnie skipped back to the table. "Fredericka has to eat a lot so she can build her cocoon and turn into a butterfly."

"Cockroaches don't turn into butterflies," Mr. Brown said. "That's caterpillars."

Hudson looked around Bonnie's room. "Um, where is the cat, anyway?"

"Hiding underneath the couch," Mrs. Brown said. "She's barely come out since Fredericka showed up."

Smart cat.

"Watch what Fredericka can do." Bonnie picked up a crayon from the table and scribbled something on a stack of paper that lay there. Hudson had been so busy staring at the bug he hadn't noticed all the paper around Bonnie's room. Each of her dolls and stuffed animals had at least one message propped in front of it.

Bonnie put down the crayon and held the paper out to Fredericka. "This is a message for Hudson Brown."

The cockroach dropped most of her food—she seemed too attached to the Cheetos to let those go—and grasped the letter with one antenna. The bug slid off her chair, dropped to the ground, and scuttled over to Hudson. Fredericka then stood on her hind legs and held the paper above her head. While Fredericka waited for Hudson to take the paper, she popped another Cheeto into her mouth.

The note read, *Welcome Home. Fredericka loves you!* Bonnie had surrounded the words with flowers.

"I bet nobody else has a trained cockroach," Bonnie chimed proudly. "I didn't even have to tell her where you were. Once you say a name, she knows where to go."

Hudson didn't take the paper. He didn't especially want Fredericka's love. "It isn't trained—it's enchanted."

The bug remained standing in front of Hudson, staring at him with flat black eyes. Hudson took a step backward, and the cockroach stepped forward, poking the paper at him. Mrs. Brown shook her head. "It'll keep doing that until you take the paper. Trust me, I've tried ignoring it."

Hudson gingerly took the paper from the cockroach's antenna. "Uh, thanks."

Without any sort of indication that the bug understood Hudson's words, Fredericka dropped back to all six legs, scurried across the floor, and climbed onto the table.

Bonnie skipped over to the table and picked up the cockroach like she was a teddy bear. "Where are your manners, Fredericka?" She sat the bug on a seat and handed her a peanut-butter sandwich. "Is that any way for a ballerina to act?"

Mr. Brown leaned closer to his wife. "The bug doesn't ever answer back, does it? I mean, does it understand English?"

"It's just a bug," she said. "A huge, ugly bug that is now our problem."

THE COCKROACH PROBLEM DIDN'T GET SOLVED THAT NIGHT. Mrs. Brown shut Fredericka in the bathroom, and they ordered pizza for dinner. Everyone had too much to talk about and too many stories to tell to worry about bugs. Even Bonnie forgot about her new pet when she found out that Charlotte was a princess.

Bonnie spent the rest of the evening talking about being friends with a princess, musing about what she would do if she were a princess, and asking if they could go visit the palace.

Hudson's parents told her no and wouldn't say more than that. After dinner, they researched cockroaches on the Internet:

The bugs lived for about a year and a half, which was about a year and a half more than Mrs. Brown wanted to house a cockroach. Mr. Brown thought they should sell Fredericka to the Guinness Book of World Records, but Mrs. Brown shot down the idea. "I don't want to be famous for having the world's largest cockroach living at my house. What'll people think about my cleaning?"

Hudson's parents were still talking about it when he went to bed. He hadn't slept very soundly at Logos—being pursued by soldiers with bloodhounds did that to a person—and he immediately fell into a deep sleep. A sleep that would have lasted all night, if he hadn't been woken up at four a.m. by something fluttering in his face.

He opened his eyes. Through the light of the streetlamp outside, he saw a giant cockroach standing on his bed holding a piece of paper in its antennae.

There are many good ways to be awakened from a deep sleep. This was not one of them.

Hudson startled, did something that resembled the backstroke across his bed, then yelled, "Bonnie!" Their parents had specifically told her not to let Fredericka out of the bathroom.

The cockroach fluttered the paper at Hudson again. He turned on his bedside lamp, squinted in the light, and took the paper. As soon as he relieved the bug of its task, it slid off Hudson's covers and scuttled under his bed.

There's nothing like knowing a two-foot-long cockroach is hiding under your bed to keep you from going back to sleep.

Hudson sighed and was about to crumple the paper up when he noticed that a small box was taped to the end of the paper. He didn't open the box. Instead, he read the message.

It wasn't in Bonnie's handwriting. It was Charlotte's.

Dear Hudson Boudewijn,

Thank you again for helping me regain my throne. I and Logos will always be in your debt. And, although Logos has a fiscal policy of avoiding debt, I don't mind this one.

I wanted to make sure you made it home safely, so I'm sending a box with another enchanted messenger cockroach. That way you can write back to me. I realize you have no way to shrink a letter down to cockroach-carrying size, so write "Yes" on something small and give it to the cockroach in the box. He'll bring your message to me.

Yours,
Princess Erica Nomira Charlotte Colette

PS. I wanted to send a prettier bug, since cockroaches are kinda gross, but my top wizard says butterflies are too easily distracted for the job, ants are too slow, and dragonflies knock into things. I considered a bee, but my top wizard says it isn't polite to send things with six-inch-long stingers.

PPS. These bugs' enchantments only last for three days. After that they'll shrink back to their normal size, so don't take long answering.

PPPS. Pokey sends his regards. He's been adopted as the official mascot of Mermaid Lake and is getting along quite well with the mermaids.

PPPPS. I miss you.

The letter made Hudson smile.

A knock came at the door, and then Mrs. Brown opened it and stepped in. "Are you all right? Why were you yelling in the middle of the night?"

Mr. Brown came in behind her, his gaze sweeping the room for danger. Bonnie came into the room last of all, her expression eager. "What is it? Did something magical happen?"

Hudson read them Charlotte's letter. His parents smiled when he got to the part about the cockroaches shrinking, and Bonnie smiled because "Fredericka has a new friend now!"

She peered underneath Hudson's bed, grabbed hold of one of the bug's spindly legs, and tugged the thing toward her. It slid from underneath the bed, all its legs helplessly flailing against the carpet. "I'm going to name you Fred," Bonnie told him. "Let's go meet Fredericka!"

Fred was not as calm as Fredericka, and he waved his antennae in alarm as Bonnie hauled him off.

Mr. Brown put his hand on Mrs. Brown's back and led her

from the room. "Three days," he reminded her. "It's only going to last for three days."

Hudson went to their computer and typed out, *Yes. I miss you too.* Then he changed the first period to a comma. He added, *We have to find a better way to talk. Have your top wizard work on that.*

He shrank the message to three-point type, which made it unreadable. Still, he printed it out and cut the sentence into a tiny strip. He set the small white box on his bedroom floor, opened the lid, and gave the piece of paper to the waiting cockroach. "Give this message to Princess Erica Nomira Charlotte Colette."

The bug took the paper eagerly, holding it in its pincers. Then it crawled out of the box, scurried across the floor, and disappeared into a closet.

IT WAS ODD TO GO TO CLASS THE NEXT MORNING. HUDSON HADN'T thought about school since he'd left Houston. In Logos, he'd had other things to worry about. But that wasn't what made going to school odd. He kept noticing things he hadn't before. The bees that hovered around the flowering bushes, swaying back and forth between blossoms like they were part of a dance. He wondered if they knew people's secrets like the bees in Logos did.

The yellow flowers that grew next to his house seemed different, too. Had their color always been so bright, so happy? The trees along the way had such thick, friendly foliage. He could almost imagine that if he climbed them, they would whisper compliments to him.

Charlotte's house was hard to pass. It stood there forlornly empty, like it knew she wouldn't come back.

Hudson's mother had called the school after he'd disappeared and said he was absent because of personal reasons. When Trevor had called their house, she'd told him Hudson went to visit his sick grandmother.

Yeah, sort of like Red Riding Hood. It wasn't the best excuse. If his grandmother were really sick, wouldn't his mother have gone, too?

Still, Hudson came up with some stories about his grandma's house in case anyone asked.

When Hudson got to school, Andy, Caidan, Isabella, and Macy were leaning up against some lockers near his. They were talking about a rematch of the basketball game they'd had a week ago. Andy predicted "total domination."

Caidan eyed Hudson and let out a snort. "Well, if it isn't Boil Boy. Your skin finally cleared up enough that you could show your face again?"

Isabella nudged Caidan, telling him to stop it, but she giggled while she did it.

Hudson spun the combination on his locker. "I never got any boils."

"Oh, come on," Macy said, chewing a piece of gum loudly. "We broke out just by being *around* you. You must have had them, too."

Andy made a face, rolling his eyes back in his head. "He must have looked like something out of a horror show."

Isabella shot Hudson a pointed look. "Really, it was totally uncool of you to go through poison ivy and then show up at the game and infect us."

Hudson opened his locker door. "You can't infect someone with poison ivy." It was a plant, not a disease. Had Isabella always been such a ditz?

Isabella tossed her hair off her shoulder. The gesture didn't have the effect it used to have on Hudson. Instead of seeming glamorous, she just seemed annoyed. "Well, you must have infected us with it. We got it after being around you." Another toss. She looked like she suffered from neck spasms. "And do you really expect anyone to believe you were at your grandmother's? That's so lame."

Hudson put his backpack into his locker. "You're right. I went with Charlotte to Logos to help her take care of some things."

Caidan raised his eyebrows and laughed. He clearly thought he'd hit the mother lode of joke material. "Charlotte Fantasmo?" he asked. "You were with wacko girl all this time?"

"It turns out Logos is a real place." Hudson took his books for first period out of his locker. "She's a princess there. She's got a castle, servants, wizards, amazing stuff."

"Does she have a psychiatrist?" Caidan asked. "Because that's what you both need."

"Or a brain surgeon," Andy said. "To fix whatever is wrong with you."

Isabella shook her head with disapproval. "You really shouldn't encourage Charlotte's weirdness. She's bad enough already."

Andy nudged Macy. "That's what she's the princess of—the Princess of Weirdness."

Andy and Caidan both laughed. Hudson shut his locker door with a thud. He didn't let the laughter rattle him. "Two-foot-long cockroaches," he said. "She can send them to visit whoever she wants. So I really wouldn't make fun of Charlotte if I were you. You don't want to get on the wrong side of magic."

"Two-foot-long cockroaches?" Andy said loud enough that several people in the hallway turned to look at him. "That's what you and Charlotte are going to have after you're married."

More laughter from the group. This time Isabella and Macy joined in. Hudson turned and headed toward his first class.

"Prince and Princess of Weirdness," Caidan called after him.

They didn't let up all day. And Hudson didn't mind.

He didn't go to the basketball game after school. He had too much homework to make up, but he didn't forget that Andy and Caidan would be there, surrounded by their friends. After Hudson finished up his algebra, he wrote each of them a note that said, *It's not nice to make fun of people.* He gave the cockroaches the messages, told the bugs to deliver them to Caidan and Andy, then opened the door and watched the insects scurrying down the sidewalk toward the park.

It was probably a mean thing to do—to Fredericka and Fred, anyway. But somehow Hudson didn't feel that bad about it.

The next day, when Hudson saw Caidan and Andy in the hallway, the two boys turned pale and hurried past him without saying a word. Apparently, they'd gotten the message.

ACKNOWLEDGMENTS

THIS NOVEL STARTED ITS LIFE AS A TWENTY-FIVE-PAGE SHORT story I wrote for a compilation. The book was canceled, which in a lot of ways should have prepared me for what lay ahead. If this book had been a person, it would have been an orphan who went door to door, barefoot in the snow, trying to sell Girl Scout cookies.

Oh sure, the beta readers loved it (a big thanks to librarians Mary Wong and Tim Loge for their encouragement), and my daughter's sixth-grade class all wanted their names in the novel, but so many agents just didn't get the story.

A land of wordplay? British unicorns? People who sold word-shaped pastries? No.

So I have to give a big thanks to Lauren Burniac and everyone at Feiwel and Friends for taking a chance on a story that didn't fit any sort of cookie-cutter mold. And a big thank-you to Anna Roberto for taking over the editing. Also, here's a shout-out to Elissa Englund, the ever-important copy editor, who caught my many grammar mistakes and changed my hurdling dogs to hurtling dogs. (Because the first would be too weird.)

I also want to thank the many talented women in my writers'

group who offered feedback on the story: Melinda Carroll, Torsha Baker, Nan Marie Swapp, Kelly Oram, Ruth Nickle, Donna Dustin, Peggy Howe, Kari Pike, Bunny Miner, Raejean Roberts, Angela Carling, and Nichole Evans (and honorary sidekick Maureen Higham).

And, of course, a big thank-you to my family, who don't complain too much about the fact that I never cook because I'm always busy writing. Hey, macaroni and cheese has never killed anyone. Probably.

THANK YOU FOR READING THIS
FEIWEL AND FRIENDS BOOK.

The friends who made

THE WRONG SIDE
OF MAGIC

possible are:

JEAN FEIWEL, *Publisher*

LIZ SZABLA, *Editor in Chief*

RICH DEAS, *Senior Creative Director*

HOLLY WEST, *Editor*

DAVE BARRETT, *Executive Managing Editor*

KIM WAYMER, *Production Manager*

ANNA ROBERTO, *Editor*

CHRISTINE BARCELLONA, *Associate Editor*

EMILY SETTLE, *Administrative Assistant*

ANNA POON, *Editorial Assistant*

Follow us on Facebook or visit us online at mackids.com.
OUR BOOKS ARE FRIENDS FOR LIFE.